The Green Flash

Kyle W. Bahl

PublishAmerica
Baltimore

ISBN: 1-4241-0725-3
PUBLISHED BY PUBLISHAMERICA, LLLP
www.publishamerica.com
Baltimore

Printed in the United States of America

For my brother, Lewie Gene Bahl, 10/22/1958–1/31/1983.
I think he would have liked this.

There are a lot of people I would like to thank, mostly Lucy, my better half, who put up with me while I spent time on this project instead of with her. Also, I would like to thank my friend and coworker, Al Calderone, who more than anyone prodded me to continue and finish this story. Without his encouragement (see nagging) this project would still be just a good idea. I would also like to give a special thanks to all of the men and women of the uniformed services, military, police and fire departments, and all others whose jobs relate to our safety and security. These people have dedicated their lives to the protection and safety of the rest of us, often at great personal cost to themselves, and we as a society truly need to convey our respect, appreciation, and gratitude to all them for their continual sacrifices.

So others may live.

Kyle W. Bahl

Chapter One

It had started out as a fairly shitty day for Alex, she overslept and got out of bed to discover she was out of coffee, then stubbed her big toe on the bathroom door. *Yeah, it's going to be just a real peach of a day. .*

After hastily getting ready for work, Alex—AKA Alexis McTeal, left her Manhattan apartment to discover one of the coldest, wettest, and basically nastiest December mornings that she could remember. She stood shivering while the doorman hailed her a cab and the nearly freezing rain dripped from her umbrella. "Some morning eh Miss Mc-T," said Bill who had been the daytime doorman during the three years Alex had lived in the building.

"At least it isn't Monday," said Alex as she stepped into the cab that had pulled up. "Amen," said Bill as he closed the door against the harsh wind. "Brookman Building," she told the driver, as the cab sped away from the curb.

Alex had been working as an accountant at Brookman for about two years, prior to that, she had been an independent CPA, mainly serving as a tax consultant. She had done all right, but old man Brookman had made an offer she had found impossible to refuse. Good salary and perks, so, Alex had accepted his offer. As Alex walked into the reception room outside her office, she took notice of the two men with five o clock shadows holding 7-11 coffee cups, an odd thing, seeing as it was eight in the morning. "Miss McTeal?" queried the taller of the two. "Yes," she answered shooting the two men a questioning look. "I m Sergeant Eggers and this," he said as he gestured to his partner, "is Detective Brady, I'm afraid were going to need a few minutes of your time. Could we please talk in your office?" *A real peach of a day*, thought Alex.

Once inside the office, Eggers was immediately taken back by the breathtaking view from Alex's windows. It was almost as though one was flying over the city. "Nice digs," commented Brady. "I've done well here and Mr. Brookman has been appreciative," said Alex with a slight edge to her voice. "Yeah, well," said Eggers, "I suppose we should get down to why we are here."

"Please do," said Alex. It was Brady who dropped the bomb. "Miss McTeal, do you know Robert Andrews, and could you please explain your relationship with him"

Oh shit, thought Alex, *what in the world would they be asking me about Bob for?* Bob Andrews was a senior associate with the law firm of, Dewy and Wilson. Brookman and D-W often collaborated on different cases, and Bob and Alex had met while working on an estate closure, which was Bob's particular specialty. They had become involved right from the beginning. It had never gotten serious, at least not for Alex, she was pretty sure Bob felt the same way. They just never brought it up, wanting to keep things simple. Alex was snapped back by the sound of Eggers voice. "Miss McTeal, would you please answer the question?"

"Why do you want to know about Bob and I, is he in some kind of trouble?"

"Just answer the question please," said Eggers. Alex thought for a second, and then matter of factly said, "Fuck you both, tell me what this is about or you can take this up with my lawyer."

"Hey, take it easy," said Brady. The two detectives looked at each other and shrugged, this time it was Eggers who spoke up. "Well, ma'am, we know for a fact that you and Mr. Andrews have been, shall we say involved for some time and from what we can gather, it's been fairly casual, at least that's the impression we got from his neighbors earlier this morning."

"Once again," said Alex, "what is this about"

"Ok," said Brady, "Robert Andrews was murdered last night, or rather early this morning at about one or two AM. A patrol boat pulled his body out of the East River this morning at about three thirty. Someone called

911 and reported a body being tossed into the river, and it turned out to be your friend." Alex felt dizzy, the room seemed to spin. *This couldn't be happening*, she thought, and she had just talked to him a couple of days ago.

"Miss McTeal, are you all right," asked Eggers. For a few moments Alex couldn't speak, when she found her voice she asked, "Do you have any idea who did it?" Brady said, "Actually, we were hoping you might be able to help us out with that, when was the last time you saw Mr. Andrews?" Alex seemed lost again for a few moments, Eggers was about to say something when Alex said, "About two days ago, we had dinner near my place and took different cabs home, I had an early one yesterday and needed to get home."

"Did he say anything at all to make you think he might be in trouble, or maybe worried about something?"

"No not at all, actually, he seemed to be in a good mood."

"What did you talk about that night," asked Brady. "Oh, nothing in particular really, Bob talked about a big bonus he was supposed to be getting, said maybe he would take a vacation this summer, I didn't take him serious, he hasn't taken a vacation that I know of in a few years, he likes making money too much, you know lawyers." Eggers had to suppress a grin. "Sergeant, you said Bob was thrown into the East River, is that how he was killed?"

"Well," said Eggers, "he was killed somewhere else then taken to the river, tossed off the bridge, the patrol boat just happened to be in the area when the 911 call came in. The only reason we found the body at all was the line they tied to whatever kind of weight they used broke on impact with the river, the end was tied around his ankles, if the line hadn't broke we may never have found him, would have ended up as just another missing person." Alex visibly shuddered then asked, "How was he killed?"

"I'm not real sure you want to know the details, but it appears that he was tortured, they, and I say they, because it would have taken more than one person to do some of the things that were done to him," said Eggers, "it would appear that his heart just gave out under the strain."

"Look," said Brady, "I think we have taken up enough of your time, here is our card, it has both our numbers on it, if you can think of anything that might help us out with this, please give us a call. And remember any little thing could be a big help." Then it was Eggers time to chime in. "Ms McTeal, I'm so sorry we had to come here like this, but, you know this is a homicide investigation and we have to cover all the bases."

"Yes, I understand," after a pause she added, "please find the people who did this, he was a good man, I really mean that." Brady said, "We'll do what we can; you got our word on that." With that, the two detectives left Alex's office and caught the elevator to the lobby. "Well, what do you think?" asked Brady. "I think the broad was telling the truth," said Eggers. "Yeah, she don't know shit, you think we should talk to her again later on," asked Brady.

"Na, I don't think this broad is gonna be much help solving a mob hit, I'd bet my badge she had no idea what Andrews was up to."

"Well, we sure as fuck don't know what he was into," said Brady, "I guess we have to find whoever blowtorched his balls and armpits and say—hey, what did that nice lawyer tell you before you finished burning him to death, yeah I'm sure they would be more than happy to tell us."

Chapter Two

Alex was sitting at her desk trying to absorb the information she had just received and make sense of it, but none of it really made any sense. Why would people torture and kill Bob, and then try to make his body disappear like Jimmy Hoffa. It didn't make any sense.

Her reverie was interrupted by the sound of her Secretary Gladys's voice over her intercom. "Miss McTeal, I need to come in for a moment if that's ok."

"Of course Gladys, come right in." Gladys entered the office carrying a package that was about the size of an oversized shoebox. "Alex, I don't know what is going on here, you can tell me if you want to, but I'm not going to ask, this package came for you by courier while you were entertaining New York's finest. I didn't think you would want to be interrupted so I smiled, showed a little leg [she has great legs by the way], and talked the kid into letting me sign for it. It's from Bob." With a concerned look Gladys said, "Just tell me what you need me to do, and I mean whatever you need. I have secretary stuff to do; I'll hold all calls until you tell me otherwis.e" With that, Gladys gave Alex a warm smile and disappeared into the reception area.

For at least a full minute Alex just stared at the package on her desk. She desperately wanted to open it, but for some reason she was afraid of it. After another minute she said aloud, "Well Pandora, here I come." It would not have been possible, not even in the furthest reaches of her imagination for Alex to realize how much her life was about to change or, how blindingly fast those changes would take place. Finally, Alex found her nerve and picked up the box and tore off the wrapper. Inside she found a jewelry box with a note on top. Beside that was a large bundle wrapped in brown paper. With a deep breath Alex opened the note, it was hand written and read:

Dearest Alex, I want to start by saying something I never had the courage to tell you before, and it doesn't really matter now because if you are reading this, it means I'm either dead or worse. I love you and have loved you from the moment we met. Ok, with that out of the way. I think I really fucked up this time but some good can still come out of it. You have two choices, you can take this box to the cops, unopened, or you can open it and change your life forever. If you open the box there is no turning back, and I have left some basic instructions inside, but you MUST decide right now, this very moment what you are going to do, call the cops right now, or open the box. Alex stared at the note in utter disbelief, "Bob you asshole, like there is any other option for a woman." Alex had the jewelry box open in a second, and as promised, there was another note inside the box. As she lifted the note out of the box Alex saw a large leather pouch. Her mind was in overdrive as she opened the note with trembling hands. As Alex opened the note, she was trembling all over. The note read:

So, you went for it, good girl! I'll start by telling you how I came to be in possession of the box of goodies that you now have. I was working on the estate closure for Hanna Richter, her husband, Karl had died ten years before Hanna, and they had been childless. Hanna Richter had stated in her will that all of her properties and possessions were to be sold at auction and that all proceeds were to be given to the international Red Cross, all personal items deemed not worthy for auction were to be donated to any charitable organization that would have them. As you recall, I had been working on this whole thing for a couple of months, well the box you now have is the bonus I was talking about at dinner the other night. I was digging through one of dear old Hanna's junk drawers when I came across a small solid gold box, with the words, All for you my love, engraved in German on the lid. Inside, was a key for a safety deposit box at the Chase Manhattan Bank. At the time, it meant nothing more to me than taking a trip to the bank to close out the account and add the contents to the inventory, was I ever wrong. As Hanna's lawyer I had complete access so I was allowed to examine the contents of the box in private. The box contained some old photos of the Richters, probably taken somewhere around Bavaria with Karl sporting his WW-2 German paratrooper's uniform, handsome couple actually; anyway, the only other thing in the box was the pouch. When I dumped the contents of the pouch out my heart nearly stopped. Alex, it is stuffed with LARGE diamonds and emeralds; I'm talking millions and millions worth. I saw those emeralds and thought of how closely their color matches your eyes. Anyway, inside the paper bundle you will find two hundred, seventy-five thousand dollars in cash, and that is where the whole thing went to shit. It didn't take long to figure how this nice old retired couple was able to live so comfortably. So here I am holding this incredible fortune in precious stones in my hand and nobody in the world knows they exist, so I made the only logical decision, keep it all and get away somewhere and live the dream. Now, the problem was what to do with them. A few years back, I had done some pro-bono work for the courts as a public defender. One of the cases I worked was this Russian kid who got busted on an extortion scam, there was no doubt as to his guilt, but I was able to get the charges dropped on a technicality. He gave me a number and told me that he owed me a big one and if I ever needed help with anything that he could be reached with the number he had given me. I guessed he had some connection with the Russian Mafia, and I figured if anybody could help me move some of the stones it would be him. Well, I used the number and was contacted in less than twenty-four hours. A meet was arranged and about two weeks before I last saw you, we met. I took a small batch of the larger stones with me to see what he might be able to do with them. When we met it was pretty obvious that the guy had moved up, his clothes and mannerisms had improved significantly. When I showed him the stones he had difficulty hiding his excitement, but maintained a businesslike manner, and correctly guessed that I needed the services of a person such as himself to unload them for me. I had taken a total of eleven stones, a mix with mostly diamonds and a few emeralds of various sizes. I told him that they were all I had and that I wanted to convert them into cash for the best price as quickly as possible. He said that it would not be a problem but I would be lucky to get thirty to forty percent of their value this way, and I told him it was more than I had now. He laughed and said that I would have to let him take all of the stones with him, and that he would contact me once he had converted the stones into cash. I really wasn't that concerned since these were only a small fraction of the jewels but I thought that I put on a pretty convincing act of being afraid of being ripped off. My new friend reassured me that I had nothing to worry about and concluded our business by adding that his cut of the proceeds would be taken off the top and he would do the best that he could for me. It took a little over a very anxious week to hear from my new friend again and I was beginning to think that I'd been had when I received a message at my office to meet at a Russian restaurant in Brooklyn, I was a little concerned about the location but it seemed logical that he would want to meet on his home turf. When I got there my friend greeted me as if we were long lost brothers. He ushered me to a table in the rear of the restaurant and once we were seated, a waitress appeared immediately and my friend ordered food and drinks for the both of us. He wasted no time getting down to business, producing a small leather attaché case and sliding it across the table towards me while flashing me a bright grin. My friend told me that there was two hundred seventy-five thousand dollars in U.S. currency in the case and that I was welcome to count it there in his presence and not to be concerned because all present were HIS people. He then went on to apologize that the amount was so small but hoped I understood that it was the best he could do on such short notice. He then told me there were ways that he could make some very high yield very short-term investments for me, I declined. He laughed and said he had assumed as much. After the waitress had brought another round of strong Russian vodka, our meal arrived and we ate pretty much in silence. It was an excellent meal, I had a shitload of cash on me, and I was starting to get a pleasant buzz from the vodka. I knew I should have said thanks and gotten the hell out of there, but I was feeling just too damned good, sort of like James bond or something. Anyway, after dinner we were joined by two exceptionally good-looking Russian girls and my friend suggested, well, actually insisted that he and his friends take me to his club and celebrate closing our deal and that it would be his treat as he had made twenty-five thousand on the deal. Alarm bells were going off in my head like crazy but my friend told me that I would be safer with him than the Secret Service. So I went and that is where I fucked myself. He played me like a true master. Between the vodka and then women, I started to get loose, too loose and like a schoolboy I hinted that maybe we could do some more business in the future. I tried to be slick but I could see it in his eyes that he had just seen right through me, he knew that there were more stones, but sensing my sudden wariness he switched to being my new best buddy again. We left the club shortly after that in a big limo and my friend asked what I wanted to do and I told him I just wanted to go home, too much vodka and I had to work the next day. That statement brought out genuine laughter; he patted me on the back and said that I could afford to take the rest of the week off. I laughed as well but said I had something that I really had to finish. As we pulled up in front of my townhouse he said something to the girls in Russian that got them giggling, and then suggested that the girls accompany me inside and the car would be sent for them in the morning at the time of my choosing. That was mighty tempting, but I was thinking about you, I'm not just sucking up because if you are reading this I am way past the point of excuses or bullshit.

It only took a couple of days before my friend began contacting me again. At first it was cordial and casual, but then he started pressing me for details as to how I had acquired the stones, and then he flat out told me he knew that I was holding out. I started seeing people following me, and I think my house was being watched. When I got home after dinner with you that last time, my house had been trashed. I had already moved the stones and the cash to a safe place. I left instructions with the person holding them that if I failed to check in for two consecutive scheduled times, to deliver this package to you. And so that is where we are. Right now you still have the choice—take the money and run, or call the cops. I hope you take the money, if things hadn't gone to shit; I had planned to ask you to run away with me, I'd like to think you would have done it. Ok, here is the way it has to work if you take the long road. Leave your office, go shopping and buy a suitcase and a few things to travel with then go to the airport and get on an airplane and head for St. Thomas in the U.S.

Virgin Islands, it's a U.S. territory so you won't have to use your passport. Be sure to pay cash for the ticket, do not use your credit card, it's too easy to track. You will have to leave everything behind, you can't go to your apartment, your new life starts the second you walk out the door of your building. I know how much you love to sail so that is what you do, you can pick and choose from the available charter boats. Stick to the privately owned boats, and avoid the big charter companies, you will have to be low key until you know that nobody is looking for you. My friend doesn't know anything about you, but I have a real bad feeling about our next meeting and it is only a matter of time until he finds me. You can travel all over the Caribbean without much hassle and it will be damned difficult for anyone to track you. Customs offices are very lax and they don't use computers, everything is on paper, all you have to do is keep moving for a while. If you need money, take one of the stones to a jewelry store down there and sell it, they should be easy to move that way, just don't go to the same place twice and nobody will notice. You can do this, I know you can, you always said you needed some adventure, well here it is, financially you are set for life, you can have or do anything, but you best get your ass in gear. There isn't anything left to tell you, Gladys can take care of your things and you can work out a way to contact her and find out if things are ok for you to re-appear, if you want to. Go get a tan and find someone to share your life with and be happy. I wanted that person to be me, but that is obviously not an option. All I can do is give you this gift and burden. Know that my last thoughts will be of you.

Alex sat looking at the box and for the first time in her life could not decide what to do. How could I have been so blind, she thought. She should have been able to sense how deep Bob's feelings for her had been, and now it was too late, he was gone. She let her mind wander and imagined herself sailing in the warm Caribbean sun with Bob, and had to admit to herself that it was not at all unpleasant. After a few moments she decided that she would have gone with him if he had had the chance to ask. The decision came quickly, Bob had died for this, what he had not said in the note was now painfully clear. If she called Brady and Eggers, Bob would have died for nothing. "Well shit, I guess I have a plane to catch," she said aloud. Alex hit the intercom button and said, "Gladys, I need you to come in for a minute"

16

"Of course, I'll be right in." Gladys came into the office and became immediately concerned by the look on Alex's face. "Have a seat Gladys; I have some things to tell you. For starters Bob is dead, he was murdered last night, I know why now, and the package he sent explained it all. I can't and won't explain, but I am going to need your help, I am going to pull a disappearing act, what I need is a discrete way of contacting you so I can find out what is going on around here. It won't be long before those detectives come back to ask questions and the less you know the better. I am going to leave from here and keep going, here are the keys to my apartment, wait at least a week before you go there and when you do, don't go alone." Gladys thought for a moment and said, "I already told you that I would help you in any way I can." Gladys wrote a number on a piece of paper and handed it to Alex. "This is my Brother Jim's number, contact him with any message you have, and he will relay any information I might have to you. Have you figured out what to tell Brookman?" Alex thought for a moment and then said, "Nothing, and if anyone asks you don't know anything either, I know you can figure out a way to explain why you are looking after my place. In fact you can say that you have had a key in case I ever needed you to pick up or drop off anything for me. I may or may not ever be back Gladys, I just can't say right now. You have been a good friend to me and I know that this is not fair to you but I don't know what else to do." Gladys said, "Whatever is going on, I trust you and I'll help any way I can." Alex went to Gladys and embraced her in a hug. Both women were near tears and Alex said, "I have to go now, but I promise that I will stay in touch, if more than two weeks go by without my contacting you, unless I tell you otherwise, it means that I can't." The two women embraced again and then Alex said, "I have to go now."

"Go girlfriend, and take care of yourself ok, I'll keep a lid on things here." Alex went through the office to the elevator, pushed the lobby button and hit the ground running like hell.

Chapter Three

Once outside the building, Alex hailed a taxi and told the Pakistani driver to take her to Macy's. On the ride there she had time to think about what was happening. She was past the confusion and uncertainty now, she would pull this off, she was confident of that, and as far as she knew she wasn't breaking any laws, with the exception of withholding evidence in a homicide investigation, but then no one would ever know she had that information. If Bob had wanted her to do anything about the Russians, he would have given her information that the police could have used. It was clear to her that Bob just wanted for her to go away and leave the whole mess behind. She had the potential resources; maybe she could do something later. The cab stopped in front of Macy's and Alex paid the fare and went inside to the customer service counter and asked the clerk to watch her package while she did some shopping. Her first destination was the luggage section where she selected a medium-sized suitcase, then to cosmetics. Alex wasn't sure, if she would use it yet but she bought some brown hair dye. She liked her natural strawberry blond but it might be a good idea to change her appearance. Alex then went to ladies wear. Alex decided she wouldn't need much here, just some jeans and couple of blouses. Alex planned to wait until she got to the island to find a hotel and buy some more appropriate clothing, the less indicators of her intentions she left with anyone she made contact with here the better. Alex started thinking about the best way to smuggle the stones and cash out of the country. She knew that she would not have to clear customs in St. Thomas but she could not carry the stones and cash on her. She would have to check them through in her luggage and take her chances, Alex didn't like it but she really had no other choice. Alex took stock of her purchases and decided that she had everything she needed for her getaway. After paying cash for her purchases, she went to the ladies room and changed out of her pants suit and put on a plain white blouse, jeans, and sneakers. She was about to put the pants suit into the suitcase then said to hell with it and tossed the whole outfit into the trash can, shoes, handbag and all. Alex stood back and looked in the mirror as she tied her shoulder-length hair into a ponytail. Even in casual clothes Alex was a strikingly beautiful woman. She stood five foot six wearing flats and had the body that came from a diligent aerobics program. Her eyes were difficult to categorize, a shade of green somewhere between the color of jade and emeralds. Alex had long ago gotten used to people, men in particular looking into her eyes with a quizzical look on their faces while they tried to figure just exactly what shade of green they were. Alex took one more look in the mirror and said, "Just another Yankee tourist on her way south to catch some rays." Satisfied that she was ready, Alex left Macy's after retrieving her package from the customer service desk and took a cab to JFK airport. She told the driver to take her to the International terminal. Alex had declined the cabbies offer to put her things in the trunk and kept them with her in the back seat. On the ride to the airport, she transferred her purchases and the cash and jewels into the suitcase. She put one of the bundles of one hundred dollar bills in her purse. Once in a while Alex would look up at the driver but he appeared to be totally engrossed in negotiating the traffic. At the airport, she paid the driver and left him a hefty tip asking him to throw away her empty boxes for her. The driver just looked at the money and shrugged his shoulders and drove off to the arrivals area to score another fare. Alex asked one of the skycaps which carrier went to St. Thomas, the skycap told her American and that he would be happy to take her suitcase for her. She accepted and allowed him to lead the way. At the ticket counter, she handed the skycap a fiver and walked up to the ticket counter. A smiling, tall brunette-haired woman asked Alex if she could help her. "Well I hope so," said Alex, "when is the next flight to St. Thomas?"

"That flight leaves in about two hours and begins boarding in about an hour and a half. Do you already have a ticket?"

"No I don't, are their any seats available?"

"I'll have to check," said the attendant. The attendant began typing on her computer and after a few seconds said, "well, I have a few seats in first class if that's ok?"

"Sure," said Alex, "make it an open return; I'm not sure how long I'll be staying." The ticket agent handed Alex her ticket and checked her one suitcase; Alex kept her small Jansport backpack as a carry on. Alex had some time to kill so she went to the terminal bar for a drink. She ordered a rum and coke and sat back in her chair and relaxed for the first time since she had gotten out of bed this morning. Shit, this morning, she thought, it already seemed like it was a lifetime ago. In just a few short hours, her life had irreversibly changed, and yet she felt a strange sense of calm, almost as if this was something she had planned to the last detail, as was her usual way of doing things. Alex ordered another drink, finished it and then went to the gate. It was only a short wait for the boarding call and Alex was glad she was flying first class, the less time she was hanging around in the terminal the better, no telling who she might run into. Alex boarded the aircraft with the rest of the first class passengers and took her assigned seat. She was pleased to have the whole row to herself and settled in for a nap. She was dreaming about the summer in Newport, Rhode Island, when as a young teen, her father had first taught her to sail. She was awakened by a flight attendant that asked if she would like something to eat. Alex hadn't even thought about food all day and suddenly realized just how hungry she was. She made her selection and watched the movie preview for the film that would be shown after the meal. After she had eaten, Alex thought about her parents. They had been killed in an automobile accident while she was in her last year of college. She had pretty much retreated within herself after that, focusing on her studies, and then after graduation, her work. She watched the movie and shortly after that the captain announced the descent into San Juan, Puerto Rico, where the plane would let off and take on passengers. The captain requested that those passenger continuing on to St. Thomas remain onboard the aircraft. The plane was off in less than forty minutes and it seemed like only minutes before they were landing in St. Thomas. Alex felt the rush of hot moist air as the door of the jetliner was opened and the ladder was moved into position. After disembarking the aircraft, Alex proceeded to the baggage claim area to get her suitcase. She was fighting for self-control as she waited for the baggage carousel to spit out her suitcase. Finally, it slid down the chute and Alex grabbed it and walked away without incident. Feeling quite relieved, she reasoned that there wasn't much smuggling to the Caribbean. Once her suitcase had been retrieved, she walked to the front curb where dark skinned West Indian cabbies were hawking for business. A cabbie approached her and said, "Where to missy?"

"I really don't know," said Alex, "could you recommend a good hotel close to the water and near a marina?" asked Alex.

"Sure," said the cabbie, "I take you to Frenchman's Reef Hotel, very nice place right on the water, has a pool, and it's close to town, everything in Charlotte Amalie close, got the old Ramada Yacht Haven, is closest marina but most folks call it rat haven now, it ain't what it used to be. A little further is Crown Bay marina, that's about the nicest one around, then you got the St. Thomas yacht club way over to the east end." Alex said, "Thanks a lot, Frenchman's reef sounds fine." As promised, it was a short ride to the hotel. During the ride to the hotel, Alex was simply reveling in the beauty that surrounded her. From the turquoise colored waters that turned such a beautiful shade of blue as the water deepened offshore, to the lush green vegetation and the way the mountains just sprang from the sea to form the island and its reef structure. As they came to the hotel, the cabbie gave Alex a card and told her to call him anytime she needed a ride and he would be her personal guide. She paid her fare and said thanks. Alex got a room on the fourth floor facing the water and paid cash in advance for a week. She got settled in time to watch the sun setting behind Crown Mountain. "Yeah, I'm going to get used to this," said Alex. For a while, Alex sat on the balcony taking the scenery in, and enjoying the cool fresh breeze. It was hard to believe that less than twenty-four hours ago, she was thinking about a report on an account she was working on, and whether or not she would make her deadline. *Well,* she thought, *there would be no more of that.* Alex didn't really have a plan as it were, just a rough idea of what she was going to do. The first thing to do would be to hire a charter boat and play tourist, sailing around the U.S.

and British Virgin Islands. With her current means, and the money she had in the bank back in New York, she could buy some property just about anywhere she wanted to. She just had to sail around long enough to figure out if anyone was after her or not. In a way she was worried about that, after all, the police had said that Bob was tortured before he died, had he told them about her, were they looking for her right now or what. It didn't really matter did it, she was gone and left no paper trail, paying cash for everything since she had walked out of her office and pulled her disappearing act. Really, the only problem Alex could see at the moment was what to do about the money she had in the bank at home, it was almost as much as she now had on her in cash. Her parents had been very well off, and had left Alex the apartment she had been living in as well as nearly four hundred thousand dollars of insurance money and bearer bonds. There was no way to access any of it without being tracked to the Caribbean. Well, she thought, I'll just have to deal with that later. Alex decided to go down to the lobby and get a drink before she turned in. In the main reception area there was a large stand with lots of brochures on the different charter boats with prices and schedules. Alex grabbed a handful and set off for the bar. She started going through them while she sipped on a rum and Coke, when she realized just how much the day had taken out of her. Alex finished her drink and was about to charge it to her room and decided to pay cash instead, as little of a trace as possible had become her mantra.

Chapter Four

New York

Mhikiail Valentnikov, more commonly referred to as Mhiki, sat at a table in one of the clubs he owned looking at the three men in front of him with utter contempt and disgust. He affixed a particularly contemptuous look at the youngest of the three, who was not only the senior man in the group, but was also the, *new friend,* of the late Robert Andrews. After making Viktor squirm for a bit, Mhiki said, "I am most disappointed with you Viktor, for many reasons, you know that don't you. Let me see, first you failed to find the rest of the lawyer's gems, of which you personally assured me there were more, then while questioning him, and I use that term lightly, you killed him you ignorant piece of shit. I should have these two pet apes of yours hang you up and use that blowtorch on you. If the lawyer did indeed have more of these gems, what he gave to you would only have been a portion of them to see what price he could get for them, or just for money to disappear with, what you are going to do my young friend, is start looking at his friends and see if anything turns up. As usual, technical support will be no problem. If more gems do exist, I want them. Now, get out of my sight before I forget that I am supposed to be in a good mood." Viktor swallowed hard before he spoke, he knew that he owed everything he had and was, to the man seated before him, Viktor loved him like a father, but also knew that Mhiki would either have him killed, or just kill him personally if he blew this one, Mhiki did not tolerate fuck ups at all, especially from what he called his staff, those whom Mhiki had allowed into the inner circle of his organization. Viktor had come to

Mhiki's attention several years earlier when he had tried to shake down one of Mhiki's restaurants. Instead of killing him, Mickey had Viktor picked up and brought to him. Surprisingly, especially to Mhiki, he took a liking to the cocky young thug. Viktor had no idea that Mhiki had owned the restaurant and even if he had, he would not have understood its significance. So, instead of a bullet in the brain, Viktor got a job, and over the years had risen quickly through the ranks within the organization. "Mhiki, if there is anything to this, I will know soon, I promise."

"I know you will Viktor, see Lexi and he will arrange any surveillance or tech support you need, this may be nothing but I want to be absolutely sure before we let it go. I have a feeling that your friend was holding back, it is what I would have done, and you believed so from talking to him when he was drunk." Mickey fixed Viktor with another hard stare and said, "A pity I could not meet him, I suggest you get busy my friend, time is money." With that, Viktor and his two goons departed the restaurant.

Outside on the street, one of Viktor's goons said, "Jesus, he must have been a scary son of a bitch when he was GRU." Viktor gave him a hard look then punched the man right on the tip of his nose. "Listen to me you idiot, he is scary now and he is pissed off, do you understand." The big Russian was holding a handkerchief to his nose trying to stem the flow of blood from the damage just inflicted by his boss. Ivan nodded his head and said, "Yes boss, I know, I'm sorry, what do we do now." Viktor looked at Stephan and Ivan for a moment then said, "Let's go to the club, I need a drink and I need time to think, we have to get something on this soon or we are all in very deep shit my friends." The GRU was and still is the largest single intelligence organization in the world. GRU is the acronym for the Russian Main Intelligence Administration. It encompasses all branches of military intelligence, satellite reconnais-sance, signals intelligence, electronic intelligence, as well as several less distinct branches that are normally found as their own organization in other countries. It also has a particularly nasty branch over which it has operational control and that is Spetznaz forces. Spetznaz, literally translated means Special Purpose. They are the cream of the crop of all branches of the Russian military and are trained extensively in all aspects of unconventional warfare, and they are very good at it. Prior to a little snag in his career, Mhiki had been a full colonel in the third directorate, third direction of the GRU, in charge of Spetznaz operations in Afghanistan during the former Soviet Unions foray in that country. Mhiki was a particularly nasty bastard and made excellent use of other former intelligence officers in his newfound career. The fact that a very large part of their former occupation was counter-intelligence made it possible for Mhiki and his people to keep the extent and methods of their criminal activities hidden from law enforcement agencies. It should come as no surprise that the majority of enforcers employed by Mhiki were former Spetznaz soldiers, as was the case with Stephan and Ivan.

After the trio arrived at Viktor's club, Viktor dialed a number he had committed to memory a long time ago. Lexi was not at all pleased to hear the phone ringing and was tempted not to answer it, he had been trying to get this petite little Armenian waitress alone for almost a week now and finally having done that, the phone was a most unwelcome intrusion. This call was coming in on a line dedicated strictly to business and could not be ignored. Lexi answered the phone, "Yes."

"Lexi, this is Viktor; I have an address for you, actually, you already know it. I need the lawyer's place watched twenty-four seven until I say different. Also, I trust you still have the address on the woman he had dinner with the night before we picked him up, watch her place too and find out everything about her, I want to know where she works, everything, you know the drill."

"Of course Viktor, I will contact you and let you know when everything is in place and keep you apprised of any progress."

"Very well, I will leave you to your work, but be advised my friend, this is very important." Viktor said nothing else and hung up the line. On the other end, Lexi thought this might be interesting, better than the surveillance for blackmail purposes that he had become so used to over the last few years. Lexi made a phone call, left his instructions, hung up then turned his attention back to the waitress. "I am so sorry my dear, business, but enough of that." The girl simply smiled as she began to unbutton her blouse.

Eggers was sitting at his desk looking through what he had on the Andrews killing, which was not much more than a dead body and a bunch of unanswered questions. Brady, sensing his thoughts by the look on his partners face said, "Well what do we do now, we already talked to everybody at his office and we got shit."

"Yeah, I know, I think we should go back to the McTeal woman's office, maybe she knows more than she was telling us."

"Couldn't hurt," said Brady, "let's go."

When Eggers and Brady Arrived at Alex's office they were surprised to find Gladys the leggy secretary in a heated discussion with a man they both assumed to be old man Brookman. "Excuse me," said Eggers, "is there a problem here, we would like to speak with Miss McTeal if we could." Brookman looked at the two detectives for a moment, then said, "And just who in the hell are you two." The two detectives shared a shrug and showed Brookman their shields. "Great, just great, now what. I really wish I could help you but Alex did not come to work today and she didn't call in either, I've had Gladys calling her place all morning trying to get hold of her and all she can get is her machine. Not only that, you two aren't the only ones who have come by looking for her today." Brady shot Eggers a questioning look and said, "Really, who else has been looking for her."

"A couple of Euro trash types, nice clothes and all but something wasn't right."

"How so," said Eggers.

"Well," said Brookman, "they claimed to work for an office furnishing firm and said Alex had contracted them to redo her office, but I don't buy it."

"Why not?" asked Brady. "Well, for one thing, we use our own people for that sort of thing and Gladys says that she hasn't heard Alex say anything about any new furniture, and if Alex was going to redo the office I should think that Gladys would know." Brady looked at Gladys and asked, "What were they like Ma'am."

"Well for starters, don't call me Ma'am, I'm not that old, and to answer your question, they were assholes." Eggers couldn't suppress a smirk and Brady was grinning when he asked, "What makes you say that they were assholes," he caught himself before he let another ma'am slip out and finished his sentence with a polite nod and said, "Gladys." She smiled, catching the gesture and said, "Well, they were pushy, you know, they insisted that I contact her immediately and didn't want to believe that I had no idea where she was, and when they left, they didn't leave a card or a number to reach them at."

"That is strange."

"What is all this about," asked Brookman. "I'll tell you when I find out," said Eggers. "So, nobody knows where Ms McTeal is or what she is doing." Brady produced one of his cards (the ones with his home number on the back) and gave it to Gladys. "I want you to call me as soon as you hear from Ms McTeal ok, and I mean any time, day or night." Eggers thought he detected a slight twinkle in Gladys's eye as she took the card from Brady. "Ok," said Eggers, "if we hear from her, we call you, same same ok."

"Gladys," said Brady, "we may need for you to come down to the station and look at some pictures. Maybe we can find your bogus furniture guys." Gladys smiled and said, "Just tell me when."

"I'll call you here at the office later after we check out a couple of other things. Let's go by her apartment and see if she just doesn't want to answer the phone today. We'll be in touch." Outside the building, two men in a telephone company van noted the time of the detectives' departure. As Eggers and Brady pulled away from Bookman's office building, one of the men in the van placed a call on a cellular phone, it was answered by one of the two men dressed as local cable TV guys who had just finished a thorough search of Alex's apartment. During their stay, the two men had installed a few rather sophisticated listening devices, in the hopes of finding out just where the hell the lawyer's girlfriend had gotten off to. The two phony cable guys left Alex's apartment and one of the two janitors noted their presence and thought it odd since he hadn't seen Ms McT all day. *To hell with it,* he thought, *none of my business.* As Brady and Eggers were en route to Alex's apartment, Eggers started in on his partner. "What the fuck was that all about?" Brady acted hurt. "Why, whatever do you mean boss."

"Cut the shit, in case you forgot, we are investigating a rather brutal homicide, and you are making moves on someone who may have information on this case."

"Hey relax man; I'm just trying to pump her for some information."

"Yeah right," said Eggers smiling, "you are trying to pump her all right, but I'm not so sure you have the best interest of the great city of New York in mind." Brady smiled back at his partner of five years and said, "Oh ye of little faith, I do what I must in the interest of fighting crime and keeping our streets safe for good and decent people."

"Have you ever been with a woman that you didn't meet on the job," asked Eggers. "God knows I try not to," said Brady, "look, this way I already have a good idea if they are whacked or not before I take them out, and there is a lot to be said for that. You and Chloe have been married for what, eleven years now and you have a perfect marriage, you the detective sergeant and her, the trauma nurse, and you both see the shittiest side of this city every day and manage not to take it home to your kids. Christ but I do love both of you, but you two are so fucking happy you just don't notice how rotten some other married couples we know treat each other, you two are the exception to the rule and don't forget how lucky you are, and tell Chloe to stop playing cupid, remember the last blind date she set me up with." Eggers had to smile, how could he forget, it had been a pretty nurse that Chloe knew from work and like a lot of women, had been interested in meeting the handsome detective. Brady stood five eleven in his socks and weighed in at about one ninety five with very little body fat. As it turns out, the only reason Chloe's friend had wanted to date a cop was to have someone to unload on and blame for all of the horrible things that she had seen people perpetrate upon one and another. Brady had sat in silence during her tirade, but when he finally got a chance to talk, Brady couldn't convince her that all of the evil rotten shit that happened in the city was not the direct result of the police not doing their jobs. After dropping the wacky nurse off, Brady had called Eggers to tell him to make sure and shoot him before he went on another blind date.

As the two detectives arrived at Alex's apartment, another cellular call was made, this time from the inside of the cable TV van parked just down the street. The man known as Lexi, also a former GRU officer who specialized in surveillance and counter intelligence answered that call. "Yes, I see, report back to me after they have left, they may or may not attempt to gain entrance to the apartment, but if they do record any conversation and forward it to me immediately over secure line." With that the former intelligence officer hung up.

Inside the building, Eggers and Brady went to Alex's apartment door and knocked several times and received no answer. "I don't like it," said Eggers.

"Yeah, me neither, want me to pick it or should I find the super," asked Brady. As the two men were making up their minds, the janitor came around the corner and was startled to see the two cops standing by Alex's door. "Who are you guys?" asked the janitor. Brady showed the man his badge and the janitor simply nodded, and said, "So, what do you guys want with Miss McT?"

"Actually, we just wanted to find out where she is and make sure she is all right, nobody has seen her since yesterday before lunchtime," said Brady.

"Come to think of it, I didn't see her yesterday or this morning either, but sometimes she would stay with her boyfriend so I didn't think much of it, but there is a strange thing though, right before you guys showed up, I saw two cable guys coming out of the apartment, but if she ain't here, how'd they get in?" Brady and Eggers exchanged nervous glances, then Eggers asked the janitor if he had a pass key, which he did. Charlie, the man said his name was, opened the door without even being asked. Once inside the trio began looking around. Nothing appeared to be disturbed, and the only things out of place were apparently yesterday's breakfast dishes and coffee cup in the kitchen sink. "Let's have a look in the bedroom." As Eggers moved towards the door, Brady pulled out his pistol and nodded. Charlie suddenly looked as if he really wanted to be somewhere else. Eggers took a deep breath and quickly opened the door and stood to one side as Brady bolted through the door only to find the room empty with the bed neatly made. "Shit," said Brady, "what do you think?"

"I dunno, let's have a look in the closets and see if it looks like she took a trip, Charlie, you can keep an eye on us to make sure we don't disturb anything ok, we just want to get an idea for what's going on here ok."

"Yeah, fine with me, this shit has me curious too." Eggers opened the closet doors and saw no gaps in Alex's wardrobe that would indicate that she had packed up and left, and that assessment was further backed up by the presence of the two Samsonite suitcases under the bed. While the trio stood back in the living room, Brady said, "I don't get it man, she just dropped out of sight completely, but we know she left the office of her own free will, and then just disappeared."

"What I don't understand is why the cable guys would be here at all," said Charlie. "What?" said Brady.

"Look at the TV, the box says direct TV, she don't got no cable."

"No shit," said Eggers, "that explains the movers as well."

"What movers?" asked Charlie. "Never mind about the movers, I'm calling for forensics, my guess is that the movers and cable guys work for the same people and came here for the same reason that we did. I want this place gone through with a fine-tooth comb." The passenger in the cable van swore viciously upon hearing this conversation and transmitted the recording to Lexi over an encrypted line as the driver sped away from the building.

Chapter Five

St.. Thomas USVI

Alex awoke Friday to one of the most beautiful mornings she had ever seen. She walked out on the balcony and watched in awe as an enormous cruise liner made its way past the hotel into the harbor at Charlotte Amalie. After standing out on the balcony for a while, Alex went down to the dining room and ordered coffee and breakfast. While she was drinking her coffee and waiting on her food, Alex started looking through the brochures advertising the local sailing charters. She kept what Bob had told her in mind, stay away from the large commercial charters and find one of the less conspicuous privately owned boats. One in particular caught her eye, it was a Gulfstar 50 named, 'PRIVATEER', and Alex had always liked the big Gulfstar's lines. She decided she would go have a look at the boat later in the day. After breakfast Alex went to the hotel gift shop and bought two bikinis, and decided that the first thing she should do was lay out by the pool and get some sun, she had no intention of walking around St Thomas looking like an albino.

Alex had something else to check out before she went to the marina, a special treat to herself. After applying a generous portion of SPF-30 sun block to her exposed skin, Alex settled into a lounger and started to read a trashy romance novel. What the hell, she thought, after all, this whole affair was about self indulgence wasn't it, and so, by god that was just what she was going to do. She lay out by the pool until about two thirty flip flopping occasionally to evenly distribute the rays. Alex went to her room and put a pair of shorts on over her bikini bottom and selected a thin white blouse which she slipped over her shoulders and tied the tail in a knot about her waist. She topped off her ensemble with a straw Panama hat, and then stopped to look at herself in the mirror. The transformation from just a day ago was almost complete. Alex looked at the reflection looking back at her in the mirror and decided with a smile, that this was someone that she would have to get to know.

Outside the lobby Alex asked one of the drivers to take her to Air Center Helicopter's office, the cabby told her it was just a few minutes away and so off they went. When Alex walked inside, she saw a couple of helicopters with men working on them but didn't really see an office. About that time a petite woman wearing a blue flight suit walked up and said, "Can I help you Miss?"

"Why, yes, I came to check on getting an air tour of the islands." The petite pilot introduced herself as Mary and asked Alex to follow her upstairs to the office. Mary rolled out a nautical chart of the U.S. and British islands for Alex to look at. "I had no idea that they were all so close," exclaimed Alex. "Yeah, said Mary, wait till you see them from the bird."

"When do you think we could arrange it, my schedule is open." Mary let out a delightful little laugh and said that she had a bird ready to go immediately and all that needed to be done was arrange payment. Mary pointed out that rental on a Bell Jet Ranger was not cheap. Alex assured her that was no problem and decided that she could see what she wanted to see in about an hour. When they walked out to the little blue and white helicopter, Mary surprised Alex by opening up the front left door and saying, "Ok hop in."

"I thought I had to ride in back."

"Well you can if you want to but the ride is a lot more fun up front. Here, let me help get you strapped in." After Mary had Alex securely strapped into the seat, she showed her how to use the Dave Clark head set. "The mike is voice activated so you don't have to do anything but talk, but wait until I say it's ok so you don't step on the radios while I'm trying to listen or talk ok."

"You're the boss; I'm just here for the ride." Mary went around to the right side of the helicopter and got strapped in. While Mary was fidgeting with the controls and starting the engine, it had become brutally hot inside the aircraft. Sensing her discomfort, Mary said, "Don't worry, as soon as I turn on the fan it'll cool off quick." Alex got a bit of a rush as the turbine spooled up to speed and the rotor system began to spin, she had never been in a helicopter before and it was something she had always wanted to do. Well here she was. Once Mary was satisfied with her instrument scan, she said something unintelligible to Alex on the radio, then using the collective lever on the left side of her seat; Mary added power and the nimble little helicopter became airborne. As they cleared the airport, Mary sharply banked the helicopter to the left and said, "That's Crown Bay Marina right down there below you, isn't that where you said the boat you wanted to hire is."

"Yeah, that's the place I guess, this is great!"

"Ok," said Mary, "where to next?"

"Hey, you're flying this thing." Mary flashed a big smile and said, "True enough but for the next hour it's your machine. Tell you what, if you're sailing out of Crown Bay towards the BVI [British Virgin Islands], let's follow the route you'll be sailing so you can get another perspective."

"Sounds good to me," said Alex. Mary did a wide sweeping turn around the inner bay of Charlotte Amalie then skirted Water Island and flew right past Alex's hotel then turned east toward St John. As they neared the eastern tip of St Thomas, Mary pointed out Red Hook and the St Thomas Yacht Club. Turning left Mary said, "Always gotta watch out for para-sailers through here, just wouldn't do to run over one. Ok, on the right is Cruz Bay St. John, great partying there, and ahead on the right is Tortola and that is where the BVI starts." Alex felt like she should say something but the view was more breathtaking than she could ever have imagined. Aside from the major islands, there were a number of other tiny ones all around the principal islands. "Tell you what, let's just go straight to Jost Van Dyke, that's it right in front of us then we cut between Tortola and Virgin Gorda." As the helicopter approached Jost Van Dyke, Mary said, "That beach on your left is white bay and in front of us is a mountain." Mary playfully whipped the little machine around the bay and said, "Picture this little harbor with over four hundred boats in it, and another hundred or so at white bay." It seemed inconceivable to Alex that so many boats could fit into such a tiny harbor. "Why on earth would people even try to fit that many boats in there?"

"Happens every year at New Year's, third biggest New Year's Eve party on the planet and the only way to get there is by boat. People literally come from all over the world to be here for it. Ok let's head for the east end of Tortola, don't talk for a minute, I have to check in with Beef Island and let them know we are coming around." As Mary was talking to Beef Island, which is actually joined to Tortola by a causeway, Alex noted the island rapidly getting larger in the windscreen. When she was certain they were about to become one with the rocky coastline, Mary banked the bird hard to the left and then pulled the nose up sharply, then as soon as they had cleared the ridge, Mary pushed the nose over into a dive hugging the terrain. For a few moments, Alex was scared shitless, and then she looked over and saw the childlike playful smile on Mary's face. At that point Alex began to relax and enjoy the ride. *God, she is having so much fun,* Alex thought, she had never gotten that much delight out of anything that she had done. As they wrapped around the east end of Tortola, Mary climbed up to three hundred feet and began to follow the south coast. As they approached a large harbor, Mary came up on the intercom and said, "That is Road Town, it's more or less the capital of the BVI, neat place to hang out." After a couple of laps around the harbor, Mary turned south and dropped down until they were just off the water and said, "See that island straight ahead, the one with the cliffs that face to the west, that's Norman Island, I want to show you the caves." As they neared the island, Alex saw an enormous bay full of boats on mooring balls, Mary saw her looking and smiled and said, "Later." Alex noticed that all along the cliff line that was a sheer drop into the water, there were dingys and small boats tied to a mooring line that ran the length of the cliff, and there were what looked like a hundred people in the water swimming in and out of the caves. Mary positioned the helicopter so that the swimmers were between them and the cliff and began to fly sideways while pointing out which caves were the best ones to swim into. Satisfied that they had a good enough look at the caves, Mary cranked a hard climbing right turn and brought them around over the mouth of the bay at about three hundred feet. "Behold the bight at Norman Island." While Mary circled the harbor slowly, people on boats were waving at the helicopter, and all Alex could do was to say, "Oooh."

"Yeah, it still has that effect on me too. You see that building over there on the beach, that is the only structure on the whole island and it's a bar and restaurant that used to be called Billy Bones, now its Pirates, and see that big old sail boat over there, that is the William Thornton, more commonly referred to as the Willie-T, great food and cheap drinks." Well kiddo, time to head back, how you liking it so far?"

"My god, I am having a blast, really, I had no idea it would be this much fun."

"Yeah, my job sucks," said Mary as she skimmed the waves heading towards the south side of St. John. The rest of the trip was spent in silence and Alex couldn't remember being more relaxed than she was right at that moment. After landing back at the pad, Alex followed Mary back into the office and paid her bill in cash and threw in an extra hundred for a tip. Alex caught a cab to Crown Bay Marina from the airport and got off right at the entrance at the beginning of the piers. She knew from the flyer that 'PRIVATEER' was in slip thirty two, so she decided to just walk the docks and look for the boat before she tried to contact Jack Schmidt, owner/skipper. She had seen a couple of people at the hotel wearing T-shirts with a picture of a sailboat on the back and the words I KNOW JACK SCHMIDT, printed underneath the picture, kind of cute she thought. When Alex got to slip thirty-two, the boat she saw was beautiful, all white with dark brown trim. All of the teak work was left unvarnished but treated with teak oil. Fifty footer, cutter rigged with all roller-furling sails, and unlike most boats that have the main sail furler coming out of the mast, this one came off the boom. The boat had a spacious center cockpit that had been customized with a hard top and zip up clear plastic windows to completely block out the elements. On the stern of the boat was a twelve foot rigid hull inflatable dingy with a center console and a Yamaha twenty-five horse outboard. And that rig was hanging from a set of electrically controlled davits. "Oh yeah, I could cruise around on that," said Alex. She was startled when a voice right behind her said, "You can if you got the money." Alex turned around and saw a big, wide shouldered, blue eyed man with sun bleached brown hair smiling at her.

Alex just stood there looking at him until the man stuck out his hand and said, "Jack Schmidt, owner and chief swab jockey of the 'PRIVATEER'." Alex shook his hand and said, "Hi I'm Alex McTeal, nice to meet you Jack."

"Madame, the pleasure is all mine, is there anything I can do for you?"

"Actually there is, I wanted to talk to you about chartering your boat." Jack looked at Alex for a moment as if considering what to do and then said, "Well, tell you what, let's walk over to Tickles, it's the Marina restaurant and bar," Jack pointed to the building and said, "see, right there."

"Sure, why not I could use a drink." As Alex followed Jack toward the restaurant she thought that Jack looked like the charter boat poster boy, big, and good looking in a rugged sort of way. She guessed him to be about six-foot even and close to two hundred and forty pounds, but he still managed to look lean. Tickles itself looked like a marina bar should look; open air with barstools three hundred sixty degrees around the bar and tables around that. Jack asked where Alex wanted to sit and she perched on a barstool. Jack smiled and sat on the stool next to her and said, "Cindy, cocktails for me and my guest." Cindy smiled and popped open a Carib beer for Jack and said to Alex, "What will you have Hun?"

"I'll have a gin and tonic with lime." Jack took a long pull on his beer and then asked Alex, "So, when are thinking about a charter?"

"Well, when would you be available?" *Just my luck,* thought Jack, *I got a live one and the damn boat is broke.* "Well, right now I'm waiting on a fuel boost pump for the gen set, that should be here in a couple of days, I had to order it off island. Then I need to hire a mate and cook, the one I had flew back to the States a couple of days ago because her sister is sick and I don't know when or if she is coming back. Whoever I hire, I need to interview and check references and so on. All the freelancers that I normally use already have other gigs and it's high season."

"How much does the boat and crew go for a week?" Jack looked at Alex for a moment and said, "It's pretty steep, eight grand a week with all provisions provided by yours truly and that includes three meals a day snacks, beer, wine, booze, scuba diving or snorkeling and the grand tour of the islands. But like I said, right now, I'm short reliable crew." Jack sat watching the gears turn in Alex's head. He could see she was thinking hard about something, then she said, "What do you pay the mate slash cook?" For a minute Jack wasn't sure if Alex wanted a charter or a job. "The mate gets two hundred a day, cash." Alex mulled that over for a minute, then ordered the two of them another round, noticing that Jack had finished his beer, then said, "Ok, so that's fourteen hundred a week out of eight grand a week and I assume that provisions come out of that remaining sixty six hundred. Here is a proposal for you. I can be the crew as well as guest; in fact now that I think about it, I would really prefer it that way. You see I'm down here by myself and I would feel kinda weird having people sail me around while I do nothing, this is my dream vacation and I want to have fun. Now before you answer, you should know that I am a fairly accomplished sailor. I grew up sailing every summer in Newport and I've done a good bit of racing. You subtract the Mates wages from the fee and I'll do the rest, and, I'll have you know, I am an excellent cook."

Jack wasn't sure what to say and Alex, sensing his consternation, gave Jack her special you can't win smile she had perfected on her father and said, "Oh, come on say yes, it'll be fun, and besides, if you say yes I'll pay you for two weeks, cash in advance." The gears in Jack's head were turning at a pretty high RPM right now, on one hand this was very irregular, but the weeks of down time had bitten into his cash reserves and he hadn't been able to book any charters through his broker. This gig could bail him out of the hole, and Alex was not at all painful to look at, in fact, she was down right gorgeous with a body to match. The temptation to say yes was very strong but sitting there looking at Alex, Jack wasn't sure exactly which part of his anatomy was trying to make this decision. Finally, Jack looked at Alex and said, "Well, if you are sure that's what you want to do, I guess it's ok with me, but I still have to wait for that fuel pump for the generator before we can get underway. We are also going to have to go over a sail plan and make up a provisions list. As I see it, it will be at least three, maybe four days before we can get underway." Alex thought about that for a minute and then said, "Does that mean we have a deal?" Jack looked into those green eyes and knew he was had. "Yes, I guess it does, Alex, congratulations you just hired yourself a boat and skipper." Alex smiled and said, "Thank you Jack, this is exactly what I was looking for, I really just want to go sailing around for a while and I'm not really into the regular tours or cruise ships, this is going to be fun." For some inexplicable reason, the old alarm bells inside Jack's head were going off. He didn't know why, how dangerous could a beautiful, single, thirty some odd year old woman with money be anyway. Yeah, right. "Look," said Jack, "here is one of my cards; it has my cell number on it, give me a call in the morning and we can meet up and I'll show you the boat, I have to go check on some other stuff right now."

"Ok, sounds great, what time should I call in the morning."

"Just make sure it isn't before seven," Jack said with a grin. Alex smiled back at Jack and said, "I'll call around nine or so."

"That should be fine; all I had planned for tomorrow was some busy work on the boat." Jack left Alex at the bar and headed for the parking lot where he got into an old Wrangler and drove off. Alex was going to leave but decided to have another drink and talk to Cindy the bartender for a while. After Cindy had brought Alex her drink, Alex said, "So, how well do you know Jack?" Cindy gave Alex a coquettish grin and said, "Not as well as I'd like to that's for sure." The two women laughed at that then Cindy said, "Actually he's a great guy, you know, never a bad word about anyone, always ready to help anyone out who needs it. He got here about five years ago and bought that boat of his for a song. Of course it was all fucked up at the time; it was a Marilyn boat, after the storm hit it was across Main Street sitting in front of the Greenhouse. Anyway, after he got her seaworthy he spent some time sailing around the islands getting to know his way around, then he hired a cook and started doing charters. He used most of the profits for the first few years customizing the shit out of that boat. It really is the best thing afloat in its class in the islands."

"You seem to know a lot about him," commented Alex. Cindy just laughed and pointed out that they were on an island in a marina community and there weren't a lot of secrets. Alex thought about that for a moment and smiled. "I guess you've got a point there, does he usually use the same crew?"

"Well, usually the same type, young, pretty, and bikini clad, it plays really well with the tourists; you know out cruising the Caribbean on a beautiful boat with the beautiful people. You thinking about doing a charter."

"Yeah, I made the deal right before he left."

"No shit," said Cindy. Alex smiled. "Yeah, no shit."

"Great," said Cindy, "who'd he get for crew."

"Just little old me, I got him to drop the price if I did the cooking and helped out with the boat, I'm an experienced sailor and I just want to go sailing around for a while. I love to sail and I really think I'll enjoy it more this way." Cindy gave her an astonished look and shook her head as if to clear it then said, "Well that's a new one, but if it works for you go for it. When are you guys getting underway?"

"Couple of days I think. Jack has to wait on a part for his generator, so I guess it'll be right after that. I'm going to look at the boat tomorrow and then we'll work out a plan from there."

"Cool, I guess I'll bee seein ya around for at least a couple of days then."

"Yeah, I guess so," said Alex, "well, I should be going now, see you later." Alex paid her tab and took a cab from the marina back to her hotel, she had a pretty good buzz going and she wanted some rest before she went out later for dinner, and maybe a couple of drinks. Cindy watched Alex leave and had to grin. Jack my boy; I think you just met your match.

Chapter Six

Mhiki sat in his office with a decidedly pissed off look on his face. Viktor and Lexi shifted uncomfortably in their chairs. "So, the surveillance on the girlfriend's apartment is blown, and we don't know anything at all about where she is, and Lexi, I thought you were a professional, that stunt with the furniture company was shit. NYPD will, no doubt find the listening devices you left in the girl's apartment, and they are looking at Europeans as suspects." Lexi cleared his throat before speaking and said, "Mhiki it isn't a problem, the cops don't know any more than we do, and the men that were sent to her office have no records so they can't be identified by any who saw them and the only person who got a look at them was the secretary. I do however; now have copies of all of Ms McTeal's credit card account numbers which were obtained from the mail at her apartment. The first time she uses one of them we will know where to look for her. Also I have one of my people checking all departing flights, trains and rental agencies, even if she did not use a credit card, we can trace her by name, technology is a wonderful thing my friend." Of course, none of this improved Mhiki's mood any, the lawyer was dead and therefore of no use, and his woman had obviously skipped town. Mhiki knew that it had been pure chance that the technicians had been blown, but he was still pissed about the furniture scam. That had drawn some truly unwanted attention. It might be best to just let the whole thing go, but Mickey had a gut feeling that the lawyer had been holding out.

"We will wait and see what your people can turn up on the girl Lexi. Until then, take no further actions that may draw attention. If you locate the girl, do nothing before contacting me; understood. Contact me immediately, now get out." Outside in the cold, while waiting for Lexi's driver, Viktor said, "It gives me the creeps when he looks at me like that." Lexi laughed and said, "If you had known him in Afghanistan my friend, you would be shitting yourself at this very moment. We need to come up with something soon and all sins will be forgiven. Cheer up Viktor, he likes you, he would probably just kill you, no muss, no fuss, as the Americans say." With that, Lexi slapped him on the back and got into his car. Viktor did not feel any better at all.

Eggers was on the phone with a buddy of his in the intel department trying to see if the local Russian mob had been doing anything unusual lately. Meanwhile, Brady was with Gladys, going through the photos of thugs with known Russian mob connections and getting nowhere. The Russian angle just felt right, this whole business just seemed their style. After a while, the three of them sat in silence for a while before Brady looked at Gladys and said, "Are you sure you don't know more about this? Because if you do, I need to know now. Your boss may be in deep shit, and we can't help her if we don't know what is going on."

"I honestly don't know," said Gladys. "Ok," said Eggers, "I guess that's about it for now, thanks for coming by. If you hear from Ms McTeal, please have her call us immediately." Gladys frowned and said she would do what she could. After she had left, Brady said, "Well, any luck with the Intel weenies?"

"No, not a damn thing, I don't think anything has happened to Ms McTeal yet because they can't find her either. Tommy said that the bugs they got out of her apartment were pretty high tech stuff; in fact he said it was the same stuff that the East German Stassi used. They were the Russian trained secret police. I want to know what Andrews was working on before he got himself croaked. Let's go by his office and see if we can make some kind of connection." At the offices of Dewey and Wilson, William Dewy, senior partner received Eggers and Brady rather coolly. "I don't know how his last case would interest you, it was a simple estate closure for an old widow, it couldn't possibly be connected. Mrs. Richter had been a client for almost eleven years; she retained us after her husband died. He died without a will and as the only living relative; Mrs. Richter was the sole heir. After her husband died, I drew up her will personally." Eggers spoke first. "Mr. Dewy, was there a lot of money involved, property, valuable art or anything like that?"

"No, the Richters were comfortable but not really rich. Karl and Hanna immigrated to the States after World War Two, and as I understand it Karl worked for a consulting firm until he retired sometime in the fifties. He and Hanna lived in the same house until Karl died in late eighty-nine and Hanna died about three months ago."

"I don't suppose you would have old Karl's social security number handy would you?"

"Detective, as you know that is privileged information." Brady cut him off before he could say another word. "Yeah, and he's fuckin dead so don't bust my balls, we wouldn't be here if we had anything else to go on. All we want to do is find out who killed him. Maybe, if we can find out why he was killed, we can find out who killed him. Seeing as he worked for you, I should think you would want to help find his killers." Dewy considered that for a moment then said, "I apologize gentlemen, as I'm sure you know this has been very difficult for me. Robert was under review for a partnership and we were very close friends, his death and the manner in which it occurred hit me rather hard." Eggers allowed a pause then asked, "Mr. Dewy, have you had anyone else, say people you don't know asking about Mr. Andrews since his death, you know, discrete inquiries that might have seemed out of place?"

"No I can't say that I have, someone from the post called and we just gave them the standard bio stuff, but that's been it. Well if you really think it might help, I'll give you a complete copy of the Richter file." Dewy pressed the intercom button on his desk and instructed his secretary to copy the file at once. "Detectives, I can only hope that you will make certain that this does not become public knowledge, I agree that client privilege does not exactly apply in a case where both clients are deceased, but potential clients may not feel the same way."

"You can count on our discretion," said Eggers. "Very well then, if you will excuse me, I need time to go over some notes prior to my next meeting. My secretary will give you the file on your way out."

Even though the lawyer had cooperated in the end, Brady, who had the typical cop's dislike of lawyers did not like this smug little bastard at all, and was somewhat rankled at being dismissed as if he and his partner were peasants. Oh well, in this guy's mind, he and Eggers were peasants. Brady thanked him for his cooperation, and the detectives exited his office. As promised the secretary had the file waiting. As she handed the file to Eggers she said, "I hope this can help you in some way, I really do, Mr. Andrews was a kind and decent man. Please, find the people who did this and punish them."

"Thank you ma'am, and you have our word, we're going to do our best." She simply nodded her head and went back to her desk.

Eggers and Brady were back at the station house looking over the Richter file and had to agree, there was nothing of any real significance there. That was until Eggers got to the part about the safe deposit box. "Now here's something interesting," Eggers said to his partner, "the safe deposit box."

"Yeah, go on."

"Well, it would appear that Herr Richter opened a safe deposit box at the Chase Manhattan Bank back in forty-six not long after he come across the pond from the fatherland. Bank records show that he accessed the box several times a year for about the first two or three years, and then only once every couple of years after that up until eighty-nine, which was the last time the box was opened until Andrews cleaned it out three weeks ago. And guess what was in the box according to Andrews's written inventory, nothing but some old photos according to the receipt. I'm going to call that prick Dewy and see if we can get our hands on those pictures. I don't think the old guy was going back there all those times to reminisce, know what I mean. I want Tommy to do a full background check on our dear departed German friend, I want to know what he did in Germany during the war, what his immigration status was when he came here, who the consulting firm he worked for was, how much he made, did he cheat on his taxes, everything we can find out about this guy ok."

Brady considered all of this for a moment then said, "Looks like that box might be what ties this thing together. I have a hard time believing that the old guy would keep that box open and inactive for the last years of his life if all he had in there were some old pictures."

"Yeah well maybe, depends on what the pictures were of. I think there was something else in the box that was maybe worth a shitload of money. No relatives to claim it and everything else of value is getting auctioned off, Andrews finds whatever it is and figures it's time to retire and tries to fence whatever it is through some shady Russian types and gets double crossed, then whacked. The fact that whoever did him is still sniffing around means that they didn't get it, whatever it was."

"Yep, that would also explain why the girl split," said Brady. "I really don't think she knew what was going on when we interviewed her, but sometime after that; I just don't know, somehow she must have gotten a hold of whatever it was that Andrews had and it either scared the shit out of her, or it was worth big bucks or both. Then she did a Houdini."

"Alright," said Eggers, "you seem to enjoy Gladys's company, pull her in. Send a cruiser over there right fucking now, if she comes nice, fine, if not have them book her on an obstruction charge. I'll have them put her in interrogation two, you watch while I start on her, me bad cop, you good cop. In the meantime I want you to get the ball rolling on the old kraut, call Tommy, I'm going to have our people start digging into the late Mr. Andrews past, somewhere in there is a connection to our East European friends."

Viktor was sitting in his apartment smoking a joint with his favorite little blue eyed plaything when the phone rang. "Yes."

"Viktor, Lexi, this is your lucky day my friend. Alexis McTeal boarded an American Airlines flight for St. Thomas in the US Virgin Islands two days ago. It took a while to discover this because she paid cash for the ticket and has not used any of her credit cards since before she left New York. Ah Viktor my friend, this is great, to be on the hunt again instead of blackmailing politicians and business executives. Anyway I will allow you the pleasure of telling Mickey, you could use some points right now."

"Thank you Lexi, I will call you back after I talk to Mhiki." While Viktor was explaining the news, Mhiki began to smile a wicked humorless smile. Once Viktor had finished, Mhiki said, "I want you to tell Lexi to start checking all the hotels on that island, she isn't using credit cards but she will still have to use photo ID for transport or accommodations. I am sure he is already doing this but tell him anyway. Also have Lexi give you one of his men, one of the good ones. Take a digital camera with you; get some pictures of the girl and anyone she is with. Remember, you are not to confront her, surveillance only. Congratulations my friend, you are going to the Caribbean. Leave on the first available flight, take Stephan and Ivan as well, Lexi can make all the arrangements, and Viktor, this was a good break, don't fuck it up." With that Mhiki hung up.

Viktor immediately called Lexi back and relayed Mhiki's message. Lexi told Viktor to pack some comfortable clothes and wait by the phone, everything would be taken care of and he could meet the rest of the group at the airport. This may work out after all Viktor thought to himself; he might just make some more money out if the deal if he was lucky. If he wasn't, oh well it did no good to ponder that possibility.

Gladys had decided that it would be better to play nice with the two uniforms that came to get her. Upon her arrival at the station she was ushered straight into the interrogation room. She was putting up a good front; at least she thought she was. After sitting alone in the interrogation room for almost twenty minutes, she began to get worried. This was of course the exact effect Eggers had in mind. He had been watching Gladys through the window since her butt had hit the chair. Eggers, satisfied that she was squirming sufficiently said to Brady, "Ok it's show time, come in on cue, but not until. She may just start talking, if she does then come right in, if not wait for the signal."

"Got it." Gladys was startled when Eggers stepped into the room. Years of doing this and the look on Gladys's face spoke volumes. Brady caught it as well and was disappointed; he actually liked this woman. "I'm sorry I took so long; there were a couple of things I had to follow up on before we get started. Can I get you anything before we start, some coffee or maybe some water or a soft drink?"

"No thank you." Bingo thought Eggers, no *hey what is this all about*, or *hey I want my fucking lawyer*, or any of that other indignant crap. Yes, Gladys would tell all. "Ok I'll get right to it. What did Ms McTeal tell you after we left her office, and do not try to bullshit me lady because I am in no mood for it." Eggers demeanor caught Gladys completely off guard, she just sat there wide-eyed staring at Eggers, not knowing what to do or say. Eggers didn't give her time to recover. Eggers was even bigger than his partner, standing six foot three and weighing in at two hundred twenty-five pounds. With his piercing gray eyes and military style haircut, he was an imposing figure. "Cut the shit we know all about the safe deposit box. We also know from other witnesses that your boss left the building less than an hour after we did. What did she tell you and where did she go?"

Outside the room, Brady felt tightness in his gut as he watched his partner grill Gladys. Even Eggers felt bad, this was a decent woman trying to protect her boss and friend, nothing but natural loyalty, but they had to find out what she knew. "I don't know anything," proclaimed Gladys with a pleading and shaky voice. "Goddamnit, that's bullshit and we both know it," said Eggers as he slammed his palm down on the table right next to the terrified woman. That was also the signal for Brady to come into the room.

When Brady entered the room, Gladys had completely broken; she was sobbing while Eggers stood over her with a scowl on his face. "What the fuck is going on in here, what did you do to her?" shouted Brady playing his part. Gladys began to really wail then and Brady signaled for Eggers to move to the other end of the table. Brady pulled a chair over and sat down next to Gladys. "It's ok," he said soothingly, "everything's going to be just fine, I promise." Gladys regained some of her composure and looked Brady through tearful, puffy eyes and said, "I swear I don't know what this is about or where Alex went, I swear to God I don't. While you were in the office one of those bicycle messengers came to the office with a package from Mr. Andrews. I didn't know he was dead until later. After you guys left, I gave the package to Alex, she was in her office alone for about half an hour. She called me into her office and said she was leaving. She didn't say where or what it was about I swear. She said if I didn't hear from her within two weeks it was because she couldn't."

"Ok, how is she supposed to contact you?"

"I told her to leave a message at my brother's apartment and my brother could relay the message. I'm so sorry; I swear I don't know any more." Just as Brady was about to say something the intercom buzzed. Eggers took the call, smiled at Brady and motioned for him to step outside.

Brady told Gladys to try and relax and that he would be right back. Outside the interrogation room, Eggers said, "She was on a flight to St. Thomas within three hours after we left her office."

"No shit."

"Yep, No shit."

"What do we do with her," Brady said, indicating the still sobbing Gladys. "Time for you to play knight in shining armor. Take her home and take one of the lab guys with you to sweep her place. Chances are it's been bugged too. Once she gets settled down, meet me back here, I'm going to see how Tommy is doing with the other info. Don't fuck around, drop her off and then get right back here."

"I am crushed, what else do you think I would do?"

"Yeah, just get her tucked in and then get back here."

"You know," said Brady, "the McTeal woman hasn't committed any crime that we know of and she is like, way the fuck out of our jurisdiction. We don't know what was in the box, and no federal judge is going to issue a warrant on what we have. So what do we do about her?"

"Well, it's like this; we still have a homicide to solve, I want to find and watch the girl because I think these mutts are going to go after her. Frankly, I don't give a shit if she gets away with whatever it was in the box. But I am sick and tired of these Russian bastards shitting on my sidewalks and getting away with it. The goombas don't even mess with them. Remember when they sent some wise guys to tell the new kids not to play on their turf; the Ruskies whacked the messengers, sent their bodies back to the boss and told them what would happen to anyone who fucked with them. They told the Dons that there was enough to go around, deal with it or move on. Christ the Italians were complaining to us about it."

"Wow, you really do have a case of the ass about this don't you. Well guess what, they piss me off too, but we can't get shit on them."

"Well," said Eggers, "maybe we can change that. I have the makings of a plan forming in the devious half of my brain." Eggers smiled and said, "Go on, take Gladys home and don't tell her that we know where her boss went. And remember, get her settled in and get back here."

"Come on Dave, cut me some slack. Do you want me to stay until the lab guys are done?"

"Yeah, do that. And Sam, talk to Lenny about doing our places too, you never know."

"Damn, you got a point, I'll have him do it in the morning. You really think they would try to bug a cop's house."

"I don't know enough about these guys to know where or even if they draw the line. The only thing we know about these guys is that they are some mean sons of bitches. Get going, I have some calls to make."

Chapter Seven

Viktor sat at JFK Airport with Stephan and Ivan while waiting for Leo [short for Leonid] to arrive. Leo was a tracker. Armed with a special laptop computer he could hack into just about any computer system. Virtually no piece of personal information was safe from Leo once he had a credit card or social security number. Leo always found it amazing how easy it was to track people's movements and dealings with a computer. Leo had learned his trade as a GRU officer working within the Sixth Directorate, which is responsible for electronic intelligence. For Leo this type of work was child's play.

Viktor stood and greeted Leo as he joined the trio. "Well," said Leo, "this should be a lot more fun than my last assignment, Lexi sent me to Minnesota in the middle of January. I used to think Siberia was bad." The foursome shared a laugh at that, and then Viktor informed Leo that this was no vacation and that they had better damn well find the girl. "Viktor my dear friend, all I have to do is get to the island and plug in my little magic box here and she is as good as found. The only problem would be if she were staying somewhere that does not keep computer records. Something like a small guest house that just uses hand written receipts and such. Once the woman is located we are only to maintain surveillance and report to Lexi, he will decide what is and is not forwarded to Mhiki. Relax Viktor this is an easy job, I know Mickey is less than happy with you now but we will fix it."

Before Viktor could respond, the boarding call for first class passengers was passed on the intercom and the group moved into the line and boarded the plane. Viktor could not shake the specter of Mhiki's face the last time he had seen it. The deep scar that ran along the cheekbone on the right side of Mickey's face, and the notch missing out of his left ear looked menacing enough. But it was Mhiki's eyes that were really spooky; when he got angry they looked dead. Mickey could turn a man's blood to ice water with that stare and Viktor had no intention of having it directed at him again.

While Brady was on his way to Gladys's apartment along with Lenny and another forensics guy that he didn't know, Eggers called Mr. Dewey to request the photographs that were in the safe deposit box. Dewey wasn't pleased but informed the detective that he would give the photos to the patrolman that Eggers already had en route to the lawyer's office. Dewey gave Eggers another piece of interesting information; Andrews had done a bit of work as a public defender earlier in his career even after he had gone to work at D-W. Well that would be easy enough to check up on.

On the way to Gladys's apartment, Sam Brady sat in the back seat of the unmarked car with Gladys looking out the window not saying anything. Gladys was the first to break the silence. "I'm sorry; I thought I was helping Alex. I didn't know what to do." Brady looked at her and frowned. After a moment he said, "Yeah well, I can't really blame you for what you did, but if you had told us the truth we could have done something to protect her sooner."

"Do you think she needs protection?"

"I don't know. Do you have any idea at all what was in the box."

"No I don't, but Alex said she knew who had killed Bob and why. I think Bob didn't want her to do anything about it or she would have told you."

"Or," said Brady, "she was too scared to talk to us so she just ran. Listen Gladys, this is some serious shit, and the players are some very serious people. When we get to your apartment, don't say a word until Lenny says it's ok. I want to be sure your place isn't bugged before we talk there." It took only a few minutes for Lenny and his partner to disable the three listening devices inside Gladys's apartment. "Ok Sam we got three bugs identical to the other ones, same installation methodology. Definitely rigged by the same guy, place is clean now but you should know something. We are most likely under surveillance as we speak unless they bugged out when we came in. You see, these are high quality devices, but they are short range because of the power source. There are two ways to use these; one is to rig a remote recording device on the premises, which is not the case because it ain't here, or in another location like next door. That would mean our guys would have to stay there or gain entry to the premises occasionally to check the tapes and that is unlikely due to the risk of detection. Most likely, they've been doing shifts in a van or a sedan, monitoring the devices and photographing whoever comes in and out."

Brady considered that for a moment then said, "So just what are you trying to tell me."

"Well, I'm trying to tell you that these guys are no amateurs and you should really watch your ass buddy. It makes me nervous when the bad guys use stuff like this." Brady took Gladys into the kitchen, thought for a second then shouted to Lenny, "Hey, you sure the phone is clean?"

"Yeah, I told ya it was didn't I."

"Ok, look Gladys, I'm going to have a cruiser park across the street from your place, that should keep these guys away, plus they know their surveillance is blown so I really don't think they will be back. I need to use your phone to call Eggers and let him know what is going on. And hey, Lenny, hit me and Sam's places this evening ok."

"Yeah, I kinda thought you might say that. And don't worry; we don't need no stinking keys."

"Just get on it ok."

Chapter Eight

Jack was up at his customary six fifteen, went for a five-mile run, came back to the marina, showered and then went to tickles for breakfast. While he sat drinking his coffee, Jack had a strange sense of foreboding about his upcoming charter. He really could use the money and this trip would be more like just cruising than work. That was the part that had him worried. *That woman is extremely dangerous*, Jack thought to himself with a grin. The problem as Jack saw it was going to be treating Alex as just another charter when he was really thinking what some would consider impure thoughts. *Ah, the loneliness of command.* Jack had done a pretty good job of not letting himself get to close to any women who would be around for any length of time. Guys know when it's time to stop asking too many personal questions about one's past, but women just don't know when to stop. Jack's past was known by very few people and none of them were in the islands and that was the way it had to be. The thing was, Jack had know idea if anyone was even looking for him or not and the only way they could find him would be by complete accident. Those few that did know his new identity and location were not the type to share information. Jack finished his breakfast and went back to his boat to tidy up the guest cabin. He wasn't there long before Alex called him on his cell phone to let him know she was on her way over. Jack made a pot of coffee and put on a Jimmy Buffet CD to set the mood. Alex arrived at nine sharp with a warm smile on her face and greeted Jack. "Good morning Mon Capitan, how is everything this morning?"

"Just fine, there's coffee if you want a cup."

"Yeah, I'd love one." Jack started to go below to get the coffee when

Alex said, "Hey, I'll get it; I have to find out where everything is anyway."

"Good point, come on aboard and I'll give you the nickel tour." Alex followed Jack down the companionway into the main salon. Alex had expected the boat to be nice but she was not prepared for what she saw. "My God is this all mahogany?"

"Yeah, well, most of it is anyway. When I got the boat, the original bulkheads in the main salon had a lot of water damage and I had to replace them or try to shore em up. I was talking to this guy at the dockyard that knew where a bunch of panels off of an old Pullman car were and I ended up getting all of it cheap. Well, anyway I replaced what needed replacing and then just kept going. The fore and aft cabins are original with the exception of some cabinets I made. It turned out to be a lot more work than I had planned on but it came out nice."

"This is beautiful, you must be proud of her." Jack just gave Alex a modest grin and finished showing her around the boat. Jack had saved the aft cabin, which Alex would occupy on the trip for last. When Jack opened the door to the cabin he had to smile when he saw the look on Alex's face. Alex was amazed at the size and beauty of it. The cabin had a huge bed with a settee on the port side and a plush reading chair with a table and lamp on the starboard side. When Jack showed her the aft head is when Alex got her real surprise. The head was a separate compartment from the shower and had a large counter and sink with a good size mirror with ample lighting. Instead of a curtain, the shower had a sliding glass door, which when Jack opened, revealed not only a shower, but also a small whirlpool bath. Alex looked at the tub and said, "You've got to be fucking kidding me." Jack looked at her with a big grin and said, "Should I take that as a sign that Madam approves of her accommodations." Alex looked at Jack and said, "Approve, I'm absolutely delighted with it, this is perfect, even better than I had hoped for. I noticed that each cabin has its own stereo system in it, that's a nice touch. Ok, time for that coffee."

Jack and Alex went back into the main salon and the galley area where Alex had to marvel at the beauty and utility of all of the work Jack had done. Alex had seen a few Gulfstar Fifties before but never one like this. Alex immediately began searching cabinets and the pantry until she had a good idea where everything was and should go. As she was getting ready to pour herself a cup, Alex hesitated and asked Jack if he would like a cup as well. "Actually, I'd love one. Cream and sugar please, and while you are at that, I'll grab a paper chart of the area and get it laid out on the dining table to look at. Alex joined Jack on the settee where he had the chart laid out and set his coffee down on a coaster and then said, "So skipper, where are we going on this trip?"

"That's up to you, I'll point out some places that I like then you decide. As you can see, all of these islands are within line of sight of each other so we can cover a lot of territory in two weeks. You know Christmas is in four days. If you want we can wait until after that to get underway."

"I hadn't even thought about that. I'm sorry, you must have plans."

"To be honest, I really didn't, I can get underway as soon as the boat is ready if you want to. I should get that pump today and it won't take any more than twenty minutes or so to install, then it's just a matter of provisions and we never have to buy too much at any given time because of the proximity of the islands."

"Ok, I think it would be nice to spend Christmas on a quaint little island where we can go ashore where there won't be much of a crowd and have a nice dinner, my treat by the way. Do you know a place like that?" Jack grinned at Alex as he took out his cellular phone and punched in a bunch of numbers. After waiting for a few seconds Jack said, "Hi Janet, this is Jack Schmidt, I know this is short notice, but do you have anything open for Christmas day for dinner, yeah I can hold, two, outstanding, see you then and thanks, I owe you one. There are occasional advantages to being a charter Captain around here."

"So where is this place you made reservations at?" Jack pointed to a tiny little island that lay south of Tortola and said, "Right here at Cooper Island. They have a little resort there with an outside bar and restaurant, the dingy dock leads right up to the club, very nice spot."

"How far is it from here," asked Alex. Jack broke out a set of dividers from a drawer in the table and began to measure the distance on the chart while Alex leaned over to watch him. Jack began to really notice Alex's perfume, and the way her breasts were straining at the thin cotton T-shirt she was wearing as she leaned over the table, quite difficult to ignore. Alex noticed how hard Jack was trying not to notice and had to fight to keep from giggling. "Exactly twenty-eight miles if we follow this course, it takes us past Cruz Bay on St.. John, then by Soapers hole Tortola, and then it's pretty much a straight shot to Cooper Island." Alex said, "Well, I guess that will work. When can we get under way?"

"As soon as you and I finish up here, I'll go and hopefully pick up my fuel pump. If you like, while I'm doing that, you can walk over to the gourmet gallery and start getting us some grub. I have an account there so you can charge everything to the boat; just remember to save the receipt. Oh, by the way, do you dive?"

"Well, said Alex, I have my PADI advanced ticket but I haven't been diving in years."

"No problem," said Jack, "among my many other talents, I'm a certified instructor, and I carry four complete sets of gear and eight tanks. There is some great diving in some of the places we're going."

"Great, this sounds better all the time. So, all you have to do is fix the fuel pump on the gen-set and we can get under way."

"Yep that's about it. Let's go get some lunch at the Greenhouse then I can go get the pump and start on that while you do the shopping. How's that sound."

"Sounds good to me, let's go."

As Jack and Alex were eating lunch, four men were checking in to Black Beards Inn in Charlotte Amalie. After settling in, Leo set up his computer and began working his magic. After only a few minutes, Leo called to Viktor and told him the results. "You see my friend, I told you, the woman is staying at a hotel called Frenchman's Reef, and it is just across the harbor from here. I suggest that you send Stephan and Ivan over to watch out for the woman while we enjoy the island a little."

"Damn you Leo, don't you take anything seriously, we don't have time to fuck around here."

"My dearest Viktor, but of course I do, we can do nothing until the woman is physically located, and our job, at least until receiving further orders is strictly surveillance. Send your minders to watch for the woman and we will have a couple of drinks and wait for them to report. You need to relax a bit my friend; you are much too young to die of a heart attack."

Viktor considered what Leo had said for a moment and said, "Yes my friend you are right. Ivan, Stephan, I want you to take the two vehicles, wait at the woman's hotel, if she shows up there, discreetly shadow her. Photograph her and anyone you see her in contact with, stay with her. If she leaves, follow her and do the same but don't loose her, understand." The former Spetznaz NCO'S nodded their acknowledgement of their orders then checked their cameras and cell phones and departed. Leo looked at the room service menu and decided to go down to the restaurant for a drink and something to eat. Viktor agreed that a meal would do him some good. As Viktor and Leo were ordering their meal they had no idea how interesting things were about to get.

Chapter Nine

New York

Brady and Eggers were in their office receiving the report on Her Richter. "Well, the guy never existed, social security number was a fake, INS says they never heard of him and the consulting firm he worked for doesn't turn up anywhere either. He was receiving some hefty paychecks from early forty-seven until around sixty-three but there is no way to find out where the money was coming from and the IRS never heard of him or his old lady." Eggers looked at Tommy for a moment and said, "The guy is a ghost eh, what about the feds, they have anything on him?" Tommy looked down at the file and said that the FBI had yet to get back to him on his request for background information. Brady looked around the room for a moment then said, "I have an idea, let's have a look at those photos from the safety deposit box."

"What are you looking for?" asked Tommy. "Among my many other interests, I happen to be somewhat of a world war two history buff, I want to get another look at old Karl's uniform." Tommy laid out the photos of Karl in his uniform and Brady began to study them, after a couple of minutes he began to grin. "What you got?" asked Eggers.

"You see this emblem, the oval wreath with the diving eagle, well that would indicate that our friend was a paratrooper. Now, German airborne forces, unlike ours were actually Luftwaffe infantry not army. "Yeah and so?" said Eggers.

"Well our boy here was Waffen SS. Look at the national emblem on the left sleeve of his tunic, the wings are straight with the wingtips angled at top and bottom to form a point, also these sleeve cuffs have no unit emblem on them, also, you see the SS Runes on the collar. And if you look at the Knights Cross he is wearing around his neck it has oak leaves, crossed swords and diamonds."

"Ok," said Eggers, "what does that mean?"

"Well, that was the German equivalent of the medal of honor. And this guy was a lieutenant colonel in this photo. I recognize this place now, it's Hitler's pad up in the mountains in Bavaria. The Waffen SS only had one division of paratroops and they fought all over the Balkans giving the Soviets hell. They were also on the raid that snatched Mussolini out of an allied prison." This guy was a heavy hitter; the SS paras were a commando unit, all volunteers and all hardcore soldiers. When this picture was taken, Der Furher was most likely just out of frame and there would have been some with the two of them together, not really surprising that they aren't here though. A picture in a German uniform is one thing, one with Hitler is another."

"Well shit," said Eggers, "so what does this tell us?"

"Could be a couple of things, maybe Odessa sneaked him in, they were the ones who helped hide and smuggle a lot of the old SS boys out after the war, or, there could be another answer. Maybe he wasn't too keen on the Nazis, a lot of these guys weren't. Maybe he turned himself in to us at the end of the war and ratted out a bunch of his buddies or had some juicy Intel on the Russians. Take me to America and I'll tell you a bunch of neat stuff. That would explain a few things. Tommy, I want you to find how many senior ranking SS Para guys got this award, the Germans were fanatical record keepers, then find out what happened to them after the war. We are going to find out just who this guy was."

Eggers scratched his chin for a moment and asked, "Should we ask the feds if they know anything about this guy or wait on Tommy?"

"I think we wait, we ask now they may just blow us off, let's see what we can find out first. Ok, now what do we do about the McTeal woman?"

"Well," said Eggers, "we can't follow her to the Caribbean, I'll talk to a buddy of mine at the bureau and see if they can look around for her, maybe they'll buy the potential material witness line until we can come up with something else." Brady was about to say something else when the phone rang. Brady answered the call and after a moment sat straight up, grabbed a pen and began making notes without comment. After a moment he spoke into the phone. "Ok, look at the photos and see if you can ID the other two. I want to know as soon as you know something, we may have to move real fast on this one, yeah, ok, and thanks. Brady hung up the phone and said, "That was Al Jones with OCU, he said one of his surveillance teams just spotted four of our Russian mutts boarding a flight for St. Thomas, think that's a coincidence? I sure as fuck don't." Eggers pounded his fist onto the table and said, "I heard you say something about ID on two of them."

"Yeah, Al's on his way over here now with what he has, says he can be here in twenty minutes. It looks like they are after the girl, what do we do now?"

Chapter Ten

St. Thomas

After lunch Alex took a cab back to her hotel while Jack went to Haul out Marine to pick up his fuel pump. Alex wanted to change clothes before she started hauling supplies to the boat and she wanted to take a moment or two to think everything through. She wasn't sure whether she would check out of the room or just leave when it was time. It would, she reasoned be better to check out as not to draw any attention to herself.

As Alex stepped out of her cab she was recognized by Stephan and Ivan. Both men took photographs and Ivan followed her inside while Stephan waited outside to make sure they didn't lose her. Ivan followed Alex towards the elevator and then sat and waited in the lobby for her to come back out. He would not follow her to her room and risk spooking her. Ivan phoned Stephan outside and stated his intention to wait in the lobby for one hour to see if she came back through or went to meet someone. In the meanwhile, Ivan phoned Viktor and reported that they had visual contact and had photographed the woman.

"Let me talk to him for a moment," said Leo, taking the phone from Viktor, "Stephan, follow the woman if and when she leaves the hotel and see where she goes, pay attention to whom she meets, and photograph anyone that appears to be a significant contact. Tell Ivan to enter her room after she leaves and give it a thorough search, we may get lucky, but tell him to be careful. If nothing is found, the woman must not know her room has been searched. You know what to do."

"As you see Viktor, things are progressing well; the woman may or may not have the stones. If she hid them in her room we will be on a flight back to New York tomorrow, if not we get to spend some more time here enjoying ourselves. Now we just wait and see."

It was only fifteen minutes before Alex walked back down through the lobby and out front to hail a cab. She had decided to wait until the boat was ready to go before she checked out of her room. Ivan called Stephan and told him to follow the woman as he was headed to Alex's room. Stephan started the engine of his rental even before Alex emerged outside. Stephan waited for Alex to pull away in her cab and then followed her at a discrete distance, all the while thinking about how much more fun this was than soldiering.

Stephan had started out in the naval infantry and had been selected for Spetznaz training. He had excelled in special operations, seeing a good deal of combat in Afghanistan, which was where he met Mhiki. Mhiki had taken a keen interest in the young soldier and had followed his career. After Mhiki decided to move to America, Stephan was among the initial cadre of people he brought in on the beginning of his new criminal enterprises. Stephan would never be management, but men like him were always good to have close to you.

While Stephan was following the woman, Ivan made short work of the door to Alex's room. As the cab carrying the woman pulled into Crown Bay Marina, Stephan phoned Viktor to inform him of what was going on. Stephan would watch from a distance in the rental and observe the woman. It was important that she not become aware that she was under surveillance. In the meantime, Ivan had completed a thorough search of Alex's room and come up with nothing. After phoning in his report, Ivan was instructed to remain at the woman's hotel and await further instructions.

Stephan watched the woman get out of the cab and go directly to a food market at the marina. After waiting for over a half hour, the woman emerged pushing a shopping cart full of groceries down the dock and begin unloading them onto a large sailboat. She was almost finished when Jack arrived in his old Wrangler. Stephan did not pay much attention to him until he noticed that Jack was headed to the same boat. Stephan took out his camera and began taking photographs of Jack and Alex. Stephan watched as Jack and Alex unloaded the stores onto the boat. After they were done, the two Americans went to the bar at the marina and Stephan followed them there to see if he could figure out what they were up to. Jack and Alex sat at the bar and Stephan sat at the table closest to them.

"Ok Alex, we are ready to go, how's tomorrow morning at nine sound, you can either bring your things today or in the morning."

"I don't really have much; I'll just bring it in the morning. So, you want me here at nine or are we casting off at nine?"

"You tell me, it's your charter," said Jack. "Why don't we do breakfast here at say eight thirty and then get underway for Soapers Hole to clear customs," said Alex.

"Works for me, why don't you meet me here at seven tonight and we can go to a place called the Old Mill for dinner, unless you had other plans."

"Oh no," said Alex, "I don't have any plans, that sounds good. Well, I need to go back to the hotel and get ready to go, so, I'll see you here at eight."

"Ok, see ya then."

Jack had one beer and Alex had an iced tea. They made some small talk that Stephan could not make out and then got up to leave. Stephan could not risk getting up to leave at just that moment so he watched as Alex went to a cab and Jack went back to his boat. Stephan quickly left a bill on the table he had been sitting at and went to his car. He had missed Alex's departure but assumed she would be heading back to her hotel. Stephan started his rental and headed back toward the woman's hotel. Just as Stephan was parking, he saw the woman walk through the front doors of the hotel. Stephan remained in his vehicle and called Ivan, who was sitting in the lobby reading a book. Ivan told Stephan that the woman had gotten into the elevator and appeared to be going back to her room. Stephan remained outside and phoned Viktor at Black Beards to report in.

After talking things over with Leo, Viktor called Stephan back and told him to have Ivan remain at the hotel and keep an eye out for the woman. Viktor told Stephan to go back to the marina and get a look at the boat and get its name and registration number, then return to the Castle to download the pictures of the woman and the sailor.

Stephan returned to Crown Bay marina and walked to the slip where Jack's boat was. As Stephan was standing on the dock looking at the boat, he heard a voice from right behind him say, "Can I help you with something?" Startled, since he had not heard or even sensed anyone's approach, Stephan spun quickly around to come face to face with Jack who stood there with a slight grin. The two men stood there for just a moment recognizing just what the other was, a hardened warrior. Stephan, with a noticeable accent said, "Oh, no thanks, I was just looking at the boats," then turned and walked away. Jack stood there watching Stephan walking away, remembering seeing him at Tickles earlier. Probably nothing, Jack thought to himself, but just the same he would keep an eye out for this one. Jack knew a professional when he saw one and the big Russian was certainly that. He had made the accent as soon as Stephan spoke. What the hell, plenty of out of work spooks and soldiers after the cold war and this was not the first one he had run into one in the Caribbean living the good life after the bad old days.

When Stephan finished briefing Viktor and Leo of the events after leaving the woman's hotel, Leo began looking through the charter boat brochures he had picked up earlier that day. "Ah, here it is, sailing vessel Privateer, owned and operated by one Jack Schmidt. Personalized charters in the U.S. and British Virgin Islands. In business for five years according to this. It would appear that the woman has hired herself a boat Viktor, we must call Mhiki and give him this news and e-mail the pictures of the boat captain and the woman at once."

Stephan said, "This boat captain looks like a hardass to me, he used to be in the business, soldier or maybe an Intel type but I could feel it, and he knew what I was, we need some more information on him."

"Correct you are my friend," said Leo, "but first we call Lexi to tell him the news, it is good that you are as alert as you are Stephan, but this boat captain should not be a problem. He is like most here, these Americans come to lose their past and start over, and as long as they have their liquor and the occasional woman they are content." Stephan gave Leo a skeptical look and said, "Perhaps, it is so, but we need to find out more about him."

Leo called Lexi to report in on one phone as Ivan was calling on another for further instructions. Viktor told Ivan that he would call back after the conference call with Lexi. "Well Leo," said Lexi, "so the woman has chartered a boat and may be getting ready to depart soon, but you don't know where she is going , or for how long. Also you don't know if she has the stones or not. They were not in her room or they would have been found, and it would seem unlikely that she would have them on her person if she does have them. At this point I do not want to risk confrontation; perhaps she is just taking some time to herself. If she does have the stones she may not have them with her, perhaps she is waiting to see if we are looking for her or not. Call this boat captain in the morning and ask about his next available charter and use your best Brooklyn accent, it is a pity but we need to keep Stephan out of his sight for the time being. You must find out how long they are going to be gone and where they are going if you can. Allow them to leave unmolested but be ready for further travel. I want you to look for a fast boat that you can rent and stay aboard, you may have to follow after them and e-mail the pictures of the woman and the sailor as soon as we get off the phone."

"Of course as usual I shall keep you informed of any developments." Lexi hung up the phone without further comment and Leo looked at Viktor with a big smile on his face. "You see Viktor, Lexi will report to Mhiki and tell him of our successes and we will soon receive further instructions. I have already looked at a boat for us among the brochures we have. If we need the boat we can rent a forty-foot power catamaran in Tortola, which is just a short ferry ride from here. Stephan was Navy before he joined Spetznaz and is an expert with small boats, he can handle the boat for us and we can cover distances much faster than any sailboat. All will be fine my friend; my only concern is how to find out where the woman and the sailor are going. I will call Mr. Schmidt and see what I can learn. In the meantime you e-mail the pictures Stephan took to Lexi. All will be fine, you will see." Leo had no way of imagining the shitstorm that would be started by four little electronic photos.

Lexi phoned Mhiki and gave him the information that Leo had passed on to him, and informed Mickey that the photos of the woman and the boat captain should be popping up on his e-mail any minute. Mhiki did not think the pictures to be important, but switched on his computer anyway. Besides, he had never seen the woman before, and understood she was quite pleasant to look at.

"Yes Lexi, I agree we should not interfere with them at the moment but I want to keep the team in place, I may want them to follow the boat. I realize that would be difficult at best but I believe it can be done. We first need to know how long they are going to be gone, and then attempt an intercept when they return if that seems prudent. Have Leo find out the likelihood of the woman being able to get rid of the jewels in that area and let me know what he says. I do not believe that she would be able to do anything down there, but that is what I pay Leo for."

"Of course Mhiki, all will be seen to; I will call as soon as I have more to report." Having said that, Lexi hung up the phone and Mhiki opened up his e-mail to look at the pictures of the woman and the sailor. Each photo was in a jpeg format and had to be opened one at a time. Mhiki opened the first one and saw the woman in profile and the man standing with his back to the camera. The woman was wearing tight white shorts and had on a thin white t-shirt obviously sans bra, and was, Mhiki decided strikingly beautiful. No wonder the lawyer had the hots for her. The boat captain was standing with his hands on hips and his head cocked to one side apparently listening to something the woman was saying. Stephan seemed to be right about one thing, the man looked large and very fit. As Mhiki opened the second photo, the man was in profile and as Mhiki looked at him, something seemed familiar. Mhiki opened the third photo and the man was facing the camera. Mhiki's heart seemed to skip a beat then he screamed in rage at the recognition of the face in the photograph, a face he had last seen many years ago in a far away but not forgotten place. Mhiki ran a finger along the deep scar that ran from just below, and to the outside of his right eye, down the side of his face, and terminating at his disfigured right ear. He was thinking about the last time he had seen that face. *Fuck the woman, fuck the jewels, and fuck everything else on the entire Goddamn planet*, thought Mhiki. "I am going to come down there and find you, and when I do, you will curse whatever god you pray to for ever allowing you to be borne."

Leo called the cellular number on the brochure and got a charter booking service that informed him that PRIVATEER would be unavailable for the next two weeks and no, she did not know where they were going and no, he could not have the owner's private number. All reservations were made through the service, and only confirmed customers were given Jack Schmidt's unlisted cell number.

Chapter Eleven

U.S. Diplomatic Mission, Peshawar Pakistan 1987

David Randal was a career diplomat who had been posted to Pakistan shortly after the Soviets had invaded Afghanistan. Most days were bad but today was pure shit; Russian soldiers had killed two CIA paramilitary types the previous day in an ambush, presumably with assistance from Afghan collaborators. It seemed that was the only possible answer. The two CIA officers were delivering a cargo of stinger missiles from Pakistan to the Mujahideen at a meeting just across the Afghan border. The mission must have been compromised; the ambush was a total success. There were only two survivors out of twelve men and both of them were wounded, one seriously. And to make matters worse, the chief of station was waiting outside his office talking to one of the new State Department spooks. Bureau of Diplomatic Security, just what Randal needed, more spooks running under foot and all over his posting.

Randal had accepted that his position here was only to add some minimal credibility to the term diplomatic mission. In reality Peshawar was nothing more than a base for the CIA's covert ops and intelligence gathering activities against the Soviets across the border. And these new guys, the DSS, as they called themselves were not your run of the mill security types. Randal didn't know what was in all of the crates of gear they had brought with them, but it was not just new cameras and alarm systems. These guys were big and looked mean as shit.

Randal's thoughts were interrupted as the door to his office flew open and Ben Hooper burst in. "Don't you ever knock?" asked Randal.

Hooper looked at him for a moment, shrugged his massive shoulders and sat down in a chair across from Randal. Hooper stared at a spot on the wall for a moment before he spoke. "Well Dave, I don't have to tell you how fucked this situation is, it could be weeks before I can get replacements for Jackson and Bell. Two damn good men and I want the balls of the man or men who sold them out. Going to be hard though, we don't know who they set up the rendezvous with. Be that as it may, I now have a bigger problem, we just got a message from our asset in Kabul, the CO of a Spetznaz unit wants out. This guy is a full Colonel in the fucking Spetznaz, I pull this one off and my days of living in shit holes like this are over. But, I need your help with this one."

"Ben, what the hell do you expect me to do, I'm a fifty-two year old pencil pusher."

"You are but those four pit bulls of yours are certainly not."

"Ben, I don't know what those guys are here for. They checked in did a security survey, replaced some cameras and told me to let them know what I wanted for them to do next and the truth is, that I don't know what to do with them. Washington says that the Marines answer to them and that they are a new special protective security detail with other capabilities. I don't know what that means but I am supposed to be in charge of them. I do know that they are paramilitary trained but I have yet to receive any guidance as to how exactly I'm supposed to use them and they just say they will keep the premises secure until I give them further tasking."

"Well Dave, that is where I need your help, I know it sounds kind of funny, but I need to borrow your spooks. I already talked to the team leader; his name is Jake Saunders, formerly a lieutenant at Seal Team 4. He says his team can cross the border and get our guy out but the order has to come from you. Our Russian friend has already picked a time and place, if we show, he comes over, if not the deal is off. There is no way I can get any company guys here and up to speed in time to pull this off, and this mission is actually within your guys' purview, protection of foreign dignitaries. If we stretch it a bit this qualifies."

Randal considered his options and had to conclude that he really couldn't lose, Hooper's ass would be out on a limb, and certainly Sanders team could end up getting their asses shot off. If these Diplomatic Security Service guys could pull this off it would be a big feather in the state department's hat; and it certainly could not hurt Randal's career either. "Tell you what Ben, I'll call the home office on this one, I don't want my ass twisting in the wind if my team ends up getting shot to shit. You say Sanders says he can do it that's good enough for me, but I still have to make a call. You go talk to the team and let them know that they have my blessing, and I'll get back with you within the next fifteen minutes with a final answer."

After Hooper had left his office, Randal inserted his key into the STU-2 secure phone and called his boss at the South West Asian desk and succinctly laid out the situation and proposal, and was given the green light immediately. It was however decided that Hooper would have tactical control of the team for the mission so the blame could be placed at CIA's feet if the mission went south. If it worked, it would not matter who had tactical control, it would still be a successful covert op carried out by the State Department's newest arm.

Randal went out to the small alcove outside of his office with a grave look on his face. The look on Hoopers face was exactly what Randal had hoped for; he thought the mission was a bust. Randal cleared his throat, looked directly at Sanders and said, "Mr. Saunders, you are a go. Mr. Hooper will have tactical control of the mission and is to provide you with all of the intelligence information, and other support you need. Let me know when you plan to depart, the home office wants to be kept abreast of events in as close to real time as possible. Gentlemen, I am a career diplomat and will leave this to the professionals, good luck." With that Randal retired to his quarters and poured himself a stiff Scotch. For the first time in his life he had just ordered men to perform an action that could very likely end in their deaths and he did not find anything pleasant about it, not a thing.

"Well boys, let's go to my office and I'll give you the details, the actual planning I will leave to you, I don't micro manage." After about two hours the plan was as good as it would get. Jake's primary concern was getting burned prior to reaching the objective. There was no way of knowing if the mission was going to be compromised or not and the fate of Hooper's last op did nothing to ease his concerns. What the hell he thought, he had left the Navy because he thought he would have a better chance of getting to the big time as a state department spook than he would as a SEAL. Besides he had been up for a promotion that would effectively have taken him out of operational status.

Jake looked at Hooper and said, "Ok, Billy and Tom will be in the number two van, they will stay about five hundred meters back when we reach the village. Everybody will have AKs, with a hundred and fifty rounds, plus a handgun with four extra mags. Billy will have the 300 Win Mag with fifty rounds; if it is going to take more than that we are most likely fucked anyway. Ed and me will approach the shop Borokovsky picked and make contact. Everyone dresses local. Tom, Billy, anything goes sideways you know what to do. We get this guy in the van and haul ass for the border that is twenty-five kliks from the pick up point. The two most likely places for trouble are the pickup point and on the return to the border. If the Sovs know what we are up to, they will wait until we have Borokovsky in custody before they hit us. You know, as an afterthought Ben can you get me two RPGs and about ten rockets each?"

"Yeah, sure, think you got enough dynamite there Butch?" Jake had to smile at that one. "Well, if we buy the farm on this one it won't be for a lack of shooting back. The Mujahideen bubbas will have coms with both vehicles and let us know if it looks like any road blocks are getting set up on our way out. Also, their guys will have Stingers just in case the Sovs try an air intercept. An Air Force AWACS will maintain coms with them and give them an advanced heads up for Helos or fast movers. I know it doesn't sound like much of a plan but it's all we can do. We just have to hope that the GRU or KGB isn't on to the Colonel."

"Yeah, and that the good comrade Colonel is on the level. This whole thing could be one big fucking set up," said Tom. Ed stood up and looked from one man to another and said, "So this ain't gonna ruin any of your social plans now is it. We have a chance to do something that will piss off the Russians and give us a wealth of intelligence information, and deal one hell of a blow to what we already know is a serious morale problem. I say the potential gains outweigh the risks."

"So, we just walk up to the guy and ask him to get in the van and then move out. The Mujahideen will be watching our route along the way; if we pick up a tail they will give us a heads up and engage if necessary. They also have the means to take out any air threat, but that is only at the pick up point or near the border crossing. If we get across the border with him we should be fine, and then Mr. Hooper can worry about getting him out of the country."

No one else had anything to add so Jake told the team to do a weapons and com check, the Op would be a go in three days, it would take that long to get the Mujahideen geared up and in place, and that was when Borokovsky had set the meet for.

Colonel Mikhail Valentnikov, GRU, Commander Spetznaz Forces Afghanistan, sat at his desk listening to his translator describe how one of his field commanders was planning to defect to the west. The Afghani fighter describing the details of the defection was the same man who had blown the CIA Stinger delivery the previous week, and was a misguidedly trusted member of the area Mujahideen. Pakta, as he was called, held no true alliance with either the Soviets or his brother freedom fighters. All he wanted to do was make enough money to move to Bahrain where life was a bit more liberal and live comfortably, maybe open a coffee shop and cater to the wealthy business men who banked there. After he was done talking, Pakta waited for the big Russian to speak but he just sat there staring into his eyes. It was a cold, dead, penetrating stare. Pakta was suddenly very afraid; this man has no soul he thought.

Outside the Colonel's office, stood another Afghani man who was not what he seemed, Raja Hasheed, a guide and tracker who worked for the Soviets was in fact a Mujahideen fighter who would pass along vital information to other freedom fighters and the American CIA. Raja felt no particular love for the Americans and did not really trust them, but they had promised to help rid his country of the hated Soviets. For now, that was enough. Raja had been watching Pakta for some time and was now certain that it was he who had been giving the Russians information, information that had resulted in the deaths of many of his brother fighters. Raja would let him go for now, he would confront him in his village tonight in front of the elders.

Colonel Valentnikov sat at his desk thinking of what to do with

Comrade Borokovsky, he would surely kill him as an example, but just how to do it was the question. He did not know exactly when the man would try his defection other than that it would be soon. To further complicate matters, he was a two day journey away by motor vehicle and he would not personally ride in a helicopter these days. Too damn many Afghanis with American supplied stinger missiles. Mhiki decided he would take three men and go and arrest Borokovsky, he would have to travel for two days to do it but he wanted to see the look on his face when he was arrested for treason. Mhiki would send a message ahead to Borokovsky's XO to keep an eye on him and to contact him immediately if it looked like anything suspicious was happening. The relatively young officer was Spetznaz to the core and a rabid Communist.

For his part, Mhiki had no real ideological position, it was all about power and privilege, and as a full Colonel in the GRU, he had plenty of both. Perhaps this event, stopping the defection of a senior Spetznaz officer from a war zone would be just the ticket for his promotion to General, and the Dacha outside Moscow that would go with it. No more field assignments for General Valentnikov.

Chapter Twelve

New York

Brady and Eggers sat looking at the surveillance photos taken of the four Russians at the airport. It was just happenstance that Al Jones who was with the department's organized crime unit was surveilling the airport looking for a couple of goombas that were expected to board a flight for Sicily when he spotted the four Russians. He recognized Leo and Viktor from photos of known Russian mob types but had no idea who the other two were; trouble by the look of them. Al looked at Eggers and said, "So, what you wanna do about this Dave."

"Well, we don't really have much in the way of evidence, we can't even get a material witness warrant on the McTeal woman but I don't think there is much doubt that these guys aren't going down there to take her to dinner." Eggers chimed in, "Hey Al, you still have good relations with the ATTF (Anti Terrorism Task Force) bubbas?"

"Yeah, Mike Nolan and I are actually very good friends, he's one of the FBI members of the New York team."

"Good, get him on the phone right now, whatever it takes, give me an intro then put me on the phone with him. We need someone in St. Thomas to meet our Russian mutts when they get off the plane and keep them under surveillance until we have a better idea of what the hell is going on. Plus, they may just be going down there to whack her. At this point, seeing as what happened to her boyfriend, I think we can safely assume that an American citizen traveling outside the continental United States, to a US possession, may be in mortal danger from foreign nationals. That should be sufficient to get our federal brothers to mobilize and cover the girl." Brady looked at his partner and smiled. Eggers looked back at him and said, "What?"

"You know, you should be a cop or something like that, you are one smart fucker." It took about ten minutes to get Nolan on the phone and after a brief conversation, Al handed the phone to Eggers who laid out the situation. Nolan gave Eggers the email address of the SAC (Special Agent in Charge) at the St. Thomas field office so he could send the photos of the Russians so the agents could spot them when they got off the plane. There were only four agents stationed on the island, but if more were needed they were only thirty some odd miles away in Puerto Rico.

Chapter Thirteen

St. Thomas

FBI Special Agents Steve Halston and Andy White were waiting at the Charlotte Amalie airport in two vehicles when the four Russians walked out the front door and took two rental cars to Black Beards Castle. It appeared that they must have had a reservation, because they went straight there, checked in and went to two adjoining rooms. Not long after they had checked in, the two big ones left in their vehicles, Andy White followed the trail vehicle while Halston remained behind. They were the only two available for surveillance at the time and would just have to make do for the time being.

White followed both vehicles to Frenchman's Reef where the two Russians parked in separate areas of the parking lot with a view of the front doors. These guys had obviously done this sort of thing before. It was not long before a cab dropped off a gorgeous blonde in tight white shorts and a T-shirt, White was looking at the woman when he noticed both Russians were photographing the woman, and then, one of them followed her into the hotel while the other one waited outside in his vehicle. White phoned Bill Reynolds and let him know that he believed he had located the McTeal woman and that the Russians had her under surveillance.

"We need at least one more guy to do this right Bill, if they split up I'll stay with the woman to make sure nothing happens, looks like they are just looking for now."

"Ok Andy, I need to get another guy on this, stay with the girl and try to get pics of anyone she meets, but remember, you have to keep from getting made by the woman or the Russians. Steve will stay and watch the Castle and the other two."

Bill Reynolds was the SAC, or Special Agent in Charge of the St. Thomas office, he had agreed, at the request of the New York ATTF to this surveillance with very little to go on. He already had two of his three agents on this with damn little info or guidance and was reluctant to commit another man but agreed to send another man, Randy Wilson to Frenchman's Reef.

Wilson called White to get instructions on where best to park and not be noticed by the Russian who was also watching the hotel. While Wilson was on his way, the woman left the hotel and got into a cab, the Russian who had followed her inside did not appear and White saw the other one getting ready to follow her cab. White immediately called Wilson and gave him a description of the other Russian and his vehicle and told him to sit tight and wait for him to reappear outside and then follow him if and when he left.

As the Russian departed, following the woman's cab, White followed the Russian to Crown Bay Marina. When he arrived there he wasn't sure exactly what to do. There were only two parking spaces open and they were right next to each other between the entrance to the marina and the little bar. White decided to get out of his vehicle, an older Jeep Cherokee, and walk to the bar and order a beer and watch from there. He couldn't risk trying to use his camera; the place was too small for the Russian not to notice him. The McTeal woman had gone into the marina grocery store next door, and the Russian was still sitting in the parking lot, so White ordered another beer. A few minutes after White had ordered his second beer; the woman came out of the grocery store pushing a cart down the dock to a big sailboat and started unloading groceries. *Now that is certainly interesting*, thought White, *looks like she is getting ready to travel.* About that time, Jack was pulling into the parking lot in his old Wrangler. White didn't pay much attention to him until he saw the guy heading to the same boat as the woman had.

White looked over toward the Russian and noticed that he was taking pictures of the woman and the unknown man with a telephoto lens. *So, the*

Russians don't know who this guy is either, thought White. Jack and Alex started towards the bar so White just sat where he was and Jack and Alex sat down just one barstool down from him and started talking about boat charter stuff. Suddenly the Russian was sitting at a table a short distance away apparently trying to listen in on the conversation. White overheard Jack and Alex saying that Alex was going back to her room and Jack was going to back to haul out marine and get a gasket that he had forgotten while he was there earlier, but he would have to go back to the boat to get the old one, and that he would pick her up for dinner at her hotel around seven.

As the two got up and started to leave, White saw a moment of confusion on the Russian's face, he had to wait until Alex had walked over to the taxi stand before he could get up to leave. White didn't have to move because he knew where everyone was going. White watched the Russian leave a bill on the table and hurriedly leave, following the woman's cab presumably back to her hotel. White sat at the bar until Jack had come back from his boat and left in his Jeep. Then he paid his tab and walked down the dock to look at the boat and note its name and USVI registration number. Then White went back to his Jeep and called Wilson on his cell phone and told him to expect the woman to show up soon, closely followed by the big Russian.

White called Bill Reynolds at the government building and told him that he would come straight over and report on what he had observed and start working on the identity of the owner of "PRIVATEER." Wilson and Halston would continue to watch their charges respectively while White and Reynolds tried to get some more information as to what the hell they had gotten involved in. Meanwhile, Wilson noted the arrival of Stephan back at Frenchman's Reef. After he had parked his vehicle, Stephan made a cellular call to someone, and then started to leave the parking lot.

Halston and Wilson had a brief exchange on the radio and it was decided that Wilson should follow the Russian as he had not yet seen the McTeal woman. White would have to return to Frenchman's Reef in order to maintain a watch on the McTeal woman.

Wilson followed Stephan back to Crown Bay Marina and was

fortunate in that there were several parking spaces open at the time. Wilson remained in his vehicle as Stephan walked down the dock directly to "PRIVATEER." Wilson was just getting his telephoto lens set up when an old Jeep Wrangler showed up whose driver also headed straight to the same boat the Russian was standing by. Wilson began shooting pictures of the two during their brief exchange.

It was less than a minute before the Russian began heading back to his car while the other man went aboard the boat. Wilson trailed the Russian until it was evident that he was turning into Black Beards Castle. Wilson kept driving since Halston was still maintaining surveillance at the Castle. White pulled over by the Greenhouse restaurant and bar and phoned in to Bill Reynolds for instructions. After several cell phone calls between agents, it was decided that Halston would remain where he was and White would have to return to Frenchman's Reef to keep an eye on the other Russian that was presumably still keeping an eye on the woman.

Wilson would return to the government building with the photos of the boat captain and the Russian. Reynolds now had two agents watching four people who could split up at any time making it impossible to keep tabs on everyone full time. The situation was further complicated by the fact that they were on a small island and the Russians obviously had experience in surveillance, so, it would stand to reason that they would also know something about counter surveillance. It would only be a matter of time before the Russians knew that they too were being watched.

Once Wilson was back at the office with Reynolds, it did not take long to determine that the owner of "PRIVATEER" was one Jack Schmidt, who had been on the island for a little over five years. Interestingly, he had no previous address, employment history, or any other information prior to his arrival on the island. Bill Reynolds decided to call Mike Nolan at ATTF in New York, they had the requisite horsepower to dig a bit deeper into Mr. Schmidt's past. After Nolan got off the phone with Reynolds in St. Thomas, he called Dave Eggers to let him know what had transpired so far.

Chapter Fourteen

Afghanistan

Raja had followed the treasonous Pakta back to his village after he had left the Russian commander's office and approached the village elder to tell him what he knew. Pakta was in his hut when five armed Mujahideen fighters came to visit him. He became visibly nervous and excited when they informed him that the elders wanted to see him and it was not a request. Pakta was searched for weapons and marched to the elders meeting tent. Raja was there looking at him with a contemptuous scowl on his face. Pakta began to shake as Raja began to tell the elders of his earlier suspicions, and of how he had followed him to the Soviet officer's camp and of their meeting. Those present were aware of the failed delivery of the all important stinger missiles, and also all knew that betrayal was the only answer as to how the dreaded Spetznaz soldiers had managed such a perfect ambush. Pakta began to sweat heavily and was looking around at the men before him when his fight or flight instinct took over. He had the presence of mind to know that any attempt to fight was useless, so he simply tried to run. He only made it about two steps before he felt strong arms grab him from behind. His last coherent thought was to marvel at the brilliance of the reflection off the knife Raja was holding high above his head, just before Raja cut his throat through to his upper spinal cord with it.

Jake and Ed were entering the nameless village that Borokovsky had selected and were looking for the little bread shop where they would meet Colonel Borokovsky for the first time.

Billy and Tom had selected a slight depression off to one side of the road a little over three hundred meters from the village as their spot from which to cover Jake and Ed. From that vantage point, Billy had placed a sand bag on a makeshift support inside the side door of the van and was tracking Jake's movements through the scope of the big 300 Win Mag. Tom had loaded a rocket into his RPG and had several more at the ready. Jake had an AK-47 concealed under his robes and was holding his .45 auto, hammer back, safety off, in his right hand hidden from view also by his robes.

Borokovsky had been watching the two vehicles approach and was walking up to Jake, each eyeing the other warily, each knowing this could be their last day if the other was not whom they were supposed to be, or, if the meet had been compromised. Just as Jake and Borokovsky were about to speak to one and other, Mhikiail Valentnikov and three other Spetznaz soldiers, one of which was Borokovsky's former number two, all stepped into view. Valentnikov shouted Borokovsky's name and began to raise his Makarov service automatic just as Jake stepped forward shoving Borokovsky to the ground. Both men fired almost simultaneously, but Valentnikov's shot went off a mere fraction of a second before Jake's. The Russian 9 millimeter round struck Jake squarely in the chest just to the left of his heart. Jake's shot, which was slightly knocked off track by the impact of the Russian bullet, struck the Russian officer in the face just under the outer periphery of his right eye socket, shattering his cheekbone and deflecting along the side of his face, bullet and bone fragments tearing a deep gouge, then tearing his right ear nearly in half.

Although not a mortal wound, the impact knocked Mickey flat on his back and left him unconscious. He and Jake hit the ground at almost the same instant. Borokovsky immediately pounced on Jake to cover him a split second before the first round from Billy's big Winchester tore through the front of Borokovsky's former XOs forehead, instantly transforming the bulk of his head into a massive cloud of pink mist. Tom cursed as he had no target for his RPG, Jake was down and too close for him to use a rocket. Borokovsky was firing his Czech Scorpion, 9 millimeter machine pistol as he lay across Jake before Billy's first target hit the ground.

As Borokovsky was firing, he could hear the clatter of an AK behind him being fired by Ed, and could actually hear the rounds whizzing past him as he watched them tear into the other Russian soldier. It was all over in less than five seconds. Borokovsky and Ed looked at each other for a second and the Russian jumped up in one swift move with Jake in a fireman's carry still holding his Scorpion at the ready with his free hand. He just said, "Move now."

As Ed, Borokovsky, and Jake sped away from the village, Billy watched for about ten seconds before tearing out behind them. Inside the lead van, the Russian noted the frothy blood coming out of Jake's mouth and could here the telltale wheezing of a sucking chest wound. Jake had a hole that went through his chest, left lung, and out his back. Borokovsky saw the first aid kit and wasted no time working to plug the entrance and exit wounds on Jake's chest while Ed was talking frantically with Billy in the trail vehicle. Tom was raising the alert on the route ahead of them. A move that was unnecessary as Mickey had told no one what his plan was, he had simply wanted to kill Borokovsky and the two American intelligence officers who were there to pick him up and then file his report.

Mickey, based on Pakta's report, had not believed that any backup would be necessary. Pakta, as a security measure had been given only slightly accurate information by his superiors who were unsure of his loyalties. Those loyalties, or rather the lack there of, were now already confirmed, and the placement of his severed head on a stake outside of his home village was a reminder to others, that collaboration with the Soviets would be dealt with most harshly.

As the two vans raced towards the Pakistan border, Borokovsky expertly tended to Jake's wounds and got an IV going. As he was securing the IV bag to the overhead in the violently bouncing van, Jake looked up to see Borokovsky looking down at him with a genuine smile on his face. He said to Jake, "Vladimir Ilych Borokovsky, I am pleased to make your acquaintance but we will have to wait for formal introductions, you have suffered a severe chest wound and I have patched the holes but you will need surgery, I think you will be fine. That bullet was meant for me and I will not let you die."

As Jake was digesting that tidbit of information, he passed out again. Borokovsky told Ed what Jake's condition was and inquired as to whether a helicopter would be able to meet them at the border to get him to a hospital. Ed told him that they had one on standby and it was on the ground, rotors spinning waiting for them at the border five minutes away. Borokovsky nodded his head in satisfaction and checked Jake's pulse again.

As the two vans crossed the border and came to a stop, the occupants were immediately surrounded by a protective wall of Pakistani Special forces. Jake was being taken out of the van and placed on a stretcher to be carried to the waiting helo when Ben Hooper ran out of the helo and approached Borokovsky. "Colonel, I'm Ben Hooper CIA, I'll need you to come with me now." The Colonel looked at the helicopter, Jake, then Hooper, then held his machine pistol down by his side and said, "Anyone who tries to separate me from that man until he comes out of surgery will be promptly shot." Hooper just looked at him and said, "Ok, have it your way, everybody, in the chopper, may I have that weapon now."

"After he comes out of surgery I will surrender my weapon to him, no one else."

Immediately after the gunfight, the only Russian not hit was Mickey's driver, who in a demonstration of superior judgment, had hidden on the floor of the vehicle until the shooting had stopped and the two vans had left before emerging to find three dead men and a badly wounded Colonel. The soldier was terrified by the crowd of Afghanis who had begun to gather around the scene, so he unceremoniously plopped the good Colonel into the truck and headed towards the nearest Soviet military camp.

While the rest of the team and Borokovsky sat at a Pakistani military hospital waiting room, Ed recounted the meeting and apparent ambush. Borokovsky told Hooper he was sure someone inside the Mujahideen had been feeding information directly to Valentnikov, there was no other way he could have been that well informed. That would be confirmed a couple of days later with the news of Pakta's severed head on a stick and a note explaining that a leak had been plugged. Borokovsky, true to his word, waited by Jake's bedside until he had awoken from his surgery.

"Thank you my friend, you took that bullet to save my life, yet we are sworn enemies. You are a brave man and perhaps someday I will be afforded the opportunity to offer you my service. Until then, I want you to have this weapon, I no longer have any use for it, I am through with killing. You are young and will be back in the game; hopefully it will protect you as it has me."

Chapter Fifteen

Mhiki was sitting at his desk shaking almost uncontrollably with rage and frustration. *Afghanistan, will I never be free of that God forsaken place,* thought Mhiki. After he had awakened from surgery in Afghanistan, Mickey had been told on no uncertain terms that his career was effectively over, and, that he would be lucky if he was not simply listed as a combat casualty.

The Soviets had decided in the end not to kill or publicly humiliate Mhiki, but he was thrown out on his ass with nothing. His whole life had come apart with Borokovsky's successful defection. After returning to Mother Russia, Mhiki had only remained in the Soviet Union for about six months before he had cut his own deal with the Americans and was smuggled out through East Berlin by a no nonsense CIA field officer. After several months of extensive de-briefing, Mhiki was granted American citizenship and given enough money to buy the first of his nightclubs by a grateful United States Government. Although he spoke fluent, though heavily accented English, Mhiki had never been to the U.S. before and it did not take long for him to deduce that the Soviet Union could never compete with the industrial might of his host country. Not only that, it was patently obvious that even the most subservient American would kill or be killed before being forced to endure the stifling economic and sociological constraints imposed by Communism. Soviet ideological indoctrination had not prepared him for the realities of an open and free society; it was, Mhiki decided, a great country in which to do business.

During his debrief, Mickey had been told that the Security Officer he had shot in Afghanistan had died of his wounds, and that the good Colonel Borokovsky was now living in an undisclosed location with a new name. Mhiki was also told that if it even looked like he was going after Borokovsky, Mhiki would become the victim of a most unfortunate accident. Freedom came with certain constraints.

Three operations had somewhat reduced the horrific effects of the .45 slug that had shattered most of the bones and torn away a goodly portion of the flesh on that side of his face. Seeing as his former masters viewed him with nothing less than total contempt for his failure near the border, not much extra care was taken to reduce the visual effects of his wounds, and it was not until nearly a year after he had been shot that a U.S. Army cosmetic surgeon had performed the first of three operations which Mhiki decided had not exactly left him handsome again, but at least people could look at him without averting their eyes in disgust. Now here he was, looking at photographs of the man who had destroyed his career and disfigured him.

Mhiki had never really hated Borokovsky, especially after he had started doing business in the States, but this one, this one was truly responsible for his disgrace and worse, his disfigurement. This man must die and die badly. What a strange thing fate is, had Viktor not met the lawyer and subsequently killed him, the McTeal woman would not have fled to the Caribbean and ended up chartering a boat from the man who had destroyed his life. Well, life was actually better now than it had ever been or could have been in the Soviet Union, even after the collapse of Communism, but that did not matter. More than anything else in his life, before or since, Mhiki had wanted to be a General, and if the insignificant fuck in these photos had not blown off half of his face, he would have been. *Oh yes*, thought Mhiki, *I am coming down there and I am going to personally kill you and the woman, in fact I am going to make you watch me kill the woman slowly, you will see her beg for death as will you when your time comes. Nothing else matters, no expense will be too great, as long as I know that you draw breath, I swear that I will not rest until I have destroyed you completely.*

Chapter Sixteen

Special Agent Mike Nolan of the Joint Anti Terrorism Task Force, New York office, was a man accustomed to getting answers, so, when the FBI data base failed to turn up anything on one Jack Schmidt, he was a bit confounded. After some further inquiries to the IRS and Social Security Administration he was even more confused, the guy simply did not exist prior to six years ago. Nolan first thought the guy might be in the Witness Security Program but he had checked that out as well and got nowhere. Even if he was in the program, there was a standard protocol to follow if it appeared he was in danger, and because he was with the McTeal woman, he was definitely in danger but who the hell is he and where did he come from. Nolan was on the phone with Dave Eggers explaining that he was not able to find out anything about the mysterious Mr. Schmidt when his secretary interrupted him with an urgent call.

"Special Agent Nolan, my name is Timothy Matthews, I'm with the State Departments Bureau of Diplomatic Security, and actually, I run it. It is my understanding that you have been going out of your way to get information on a man named Jack Schmidt."

"Well, yes, I am why would that interest the State Department's spook division."

"Ok Nolan, it is imperative that I, me, personally know exactly why you are trying to find out about this guy and everyone else who is interested in him" After Nolan explained the situation, Matthews uttered a curse and told Nolan to get Brady and Eggers and meet him at the VIP terminal at JFK in two hours, it would take that long for him to get there by helicopter. Nolan was to secure the use of a little known federal command center at JFK for a conference as soon as Matthews arrived, and everyone would have to wait until then to get any more information. Also, Nolan was to have surveillance placed on one Mikhail Valentnikov, former GRU Officer now residing in New York, follow do not intercept. Matthews would be at the airport at eight PM sharp. When Nolan asked what was significant about this Valentnikov character, he was told to just do it if he wanted to hang on to his job.

Fuck, thought Nolan, what was going on here. Nolan got in touch with Brady and Eggers and filled them in on what little he knew. Using his ATTF horsepower, he had secured an address on Valentnikov and had Task Force agents on their way to his residence to initiate surveillance. The agents were advised that the subject was a former intelligence officer and commando, so they would have to be especially careful to avoid detection by their quarry. Nolan's next call was to St.. Thomas resident SAC, Bill Reynolds. Nolan told him to have the marina and the Russians' hotel watched, the important thing now, was to see when Jack and the McTeal woman left, and what the Russians were up to. Reynolds was to take no other action without first contacting Nolan.

Nolan, Brady and Eggers were sitting in the command center waiting for Matthews to show up. Nolan asked if either of them had ever heard of Valentnikov before. "Well," said Eggers, "we know he is a real bad guy, we believe that the Russian mutts that are in St.. Thomas now work for him. We don't have any real proof of that but it is what we believe. He got here about fifteen years ago from Russia and bought a night club with cash. After about six months, he bought two more. His business has expanded considerably and we are certain that he is running a large criminal enterprise but we can't prove shit, too many layers between him and the street soldiers. We would certainly like to know more about the guy, but we've never been able to get any wire tap or surveillance warrants due to lack of evidence, which we will never get without the wire taps or surveillance."

"Well, you got it now," said Nolan, "the State Department has provided a Federal John Doe warrant for full physical and electronic surveillance for suspicion of seditious activities and other egregious crimes against the United States of America. That gentlemen, gives us the legal justification to do just about any damn thing we want. As soon as my guys have made visual contact with Valentnikov, they will let me know." Eggers asked, "So, what is the deal with this guy Schmidt, you said shit started happening when you started checking him out." Before Nolan could answer, three men strode into the room, one of them looking to be in his mid fifties with an obvious air of power and authority, and the other two who were in maybe their early thirties and both looked like very unpleasant men. Matthews spoke first and said, "Which one of you is Nolan?" Nolan introduced himself, then Eggers and Brady. After the introductions, everyone but the two as yet unnamed gentlemen sat down at the table. As Matthews was getting ready to speak, he noticed that Eggers was looking at the two security men. Matthews said, "Don't worry about them, they are deaf and blind unless told to be otherwise, but what the hell, meet Bill and Bob. I don't get out of the office much and the boss insists that I have company when I do, just goes with the job. Ok Mike, you want to know just who the hell Jack Schmidt is and what does he have to do with a former GRU Colonel."

Eggers and Brady traded a look and Matthews said, "That's right we know who and what he used to be, we had a hand in getting him his citizenship after CIA got him into the country. But that can come later." Bill or Bob, whichever, walked to the opposite end of the room and pressed a button under the end of the table and a panel opened on the table to reveal what looked like a video player while at the same time a screen lowered from the ceiling at the other end of the room. Bill or Bob took a CD out of his jacket pocket and put it in the machine and picked up the remote.

The first picture was of a man in his mid to late twenties in a Naval officer's uniform with the large, unmistakable eagle, trident, and musket insignia of a Navy SEAL over his left breast pocket. "Gentlemen, meet Jake Saunders, aka Jack Schmidt." Bill or Bob advanced a frame and there were more pictures of Saunders/Schmidt that appeared to be a progression of ten to fifteen years ending with the recent pictures shot in St. Thomas at the marina with the McTeal woman. "Saunders was a Navy Seal and got out in eighty-five and came to work at State. We had recently started up a new unit of the Bureau of Diplomatic Security known as the

Diplomatic Security Service or DSS, I'm sure you have all heard of them but in the eighties very few did. Anyway, their mission then, like now was the protection of senior state department officials, foreign dignitaries visiting the United States, running physical security at U.S. Embassies and diplomatic missions abroad, as well as being the principal investigating agency for visa and passport fraud.

Saunders' first overseas posting was at the diplomatic mission is Peshawar Pakistan as the staff PSO (Protective Services Officer) in eighty-seven. Now that particular post, at that time, was basically spook central. Most of our clandestine and covert operations folks were running some sort of ops out of there. Just before Saunders got there, a CIA Paramilitary team got shot up delivering a batch of stingers to the Mujahideen. Right after that, and coincidentally coinciding with the arrival of Saunders and his team of three more DSS Agents, the CIA Chief of station got word that a Soviet Special Forces Colonel wanted out and wanted us to go into Afghanistan to pick him up. Well, CIA didn't have anybody that could pull it off in time so we used Saunders' team. Apparently the meet was compromised because they were jumped at the meet. All hell broke loose, the head of Spetznaz forces in Afghanistan at the time was a GRU Colonel and he personally took charge of the ambush. He and Saunders actually shot each other; Saunders caught one in the chest about an inch or so from his heart, blowing through both sides of his left lung. His shot hit the Russian in the face and took him out of the fight but did not kill him. There was a brief firefight and when it was over, the only functional Russian was the GRU guy's driver. The Spetznaz colonel is actually credited with saving Saunders' life, and the bullet Saunders took in the chest was meant for the Spetznaz Colonel. We got our guy out and back to the States. Saunders was sent back to the States where he recovered and served in various capacities prior to being assigned to the New York office heading up an investigation involving the Galliano Crime family and their involvement in immigrant smuggling, fake visas, and passports.

Saunders was working undercover and when it came time to make the bust, old man Galliano's son Vito was there. A gunfight started and Saunders put a couple of forty-five rounds into Vito's head, big mess as

I'm sure you can imagine. Four days later, Saunders and his wife and little girl are going to go see a movie, well, Saunders is the last one out of the house and his wife and little girl are already in the car. As Saunders is watching, his wife leans across the seat and turns the ignition key and the whole thing explodes. The force of the explosion blew Saunders back onto the front porch and against the wall knocking him unconscious, and totally destroyed his wife and little girl. He was in the hospital for two days before he just walked out. Nobody saw him for five days, and in that time, old man Galliano, a couple of his Capos and a bunch of his soldiers met with a series of most unfortunate accidents. After that, all five families had kill on sight contracts out on Saunders, he had whacked a Boss and the Italians went ape shit. We were not able to prove that he was the one taking out the Galliano family, but it made sense. We got him to come in.

Two weeks to the day after his wife's death, news was released that Jake William Saunders' bullet ridden body had been pulled out of the Hudson River, and that he had apparently been killed in retribution for the killing of Vito Galliano during a high risk felony arrest. Of course there was no body pulled out of the river, and it was an FBI confidential informant who took credit for the phony hit and claimed the bounty. That not only made him rich, but it got him closer in, where he, over the next couple of months got made, and was able to help do considerable damage to La Cosa Nostra from the inside. Jack Schmidt was born the same day that Jake Saunders body was supposedly fished out of the river. He then retired quietly to the Caribbean until now.

"Holy shit," said Eggers, "I remember that mess, all that was said at the time was that a federal agent and his family were believed to have been killed by the Goombas. We thought Galliano was ordered taken out by the commission because of all the bad press." Matthews said, "It is important for a lot of different reasons to keep a lid on things as I'm sure you can deduce on your own. You see, the GRU Officer he shot in the face in Afghanistan was none other than your Mhikiail Valentnikov; evidently, his people were after the McTeal woman for unknown reasons related to your investigation Detective. She just happened to charter a boat from Saunders, and by now Valentnikov has seen pictures of Saunders/Schmidt. We had told Valentnikov that Saunders died of his wounds in Afghanistan. Also we never told him his real name. After Valentnikov got out of the hospital, they shitcanned him. Tossed him out on his sorry ass with nothing, no pension, nada. Needless to say, he was pissed. So, about six months after he gets back to the good old USSR, he contacts someone at the U.S. Embassy in Moscow and tells them that if we will get him out and to the U.S., he would give us anything and everything he knows.

"Had it not been for the botched episode in Afghanistan, this guy would have been made a General in short order, it was just too good an offer to turn down. Win, win for our side twice, we got a wealth of information on Soviet Spetznaz structure, training, and tactics, everything. Then, just months later, we get a very disgruntled, very senior spook who tells us everything we ever wanted to know about the GRU. It was a gold mine, countless dollars and human lives were saved with the information we got out of those two, it was one of the greatest intelligence coups of the whole cold war and we owed every goddamn bit of it to Saunders, and that is why we turned a blind eye to the assassinations of a few Mafioso scumbags, fuck em, they killed his wife and little girl. Now Saunders has no reason to believe that he would ever have any trouble with the Russians, they all thought he was dead, he does remain a little concerned about the Italians, but they too believed he was dead. With the information I have just given you, there are still less than a dozen people that know who and where Saunders is, and we are going to stay out of it completely. The deal I cut with Saunders was off the books, Jake Saunders is officially dead and buried, and we will not acknowledge any of this, understood.

"Mike, here is a phone number I want you to have, it belongs to a man called VI Borden, I believe he is called now, former Spetznaz, he is a civilian employee at the Naval Special Warfare Development Group at Dam Neck, Virginia, he's the one Saunders got out, give him a call and let him know what is going on Mike, you can tell him everything. As for us, we never had this conversation, and we will not get involved, I have no interest in the McTeal woman or why Valentnikov and his people are after her. What I do know, is that Saunders is owed a debt for what he did for his country and his proximity to this woman has placed him in grave physical danger. How you handle this is up to you, but it is now the position of the powers that be, that Valentnikov has outlived his period of usefulness. The federal warrant you now possess gives you and NYPD full license to go after Valentnikov and all of his various businesses and associates."

Eggers was trying to get his mind in gear when Brady said; "Can I ask you a couple of questions?" Matthews smiled politely, said, "No, there will be no Q&A here gentlemen, it is now up to you how you will proceed, Detectives, you can now dismantle Valentnikovs entire operation, in that, you will receive the full backing of the Justice Department, they don't know why they are going to cooperate fully, but nonetheless, they will. Mike, you are to personally head the investigation, official and unofficial. Headlines are to be kept to a minimum, this all needs to be cleaned up quietly. Detectives, the only reason you two are here is so that you understand that this is going to get cleaned up with or without you being involved. Detective Eggers, you should be receiving a phone call within twenty-four hours from interested parties who will be able to help with your investigation. They have the advantage of not being hindered by legal niceties. Do either of you have a problem with this; I need to know now if you do. This is just the way some things have to be done, and will be done for all the right reasons." Brady and Eggers looked at each other and shrugged their shoulders and Eggers said, "We don't care much for Mafia types, don't matter to us what their ethnic background is. One thing though, while you are here, there may be something you can help me with that relates directly to this situation." Matthews said nothing so Eggers continued. "This whole thing got started after the McTeal woman's boyfriend who was a lawyer and who was murdered, took something out of a safe deposit box belonging to one Karl Richter. He was dead and the lawyer was just clearing out the estate, whatever got him croaked was in that box. I don't really care too much about that right now but we can't find anything out about Richter, it appears that he was *born* in forty-seven here in New York, but we also found pictures of him in a Waffen SS uniform with the rank of colonel also wearing the Nazi equivalent of the Medal of Honor. Maybe you can help fill in that particular blank. It all starts with him from our perspective."

"Ok," said Matthews, "I'll look into it and have someone contact you. Now, back on subject, Mike you are to provide the people who are going to contact with any and all information they may require. A pallet of equipment has already been sent to St. Thomas from McDill AFB in Florida in a USAF C-130 for those men to pick up, you need to call Bill Reynolds and tell him that there will be some men coming to pick up the big box of goodies I sent for them and that he and his men are to share any and all information they have with them. They will be carrying federal credentials. After that, the Caribbean end of things will take care of itself. One of the men, Billy Chalmers, AKA Bob Moore is on the first flight to St. Thomas in the morning and will try to contact Saunders personally, can't risk a phone call due to the nature of the people after him, we have to assume that his cell phone is being monitored. He already has pictures and the location of Saunders' boat as well as photos of the woman. Also Bill Reynolds will have to agree to play ball as well. It involves more looking the other way than anything else, and, if this turns out the way I think it will, there may also be a couple of, "Gee, we just can't figure this one out," scenarios called for. These guys know how to be discrete, but as they say, shit happens. Mike you can turn it off right now and nothing will ever come of it. It will not affect the Federal Warrant, but it will mean that Saunders and the woman will be dead in seventy-two hours or less. There are no grounds to take them into protective custody, and as yet, no grounds to apprehend any of the Russians. Also they could be leaving for British territory or in any direction for that matter, at any time. Again, I was never here. If you check, there will be no record of my flight arriving or departing here, and numerous witnesses will account for my whereabouts during this time frame. And similarly, nothing that happens from this point on can possibly come back on any of you, all you will do is provide some information to some people who will identify themselves to you as Federal Agents, no one will ever be able to ask them anything because they do not in fact exist, but hey you didn't know that. Gentlemen, I leave you to it." Then Bill or Bob took the disk out of the video and then the three of them just walked out.

Mike looked over at Sam and Dave and said, "I am really not certain what the hell we all agreed to, but I think it means that somebody just let some big bad dogs loose." Eggers said, "If he can tell us about the old Nazi it will give us someplace to start with trying to figure what got this whole thing going."

"Who gives a shit anyway, we can get all of these assholes now, we just have to wait for the surveillance to get in place, get the info we need to make a case and nail these guys, at least the ones that don't get whacked over the next few days," said Brady. "Yeah, but I still want to know about old Karl and maybe find out what was in that box," said Eggers. Mike said, "I am going to call this Russian that works for the Navy right now and see what he has to say, then we can figure out what to do next. In fact I believe I will suggest he get here immediately, I can send a helo straight to the pad at Dam Neck. I also have to call Bill Reynolds in St. Thomas to tell him about his visitors. Congratulations boys, you just became part of a federal task force, I'll call your Captain and square it with him. I want to play this close to vest guys, no one gets in that does not already have knowledge of the case and we limit their exposure in as much as is possible. I hate to do this but I am taking charge of this investigation, from here on, it will be a joint ATTF NYPD operation that for reasons of national security must and will be kept as low key as possible. I can explain visits and conversations that never happened to my boss, he knows how that shit works, as for your Captain, he only finds out what he absolutely needs to know. Look it is getting late, you guys knock off for now and meet me here tomorrow morning at nine, we can use this place as a CP for this thing in order to help keep it secure. Have all of your files on this transferred here and make sure anything that you have anyone working on in relation to this gets sent here, I'll give you the secure fax number and we can get both of you set up with desks. I don't know how long this will take but we are all in it until it's done, ok."

With that said, the two detectives went home to think about what had just transpired. It appeared that hunting licenses had just been issued for some rather nasty Russians. Nolan called the number that Matthews had given him for the former Spetznaz Colonel. All he had to say was that Saunders was alive and in trouble and Borden said he would meet the helo at DEVGRU's pad at 0600. The helo would take him to NAS Oceana where an FBI Lear Jet would be standing by for him and he would arrive in the city by 0930. With two calls, the helo would be cleared in to the pad in the morning. The only question Borden had was about weapons on the flight. Nolan assured him that would not be a problem and in fact stated that it would be a good idea, and that they would have a lengthy conversation in the morning.

Chapter Seventeen

Jack pulled up in front of Frenchman's Reef promptly at seven and Alex was waiting for him outside at the hotel entrance. She was wearing a white sun dress and looked absolutely stunning. A fact not lost on everyone else who was there watching her. Ivan was sitting in his rental car across the parking lot, and Agent Halston was watching them both. As Jack came to a stop in front of the hotel Alex flashed him a smile and climbed into the Jeep. "So, we're going to the Old Mill," said Alex. "That is correct Madame, I think you'll like it, after we eat I'll take you up into the old tower. It has a 360 degree view and it looks down on the bay. The food ain't bad either. Nothing fancy but it is tasty. And by the way, the gen set is up and running just fine so we can get underway in the morning."

"Works for me," was all Alex said. Alex was amazed at how steep the road was leading up Crown Mountain towards the restaurant. At the restaurant, Jack selected a table on the upper deck and they were the only two people there, that put Halston and Ivan in a bit of a pickle as neither wanted to be seated on the otherwise empty deck in plain view of the couple. Halston sat at the downstairs bar where he could watch the exit and parking lot and saw Ivan return to his vehicle, presumably to wait for the pair to leave. Jack and Alex both ordered drinks and each decided to have the blackened Tuna steaks. "So, where are we off to tomorrow Mon Capitan?"

"Well," said Jack, "I was going to ask you that. Tomorrow is Christmas Eve and we have dinner reservations at Cooper Island for Christmas, so I was thinking we could go to Salt Island which is right next to Cooper and do a couple of really nice dives and then go on over to Cooper and pick up a mooring ball for the night. I took the liberty of reserving the mooring for both nights, and then we can get underway the morning after Christmas. We do need to stop by Soapers Hole on Tortola on the way to clear customs but it's on the way."

"Sounds good to me," said Alex. "Tell me about this dive."

"Sure, did you ever see the movie, The Deep, with Nick Nolte and Jacqueline Bissett?"

"Of course I did, that's what got me into diving. I figured if she could do it, I certainly could. What does that movie have to do with our dive tomorrow, didn't that story take place in the Bahamas?"

"Ah, a very astute observation Madame. Yes the story took place in the Bahamas, but the diving scenes were shot in five separate oceans and the actual wreck they were diving on was none other than the R.M.S. Rhone. It sank just off the eastern tip of Salt Island in a hurricane back in 1867. She was one of the first steam powered ships around. The wind drove her into Black Rock right there at Salt Island and opened up her hull, when the cool sea water hit her boiler she blew in half, killing all but 22 of 145 souls aboard. The inhabitants of Salt Island helped save the ones that made it and the Queen of England gave the island to its inhabitants for the annual payment of 10 pounds of salt as an act of gratitude. Anyway, we dive the bow section which is at about 75 feet for about a thirty minute dive, then we can do lunch on the boat and chill for a bit and off gas, then do the stern section which is at about 35 feet, and we can hang out and burn a full tank. After we clean the gear, we motor across to Cooper, and that is only about a ten minute trip." Alex thought for a minute and said, "Cool, sounds great, can you go inside the wreck?"

"Yep, sure can, you can't really make anything out that still looks like a ship though, 140 years on the bottom have pretty much taken their toll. Lots of fish and critters though. In fact, if you're lucky you'll get to meet Fang."

"And who would Fang be?" asked Alex. "Well, Fang is one of the biggest cudas I've ever seen, he hangs out inside the wreck. He's been there so long I believe he thinks that divers are his pets; he's no threat but the first time you see him it will get your heart going a little faster." The two ate mostly in silence, savoring the flavor of the freshly caught tuna.

After they had finished their meal, Jack paid the tab, despite a polite protest from Alex, then Jack said, "Let me show you the Mill Tower, it's a great view from the top and the climb up is kind of cool too." As Jack and Alex climbed the spiral stairs they came to the second floor and Alex noted that was a small area with a couple of comfy looking lounge chairs and a table with a reading lamp, on the next floor was a sofa and a coffee table with lamps as well, finally, at the top, there was a sofa that went all the way around the tower wall 360 degrees and there was a windowless opening that went all the way around. Alex walked over and kneeled on the sofa next to where Jack had stood and looked out over the harbor of Charlotte Amalie.

"Wow, what a view, how long has this place been here?" asked Alex. "It's over 200 years old, they have added a lot of stuff, but I like eating up on the deck and if you catch it just right like we did, you can have a private dinner on the deck. Well, I should probably get you back to your hotel, big day tomorrow. Do you want me to come pick you up in the morning?"

"No, I'll just take a cab after I check out. I'll just bring my stuff with me in the morning and we can get underway right after we eat."

"Good enough, and lunch will be right after the first dive, but we can snack on the way to Salt Island after we leave Soapers. With that said, let's get you back to your room." As Jack and Alex were leaving, Ivan pulled out of his parking spot after Jack's Jeep and Halston after that. Halston was upset that he had not been able to listen in on any of the conversation that Jack and Alex were having, but then neither had the Russian.

Agent White was watching the hotel and Wilson was positioned at the marina. All noted the time when Jack dropped Alex off and went straight to the marina and his boat. Reynolds told his people that he wanted one agent at the marina and hotel no later than 0700. Halston would go to the hotel and White would go have breakfast at the marina and keep an eye on Schmidt. The Russians on the other hand had bigger problems. As soon as Ivan had reported that the sailor had dropped the woman off he was told to return immediately to Black Beards, when he arrived there, he was not at all happy with the news.

Viktor and Leo sat in their room pondering the recent call from Lexi, Mhiki was going to arrive on the 1130 flight from New York in the morning and Viktor and Leo were to meet him at the airport. According to Lexi, Mhiki was in a very dark mood. He did not know why Mhiki had decided to go there himself, but he was told not to ask questions, just do what he was told if he wanted to keep his balls intact. H e also ordered Lexi to FedEx five 9 millimeter handguns to the hotel address along with two Draeger rebreather type SCUBA rigs. The handguns would not be a problem if they were clean of any residue, and were shipped without ammunition. The box would be labeled as boat parts, and they could purchase ammunition there on the island. With that done, Lexi had made the flight reservation, informed Mhiki, and then called Leo.

"Why is he coming here Leo?" demanded Viktor. "What the hell is going on. Lexi said he is pissed about something but what, we are doing our jobs. Stephan, first thing in the morning, call and reserve the boat in case we need to move quickly. We will have to wait until Mhiki arrives to get it, I need you, Ivan at the marina watching the boat no later than 0600 and report all movements to me. That will leave the woman unobserved but we know, or expect her to show up at the marina. I don't know what is going on yet but I want to be ready for whatever."

Billy Chalmers would be arriving in St Thomas an hour before Mhiki, information he received from the New York FBI who had wasted no time in beginning their electronic surveillance of Mhiki after the receipt of their warrant. Billy had not seen Jack in years but they had remained good friends after the Afghanistan assignment, serving together for a couple of years as Personal Protective Officers on the Visiting Dignitary Security Detail out of D.C. They had lost touch after Jack was re-assigned to New York. Billy's main concern was being able to contact Jack before he got underway. It would be difficult to locate him while he was island hopping and as yet, he was uncertain of the opposition's intentions, and his two companions would not arrive until Christmas day.

Both were good men to have with you in a scrape. Dan Wilcox was a former Special Forces soldier and retired from the DSS, and Will Evans was a former DSS and then CIA Paramilitary type. Both were fiercely loyal and both good friends of Jack's, who like everyone else, thought he was dead. It did not take much goading for the two retired spooks to accept their current mission once Billy had laid it out for them. They were to protect Jack and the woman, and if necessary kill all of the Russians, discretely as possible of course, but the inference was there that they should never return from the Caribbean. The three men would be carrying DSS credentials under false names, and after this was all said and done if anyone were to enquire about them, the answer they would get would be, "Who, we don't have one of those."

The first thing Billy had to do was to get a SITREP from Bill Reynolds and secure the box of goodies that Matthews had sent ahead for them. If Reynolds knew what was in that box he would positively shit, thought Billy. There were four Limpet mines, three H&K MP-5K Machine pistols, three Glock 23, .40 caliber pistols, all equipped with suppressors, and a significant amount of ammo for each, several different types of knives, three sets of ANVIS-6 night vision devices, assorted SCUBA gear, 3 clean, encryption capable cell phones, four secure voice walkie talkies, one laptop computer with a navigation program loaded into it that had wireless satellite connectivity, three GPS receivers with chart plotting capability, three satellite tracking devices, and $100,000 in cash. Also, a previously confiscated 39' Donzi Cigarette boat with modest sleeping accommodations for four, with an RI B, type dingy on the swim platform, and twin 500 HP inboard engines was being delivered to American Yacht Harbor marina on the eastern tip of the island, compliments of the U.S. Customs service. It had been decided to use a different marina as not to be seen by the Russians loading boxes of gear onto the boat at the same marina that everyone had under surveillance.

Mhiki just wanted to find and then kill Saunders, he knew that it was possible that the woman and sailor might be gone when he got there, but they could rent a boat and follow or find them. If they could not be located, Mhiki could wait for them in St. Thomas and kill them when they returned if he was unable to locate them sooner. Mhiki had no idea that he was now under surveillance and that federal agents had his residential phone tapped and were now listening in on all of his cell phone conversations. Mhiki had a rough idea as to how to kill Jack and the woman, the stones did not matter now, Mhiki was here to kill the man he perceived as having ruined his life and nothing else mattered for the time being. An unfortunate explosion on their boat would be nice, Mhiki could not chance shipping explosives to the island, but Stephan could build a bomb out of just about anything, he would just have to see how it went.

Jack was up at 0600 and went for a long run; it would be his last chance for a couple of weeks. He was back at the boat and showered by 0700, and decided to get the boat ready while he was waiting for Alex. Jack did a walk around down below to make sure everything was stowed for sea and then went back on deck and re-checked his jerry cans of fuel for the dingy, and double checked all of his scuba tanks to make sure they were all at 3000 psi. The weather was supposed to be beautiful for at least the next week. This was all observed by Ivan and reported to Leo, he told Ivan to just stay where he was and take no action.

The winds were going to be unusually light for the time of year. The usual Christmas winds, as they were known, had yet to materialize this year. A 10 knot wind would not move the big Gulfstar at more than about 5 knots or so. 15 to 20 knots would move her at 7 to 10 knots plus depending on sea conditions.

At precisely 0600 the FBI helo landed on the pad at DEVGRU's compound at NAB Dam Neck. VI was greeted by an agent who asked to see some ID and when satisfied, took VI's two bags and put them in the bird and opened the passenger door for him. Once VI was strapped in the pilot wasted no time in taking off, once airborne, the agent who had helped him handed him a set of headphones with a boom mile. "Good morning sir, it'll only take about ten minutes until we're on deck at Oceana and the Lear is already turning, as soon as you are onboard you guys can get going. There are coffee and Danish rolls on the plane if you want them on the flight to New York which will take about an hour and forty-five minutes. Another agent will meet you on the ramp there and your briefing will take place in a command center at the airport. Any questions?" VI thought, *Hell yes I have questions*, but figured those could wait for the briefing. "No, thank you," was all VI had to say and not long after, they were landing on the ramp right next to the waiting Lear Jet.

As VI was getting out of the helo, he saw the door open on the Lear and another agent stepped out to help with his bags and motioned for VI to get in the plane. After VI was seated and strapped in, the agent gave the pilot a thumbs up and moments later they were rolling. VI was impressed;

the jet taxied right onto the runway, did its run-up and then took off. Nothing was said during the flight until the aircraft was approaching final into JFK. The agent informed VI that he would escort him to the command center once they were on the ground. Despite what Nolan had told him, VI was a bit concerned about the contents in his one bag. After landing, the Lear taxied to within a few feet of a door on the far side of the terminal marked with a **Warning Do Not Enter** sign and a uniformed NYPD officer was standing outside. As promised, the agent escorted him to the command center.

While they were waiting for Borden to arrive, Nolan got a phone call from a man named Rick, he said he was traveling with another gentleman and they had been sent by Matthews. Rick left a number and told Nolan that they would be available for two weeks, after that, the number would no longer work.

After VI was escorted inside, Nolan introduced himself first, then Brady and Eggers. Nolan said, "Ok, this is why you are here, Valentnikov will be here in the airport boarding a flight for St. Thomas in about an hour, we can't and don't want to stop that, I have an address for you, it belongs to one Alexei Sergeyivch Yoskov, AKA Lexi. He is basically Valentnikov's second in command, also he is the central contact point, get him to suspend all contact with the people in St. Thomas so they are cut off with no outside help, no one on this end answers the phone."

"And I am to just ask him this and he will do it?"

"I did not say you had to ask nice, also here is a file I want you to look at before you go for your visit, all materials must remain here though. I want you to get as much information about Valentnikov's infrastructure as possible; we want to completely shut down his criminal enterprises. We already know it includes narcotics, gambling, prostitution, loan sharking, and blackmail. Valentnikov is finished, actually, he will most likely not return from the Caribbean, the men that were sent there have orders to protect Saunders and the woman by whatever means necessary, or deemed most effective. In fact you know the team leader, you met him in Afghanistan, his name is Billy Chalmers." VI looked at Nolan and at first showed genuine surprise, and then a wide grin appeared. "If that is so, you will not have to worry about the Russians there. And what are Billy's instructions."

Nolan said, "He will only kill them if it appears to be the best means of handling the problem."

"Let me tell you something," said VI, "if Valentnikov is there, killing him will be the only way to keep Saunders safe. I know Mhiki, I served under him in Afghanistan, he is the reason I defected to the west, he is the most utterly ruthless animal I have ever come across in my entire life, the man has no soul that I can discern. The things he made Spetznaz Forces do in Afghanistan had not been seen since the SS Einsatzgruppen wreaked havoc in Europe forty years before. I left because I was a professional soldier, and the things we were doing, were not the actions of men of honor. What I cannot believe is that he was ever turned loose in this country."

"What about you?" asked Eggers, "As I understand it you were a full Colonel in the Spetznaz, and you personally carried out these orders and now you work for the U.S. Navy."

"Good point Detective, I defected because I do have a soul and our actions weighed heavily upon it. After I came over, I did everything I could to help defeat the Red army in Afghanistan as a matter of conscience and personal atonement."

Brady asked, "What exactly is the Naval Special Warfare Development Group and what do you do there." VI looked over at Nolan who nodded as if to say "ok," a gesture that surprised the two detectives. "Well," said VI, "it is actually Seal Team Six, made famous by a series of novels. According to the Navy, it does not exist, though its existence has become rather common knowledge. Their primary mission is counter terrorism. They, along with Special Forces Operational Detachment Delta, more commonly referred to as Delta Force; make up JSOC, or Joint Special Operations Command, which has a completely different chain of command from all other special operations units. What I do there Detective, is teach unarmed combat and knife fighting skills to the new guys, you see after I was done debriefing, I genuinely wanted to do something to help stop the spread of Communism and terrorism, you see, I had seen the evils of both as I had participated in them. I was slowly integrated into the community at first, and more as the people in charge began to realize the depth of my commitment to this cause, I am now a

U.S. citizen and perform a service to which I am uniquely suited. I have a pleasant disposition, but know that I am a genuinely dangerous man, I say this not as a boast, but as a fact, why else would a former Soviet Spetznaz officer be training U.S. counter terror forces."

Everyone looked at VI and had to admit he had a pleasant enough demeanor and spoke English without accent, something he had worked very hard at over the years. He was an American now, and all of the Team guys that knew him, knew his past and actually respected him even more for it. What VI had not told the three men was that he had never been physically bested, in combat or training, and that was why he was teaching the best of the best. The most common comment after VI's two week training course was, "I would hate to see him pissed."

"Well," said Nolan, "after we finish here, a taxi will take you to see Lexi, the cab is one of ours and so is the driver, he is one of our best CT Agents and will serve as your back up. He answers to you, we don't care how you achieve your objective, but the thugs in St. Thomas have to be isolated."

"Very well," said VI, "I think I can get most of what you want in a day with one visit."

"Do you need any equipment," asked Nolan. VI opened his one bag and produced a Smith and Wesson 9MM pistol with an integrated suppressor commonly referred to as a hush puppy in the teams. He also had four boxes of ammo and four magazines, two of which had the butt plates painted yellow; those were for the special loads. Its primary use in the field was to take out guard dogs and sentries. When loaded with subsonic rounds, the bulk of the noise created by the weapon was from the sound of the slide cycling. He also produced three knives of various sizes and said that he had all that he required. A phone rang and Nolan answered it, after a moment, Nolan hung up and motioned everyone to a video monitor. "There he goes, that's Valentnikov boarding his flight. Mr. Borden, look over that file, ask whatever questions you have, then it's time for you to pay Lexi a visit."

Alex was up at 0700 and drank some coffee and packed her things and then went to the lobby to check out of the hotel. At the counter she had the duty manager retrieve her box from the safety deposit box and placed it in her small suitcase. She decided to go to the marina early; she didn't think Jack would mind. Alex let the bellman carry her bags outside and hail her a cab.

Alex arrived at the marina at just a little after eight. Jack saw her getting out of her cab and walked over to greet her. She was wearing those tight white shorts again with a relatively sheer white bikini top and her straw Panama hat "Good morning," said Jack, "let me get those bags for you, we can put them on the boat and go get a bite to eat, then we're off. The boat is ready to go; all we have to do is fire up the motor and cast off."

"Great," said Alex, "as they were walking to the boat, I'll stow this stuff back aft then we can eat." As Jack and Alex were walking to the boat, Ivan was on the phone with Leo informing him that it appeared that they would be leaving today; he also noted that the only bags she had were the ones that he had searched in her room previously. Leo told Ivan to keep watch but to stay out of sight as much as possible. Special Agent Andy White was seated at the counter at Tickles drinking a cup of coffee and reading the *New York Times*. Wearing shorts, sandals, and a grey Hawaiian shirt to conceal his Glock 22 pistol, he looked like part of the usual scenery.

Jack and Alex ordered and ate and talked about everything except where they were going before they got up and left for the boat. White knew that he needed that info to pass along to Chalmers/Moore. As White and Ivan watched, Jack started up the motor on the big Gulfstar. On the boat, Jack was standing at the helm and told Alex, "Ok, go ahead and toss the starboard spring line first, then get both stern lines off, just leave them tied to the dock, we'll use them when we get back." After Alex had done as she was told, Jack said, "Good, now get the port side bow line first, then get the starboard side and tell me when we're clear so I can back us out of here."

Alex did as told and called clear, then Jack pulled the shift lever back into reverse, and gunned the throttle for about two seconds then throttled back and shifted back into neutral and the boat began to move backwards out of its slip. Just as the bow was clearing the end of the dock, Jack hit a switch on the console and Alex could hear a hydraulic motor kick on and the bow instantly began to swing to the right pivoting the boat as if the center of the vessel were on a pin. Before the bow was lined up with the entrance to the marina, Jack switched off the bow thruster and shifted the boat into forward gear and advanced the throttle slightly. The big boat smoothly began to make way for open water. After clearing the marina entrance, Jack turned to the left to skirt between Hassle and Water Island. Jack steered the boat through the channel between the two small islands then turned south for open water.

Jack kept the speed to about four knots and told Alex to get the fenders off the starboard side and stow them in the locker under the cockpit seat behind the helm. Alex had to make two trips to retrieve the bulky inflatable fenders and Jack noted her ease of movement, it was obvious she had done all of this before. Jack was watching his wind speed indicator and noted that they only had about 4 knots of wind. Even after turning out of St. Thomas harbor, the ocean looked like a mill pond.

"Are we going to motor there," asked Alex.

"Yeah, looks that way, maybe after we clear customs at Soapers we can get some sail up for the trip to Salt Island, with some wind it's a real nice run. Just have to wait and see. I'll throttle up a bit so we can make some time on the way to Tortola." Jack advanced the throttle until he was making seven knots, the bow of the boat slicing cleanly through the calm clear Caribbean water. Alex had moved up to the bow and sat down with her legs hanging over the port rail and sat in silence as she watched the island of St. Thomas pass by on the port, or left side of the boat. Jack entered a couple of waypoints into his navigation computer and switched on his auto pilot. Alex was initially startled when Jack sat down next to her. "I forgot you have all the wiz bang NAV gear."

"Yep, I don't really need to drive for about twenty more minutes, you see those rocks sticking out just above the surface out there just off the starboard bow, we'll be turning to port right before we get there and turning through current cut, or puke passage as it's known. When we have normal winds around here you get the Atlantic and Caribbean currents colliding right after you pass through the cut, it can make for a pretty rough ride for about ten or fifteen minutes, after that, you get into deep enough water that the surface doesn't get so stirred up. After we take that left and pass through the cut it is like sailing into a different world, you can see most of the BVI, and then you can just pick an island, point the bow at it, trim up the sails and go."

"You know," said Alex, "your job really sucks big time. This really is wonderful Jack."

"On one of my first charters here, we were motoring through the cut just before sunset, we got through the cut and the sun was setting off the port side and the full moon was rising off the starboard side and they were at the same height above the islands, the sun over St. Thomas, and the moon over St. John and they appeared to be the same size. It was the most beautiful thing I had ever seen. The water was calm like it is now and the reflections of the two merged on the water in the sound, absolutely magnificent. You could spend your whole life sailing and never see anything like that. There were three other people on the boat that day and we had at least two video cameras onboard and no one thought to go below and get one, we were all just mesmerized by the sight of it. Oh well," said Jack, "I will always have a perfect picture of it right here in my head." Alex was watching Jack as he told the story and could see that it was more than just a sea story, that the experience had moved him and she found herself wishing she had been here with him to have shared such a moment with this man.

Alex did a quick reality check, was she going soft for this guy already, *God,* she thought, *you just met him.* Her thoughts were interrupted when Jack said, "Well, gotta go shut off the auto pilot and start driving this rig again to get through the cut." Jack walked back to the cockpit and stepped through the front window which was made of a soft clear plastic called, Eisenglass. The boat had a fully enclosed cockpit with two large Eisenglass windows in front with zippers so they could be rolled up and secured to the overhead, or rolled down and zipped in place on either side of the centerpiece that ran from the cockpit overhead to the front lip of the cockpit, also several more roll up windows lined the entire cockpit area so it could be completely closed in from the elements, or all of them could be unzipped and rolled up to get plenty of airflow just like an open cockpit boat. Jack killed the auto pilot and called for Alex to come back to the cockpit, when she got there Jack said, "See that big rock sticking out of the water in the middle of the passage, the place we go through is to the right of the rock between that and the shore on the right." Alex looked at the cut and was amazed the "CUT" as it were was maybe seventy-five feet wide and you could look at the water and tell you had to be dead in the middle of it not to smack the keel of the boat on the bottom.

"Tight squeeze," said Alex, "I can just imagine it when it's rough out."

"Yeah," said Jack, "even though, it doesn't get real bad until you get to the other side of it. Maybe it'll be nice and nasty for us on the way back so you can get the full effect." Alex just shot him a menacing look then grinned and said, "Maybe so, I'd like to see what you look like with green gills."

"Ha," said Jack, "why don't you do something useful and go get me a small Gatorade out of the fridge," grinning himself.

"But of course Mon Capitan, anything else you need while I'm down below?"

"Nope, that ought to do it." As Alex went down the companionway steps Jack could not help looking at her butt, a damn nice butt at that Jack thought to himself. When Alex came back topside, she had a drink for both of them. "Now," said Jack, "over to our left, is St. Thomas, and to the right is St. John, that bay on the right where that big ferry just pulled in is Cruz Bay." As they passed the mouth of Cruz Bay, Alex saw a beautiful beach and asked Jack what it was called. "That Madame, is Caneel Bay, if you're lucky you can pick up a mooring ball. If you want to go to Cruz Bay we can snag a ball or anchor here and Dingy over around the point. Between the ferry's going in and out and shallow water, I won't take the boat in there unless I'm going to the service dock. Ok, see that long skinny island up there on the left, then the smaller one on the right."

"Ok," said Alex.

"We're gonna go between the two of them then hang a right into Soapers Hole, also referred to on Tortola as the West End." As Jack rounded Little Thatch and headed into the mouth of Soapers, Alex was again awestruck with the beauty of it. Jack looked over at her and said, "Very well Madame, time to earn your keep, look in the port lazerette that's under the cockpit cushion right there, and you'll find the boat hook and a forty foot length of line, take the line up to the bow and tie one end off to the port bow cleat, then coil the excess. When I find a clear mooring ball I'll need you up on the bow with your hook. Usually, I would run into the wind but since there isn't any today, I'll just run straight at it. When we get to the ball give me a stop signal like this, Jack raised his right arm up with his elbow out ninety degrees from his body and his palm facing out. When we get to where you can grab the line coming off the ball with the hook, close your hand into a fist, that's how I know when to stop the boat. Once you grab the line that's attached to the top of the ball, pull it up to you and grab a hold of it then take the end of the line and run it through the eye in the mooring line, then cleat it off to the starboard cleat. Simple, right."

"Sounds easy enough," said Alex, actually she had done this several times before but she really wanted to do this well, she wanted to impress Jack with her seamanship skills. Alex got the line and boat hook out of the laz and headed up to the bow and laid the boat hook against the toe rail that ran all around the boat and cleated the line off on the port side then coiled the line up between the two bow cleats. When she was done, Alex looked back at Jack and gave a thumbs up sign. Jack spotted a ball near the customs house and pointed it out to Alex. Jack throttled back to a crawl and approached the ball directly. As he was almost to the ball, Alex gave him the stop signal and got the line with the bow hook on the second attempt and hauled it aboard. As soon as she had a grip on the line, she let go of the boat hook and ran the bitter end of the pendant through the mooring line and quickly cleated it off on the starboard side. When she was done she looked back at Jack and said, "Got it!"

Jack smiled and said, "Ok, taking tension," and then put the shifter in reverse and gave the throttle a quick bump, then went back into neutral. The boat moved back slightly and as it did, the eyelet on the mooring line took the slack out of the coiled line until the mooring line centered on the pendant and then held fast. Jack walked up to the bow where Alex was standing and looked at her handy work and was pleased to see that she knew what she was doing, and that both ends of the pendant were properly cleated off. "Good job," said Jack, "now we can launch the dingy and go over to customs, be sure to bring your passport and ten bucks for entry fees. We can clear out on our way back to St. Thomas and then all I have to do is make a call to clear back in to the U.S."

"Ok, I'll go down and get my stuff, do you need a hand with the dingy."

"No, but I want to show you how this works so I'll wait till you come back up." When Alex came back on deck Jack was hooking the ladder to the starboard side of the toe rail just forward of the cockpit. When he was done he said, "See where that goes, it's stowed in the starboard laz, now let me show you how to launch the dingy." The pair walked aft to where the dingy was stowed on the electric davits with the bow to port. Alex noted that there was a coiled line tied off to the starboard stern cleat and the other end was tied to the bow ring on the dingy. Jack said, "Ain't technology cool," as he opened a plastic box on the stern rail and pulled out a control box. "Ok, you see the two lines that go from the stern cleats to grab line on the side of the dingy, I'm gonna lower the RIB a couple of inches to give you some slack, then I want you to undo the two snap hooks." Jack pressed a button on the control box and the dingy lowered a few inches and Alex deftly unclipped the two snap hooks and then Jack hit the button again and lowered the dingy all the way into the water. Once the dingy was in the water Jack grabbed the davit line on the stern of the dingy and slid down into the boat and unhooked the dingy from the davit hoist lines then said, "Ok, Alex, take the control and raise the hooks until they are about two inches from the top pulley." After Alex had raised the hoist lines, Jack turned the key on the dingy console and hit the engine trim switch and lowered the motor into the water. After squeezing the primer bulb on the fuel line, Jack fired up the twenty-five HP Yamaha outboard engine, untied the bowline from the stern cleat on the boat and hand walked the dingy around to the ladder and told Alex to climb in. The whole process only took a few minutes.

Alex sat on the bench seat next to Jack and said, "This is truly decadent, I'm used to having to either inflate the dingy on deck, then manhandle it over the side, then take the motor off the stern rail and mount it on the transom, or drag it around behind me everywhere we sail, I like this."

"Yeah, I really like this setup, I almost never tow the dingy, and it's just too easy to use the davits and hoist. Give us a little push off the boat will you and we'll get going." Jack pointed out the customs house and soon they were tying up at the floating dingy dock. Alex leapt out of the dingy and cleated it off without Jack having to say anything. As they walked up the stairs to clear into the BVI Alex asked how long it would take. "Depends on how many people are ahead of us, usually not long though." A moment later that hope was dashed when they saw the line, at least fifteen people in front of them and the captain on a first time charter was unwisely arguing with the customs official. It took almost forty minutes to make it through the line and fill out the requisite paperwork and get their passports stamped. Though Jack never complained, Alex could see that he was pissed about the delay.

When they returned to the boat, Jack let Alex climb up the ladder then repositioned the dingy at the stern of the boat and said, "Grab the control box and lower the hoist lines to me." Alex did as she was instructed and Jack reconnected the hoist lines to the lifting pendants on the dingy. Then he turned on the bilge pump for a few seconds, then raised the lower end of the motor out of the water with the engine trim switch, and then told Alex, "Haul us up." Alex decided the davits and hoist must be hardy enough to handle the weight so she hit the switch and lifted Jack and the dingy to about the point that Jack had lowered it initially to connect the securing hooks. Jack climbed out and attached the clips to the grab line on the side of the dingy and told Alex, "Ok, take tension on it, just enough to keep it from being able to swing fore and aft." Once she had done that, Alex stowed the controller back in its box. Jack coiled the bowline up next to the stern cleat and said, "You ready to get out of here?" Go ahead and leave the bow pendant rigged after we cast off, we'll be using it a lot on the trip, just coil it up between the bow cleats like you did before. I'll start the motor now, then when I give you the ok sign, uncleat the starboard side then pull the pendant line through and give me a thumbs up when we're clear to maneuver."

"Sounds easy enough." Alex was walking forward as Jack started the engine and watched the amp meter and oil pressure come up, then after doing a traffic scan in the area around the boat, gave Alex the ok sign. Alex pulled the pendant line through then gave Jack the thumbs up. Jack let the boat drift back for a few seconds, then, after checking for traffic again put the shifter in forward, gave it some throttle and cranked the wheel hard over to starboard and turned for the mouth of the harbor. As they were heading out, Alex saw Jack looking at his watch with a slight scowl and knew they were behind schedule.

"We have to pass Norman Island on the way to Salt right?" "Sure do," said Jack, "why?"

"Well, I was thinking we could just go to Norman and snorkel the caves today, and dive tomorrow before we go to Cooper." Jack smiled and said, "Whatever Madame wishes, I am but your humble servant. After we clear little thatch there, we'll see if we have enough wind to sail now." As the boat cleared Little Thatch, Jack noted that the winds had come up to about ten knots or so, so he decided to hang out the laundry. Jack said, "If you think the dingy is decadent, wait till you see this." Jack swung the bow over to starboard into the wind and hit another switch on the console and the mainsail ran itself out of the boom and up the mast in a few seconds. After the main was up, Jack turned the boat on heading towards the distant Norman Island then hit another switch and the port Jib winch in the cockpit began to turn and the jib began to unfurl and pull the trailing edge of the huge headsail back past the mast. Jack made some manual trim adjustments and killed the engine then switched on the autopilot.

"Oh my God," said Alex, "that is so cool; you can do everything from right here in the cockpit. I noticed that you already had the starboard jib sheet off the winch." "Yeah," said Jack, "I knew we would have the wind from starboard on the first tack so I took tension on the port sheet and slipped the starboard one off the drum."

"Ok, but do you have to tack manually."

"Partially," Jack said as he pointed to his control console, "these two switches control the main sheet, that one is a high speed winch and sheets the main in or out from center line, the jib winches as you can see, are unidirectional and self tailing. To tack, as I bring her into the wind, I sheet the main in so the boom centers with the boat, then you take three wraps around the opposite jib winch with the lazy sheet, then lock the sheet under the tailer, then spin the working sheet off the drum so it's free, you see the line chock behind the winch, it keeps the lazy sheet from getting away from you. Then as I fall off the wind line on heading, I start taking

112

in on the working sheet and bring the jib across until I think it's about right, then I hit the winch for the main and let the boom go over until the telltales on the leading edge are lined up straight back on both sides of the main. That's why the roof top in the center is Plexiglas with the nifty sliding door to block the sun when you want to. Otherwise you would have to step outside the cockpit to check the trim on the main."

"And you set all this up yourself huh. I know the hardware is all off the shelf, but you designed and built the hardtop and did all the running rigging routing yourself and built that console right?"

"Well, I did have help you know, but yeah I did most of it on my own, the really hard stuff was the work down below."

"This is a magnificent boat Jack; you have every right to be proud of her and what you've done. This is going to be a great trip. How long till we hit Norman?" asked Alex. The fifty footer was barely heeled over to port and they were only making five knots, Jack guessed they would be looking for a mooring ball in the Bight in about an hour and a half or so, and so informed Alex.

Alex went below and came back topside with a beach towel minus her shorts revealing a white thong that matched her top. "I'm going to go and catch some rays on the way there if you don't mind."

"Not at all," said Jack, "have at it." Alex stepped out of the cockpit and went just forward of the mast and laid out her towel and then lay down on her stomach with that perfect little butt of hers directly in Jack's line of sight. *Women are just plain mean,* Jack thought with a smile.

Andy White, FBI, met Billy at the airport in the van that Billy's team would use while on the island. The two men introduced themselves, Billy using his Bob Moore alias. "They left the marina at about eight thirty this morning and all we know is that they were heading somewhere in the BVI. According to his booking agent, he doesn't use his boat name on the radio while he has a charter aboard; he usually uses Captain Jack as his call sign, that way he can't get hassled by anyone trying to make a deal."

"Well, what happens if someone needs to contact one of his customers?"

"If they want to be contacted, his booking agent will have the cell phone numbers of the client, and if they so desire, they are allowed to call.

Remember, these people are paying eight to ten grand a week not to be bothered. The booking agent has a number for Schmidt's cell phone but says he's not that good about answering calls, he usually gets back to her in a couple of days, he doesn't like being bothered while he has guests aboard. You can cover a lot of territory with the boat we got you, it'll do about seventy, but you kinda need a place to start."

"Ok," said Billy, "give the booking agent this number and tell her it belongs to an old buddy from D.C. from the Muller's office, it's my cell number, hopefully, he'll call soon. At least the Russians will have an even harder time finding them. You did tell the booking agent not to put any other calls through right?"

"Yeah," said Andy, "she is to take the message then call us, but not do anything else, the only messages Schmidt gets will be from us."

"Are those boxes in back my stuff?" asked Billy.

"Yeah, if you want we can take it straight to Red Hook where your boat is and get it stowed now. There is a team that will initiate surveillance on Valentnikov when he gets off his plane; we assume he will go straight to the hotel when he gets here since the boat is gone."

"Yeah might as well, you guys will keep me informed as to their movements so let's do it."

"I understand that your guys won't get here till tomorrow."

"Right," said Billy, "we didn't get much lead time on this but I want to be ready to haul ass as soon as they get off the plane. Neither man said much on the drive across the island, Billy didn't want to talk much anyway as the ride up and down the island to Red Hook was on steep and decidedly shitty roads which White negotiated with a familiarity closely resembling wreckless abandon. Billy was amazed that it took forty minutes to navigate the road from the airport to Red Hook. When Billy and Andy arrived at the marina, Andy backed the van down by the dock and Billy got a look at the boat he would be staying on for the immediate future. The boat was thirty-nine feet long and had a very sleek and sporty appearance. Andy told him the boat was factory rated at fifty-five knots but its previous doper owners had made substantial upgrades that enabled her to hit seventy on flat water. There was sleeping space for four but there would only be three staying onboard.

As Billy looked around down below he was surprised to see that the interior was plushly accommodated and not gutted out, and mentioned that to White. "They didn't use this one for smuggling, this was one of the guy's toys, they confiscated this and a sixty-five foot Nauter Swan sloop. Didn't really hurt him much though, he'll do four years in some club fed, then go back to the Caymans and make a withdrawal. Whoever hid his money was damn good at it." As White and Billy were loading Billy's gear onto the boat, White's cell phone rang. "Yeah, ok, got it, straight to the hotel, later. That was Halston, your guy got here and was met by one of the other Russians and went straight to the hotel, we'll know what their plans are shortly, Randy Wilson is sitting across from their room with a laser mike and some recording equipment so we will hear and record anything said in the room."

"Good, that'll be a big help," said Billy. White said, "We couldn't get into the room to plant a bug because there is almost always someone there but you can't hide from the laser."

A laser mike is a sophisticated device that when focused on the window of an occupied room, the laser beam reads the vibrations of sound waves on the window and acts as an amplifier enabling the surveillance team to hear conversations in the room as clearly as if a microphone was hidden in the room.

As Mhiki was leaving New York, VI Borden and his driver pulled up in front of the Little Armenia Restaurant which was Lexi's office of sorts. VI said, "I'll go in, if I'm not out in forty-five minutes and haven't called you on my cell, something is very wrong."

"You sure you want to just walk in there by yourself and start dictating policy to this guy."

"Oh yes, I'm sure, you see, you are a law enforcement officer and cannot be compromised by what I may be required to do to get Mr. Yoskov's attention. I should be fine; I have been in this game for a very long time my friend." VI took the Smith and Wesson out of his waistband and chambered a round, then made sure his Tanto styled knife was easily accessible and said, "Showtime." VI stepped out of the cab and went through the front door. As soon as he was inside, he saw two large men seated on a sofa at the back of the restaurant by the door he assumed to be to Lexi's office. As VI purposely strode toward the two men, they both stood up and the largest one said, "We're closed, what do you want?"

"I am here to see Lexi, you will permit me to enter and see him, my business is with him alone." The two men exchanged a look and the larger one said, "Who are you and what is your business with him?"

VI said, "Gentlemen, please, you do not want to make this difficult," and moved towards the door. When he did, the big thug reached out to grab VI and when he did, the attack came with almost incomprehensible speed. VI grabbed the big man by his right wrist twisting it outward with his left hand, and pulled the man off balance pushing his right arm down and pulling him forward at the same time. As the man began to lose his balance, VI swept his right arm across striking the man's elbow with the palm of his hand, shattering the joint, then pivoting his whole body underneath the man's outstretched arm, came around beside and to the right of the big thug and then kicked his right leg out from under him, then using their combined weight and momentum, drove the side of the falling man's head into the corner of the solid oak coffee table that was next to the sofa where the two men had been sitting. The sound was similar to that of someone striking a melon with a hammer as the big Russian's skull caved in from the force of the impact. The event happened with incredible speed. Before the big Russian's body had even hit the floor, VI had drawn his Tanto blade and started a half pirouette to his right, the nasty blade parallel to his forearm. The other thug barely had time to react and was in the process of trying to draw his pistol when VI's blade hit him in the throat just above his collar bone. As the blade struck bone and spinal cord at the back of the man's neck, VI twisted it sharply and withdrew the knife. VI grabbed the man by his shoulders and eased him to the floor. A look of shock, fear, and the realization that he was about to die spread across his face. VI looked into his eyes said, "All you had to do was let me in." VI stepped across the dying man, opened the door, and walked through a vestibule into Lexi's office and closed the door behind him and stood with his arms folded across his chest.

Lexi, believing it was one of his goons did not immediately look up but the other man in the room was getting to his feet when Lexi looked over at VI. The bodyguard looked at Lexi and Lexi held his hand out as to say, hold on a moment. "Who are you and what do you want here," demanded Lexi, and where are the two men who were outside?"

"Who I am is not immediately important, and as to your two men, one is dead and the other is drowning in his own blood as we speak." Lexi's face went pale and the bodyguard went for his gun. He never had a chance. VI had been holding his pistol behind his left bicep as he stood with his arms crossed. The bodyguard never cleared the holster with his weapon. As VI's arm extended, the Hush Puppy barked twice, the two rounds striking the man in the forehead almost in the same place. The subsonic rounds did not have the energy to go through both sides of his skull, but even so, a geyser of blood erupted from the holes in the man's forehead, probably from a ruptured artery. The man fell straight to the floor as though someone had turned him off with a switch. Lexi was thoroughly terrified now, especially since his view of VI was somewhat obscured by the opening in the business end of the suppressor now trained on his own forehead. VI looked at Lexi and said in a rather casual voice, "I am not going to have trouble with you as well now am I? I came here to have a simple conversation and I have had to kill three men in less than two minutes. Now sit down and keep your hands in view, any sudden movement will result in your death, and my visit here will prove to have been a waste of time."

Lexi did as instructed, he did not understand any of this but he wanted very much to stay alive, and would do nothing to provoke this stranger as long as he appeared in the mood to talk. VI sat in the chair across from Lexi's desk. "So Lexi," said VI, "your life is about to change and your destiny is in your hands. As we speak, your boss Mhiki is on his way to St. Thomas. You are to cut off all communications with him, you are going to sit here with me and have every phone number that he may try to call here turned off, disabled as it were, he is to have no communication with anyone from your organization for any reason at any time from this point on, do you understand me?" Lexi looked at VI and said, "Or what, you will kill me."

"No, no, of course not, I will sit here with you while some of my associates rape, savagely beat, and then kill your wife and sixteen year old daughter and bring their severed bloody heads here for you to see. Then

I will start by shooting off your testicles, and, once again tell you what it is that I expect of you." Of course VI had no associates that would harm Lexi's wife and child, but Lexi had no way of knowing that, and, having just dispatched his three best men as though they were mere annoyances, Lexi had no intention of pissing this man off. "You see Lexi, Mhiki will not be returning from the islands, associates of mine will see to that, you are in a unique position to assume total control of all of Mhiki's legitimate enterprises, all criminal activities will of course cease immediately. Federal authorities have began surveillance of most of your combined businesses and the slightest infractions will be dealt with by the full weight of the United States Justice Department, all involved will be convicted and all assets seized by the State."

"Or," said Lexi. "As I said, all legitimate enterprises will fall into your hands, as I understand; you will be able to continue to live very well, as will the associates you should choose to retain. I must add however, that you must choose wisely and carefully, if I find out you have gone back to your old ways, the very hand of God Almighty himself will not be able to keep you and your family safe from my associates."

"Why are you doing this, what are you getting out of it?" asked Lexi.

"As to why, I am keeping a promise made long ago to a friend, as to what am I getting out of it, nothing, other than honoring my word, it is that simple to me. You should also know that I will maim, torture, and or kill as many people as necessary to keep that promise. You see, I am a ghost, I am completely non existent and you can never hide from me or those who will come for you if you do not do as I say. Simply put, live a full life with all its amenities, or, die a horrible death, make no mistake, those are your only options."

"Do you work for the government?"

"No, who I do or do not work for is none of your concern, and please spare me any talk of your rights being violated. As I have explained, if you do not comply with my instructions, implicitly, a great deal more than your rights will be violated. I want a complete list of all of your combined holdings in case my associates have missed anything, also, you will give me your telephone contact list, land and cellular, I will then make a phone call and all of those lines will be immediately disconnected as will your email accounts."

"If you have all of our lines disconnected, how am I to contact my people to issue new instructions."

"You are a resourceful man; I trust you will find a way. Also, first order of business, I need the cellular numbers of all the men in St. Thomas, those will be left functional and monitored. And speaking of cell phones, this one is for you. VI reached into his jacket pocket and produced an ordinary looking cell phone and a battery charger and laid it on Lexi's desk. You will keep this phone with you at all times until told otherwise, the battery must not be allowed to discharge, the penalty for noncompliance is death. As long as you are shutting down the criminal portions of your businesses, no actions will be taken against you for conversations about or information pertaining to them."

"We have a great deal of money on the street in loans, what about that."

"You will have to absorb the loss, it all ends here and now, or, I start by having my associates pay your lovely wife and daughter a visit." VI punctuated his last statement by taking out his own cell phone as if to dial a number. "No, no for God's sake," cried Lexi, "ok, ok, I'll do as you say, please, put the phone away." VI looked at Lexi and knew that he would cooperate, he was not a hard man, he had never personally killed, he always had that sort of thing done for him. Now faced with his own mortality and that of his family, VI saw the exact moment that all of the toughness left the man, he would be compliant and if not, he would be someone else's problem. After VI had the complete list of everything that Valentnikov had interest and or involvement in, and all communications had been severed, VI told Lexi, "I may contact you again soon if I have more questions, or if I need your assistance. And remember, if that phone goes off line or if you engage in any attempt at trickery, or fail to answer that phone at any time, night or day for any reason, death will come swiftly."

As VI was starting to leave, Lexi said, "What about them?" indicating the bodies of his former employees. VI smiled and said, "Not my problem is it," and casually stepped over the bodies and walked out the door. As VI got back into the cab, the driver said, "So, how'd it go?"

"Very well I should think, I found Mr. Yoskov to be most cooperative. Let's go back to the airport, I have more information for Agent Nolan that I think he will find useful. Lexi stood looking at the bodies of the men that his visitor had killed so effortlessly, his own mind and body wracked with fear. He would do anything this man wanted him to do, this stranger, thought Lexi, makes Mhiki look like a cub scout.

As soon as Mhiki entered the hotel, Halston switched on the laser mike. Mhiki turned to Leo and said, "You were unable to obtain the sailor's destination and the charter agent will not contact him on your behalf, so, we must find him ourselves."

"Yes," said Leo, "we have made arrangements to rent a forty foot power Catamaran on the Island of Tortola, it is much faster than the sail boat, but we can not get the boat until tomorrow afternoon, it is peak season here and we were actually lucky to obtain the boat at all." Leo laid out a nautical chart of the U.S. and British Virgin Islands for Mhiki to see, "Here is where we must go to acquire the boat and as you can see, they could be anywhere in these islands. We can simply drive the boat around and monitor the VHF radio and hope he uses it and reveals his location, or we can attempt to locate them visually."

Mhiki thought about it for a moment then said, "If she was going to try and move the stones, she would need to go to the most populated areas with the most high end shops. That would be in the same place as we need to get the boat, or here on the Island of Virgin Gorda at the Bitter End Yacht Club, the rest of these islands are inconsequential rocks dotted with bars and such."

"True," said Viktor, "but what if that is all the woman came here for?" Mhiki shot him a hard look and paced about the room for a bit and said, "How do we get to where our boat is?"

Viktor said, "We can catch a ferry from here at the waterfront that takes about forty minutes, the boat will be ready for us when we get there, it will be rented in Stephan's name and he will have to be given a safety and rules of the road brief and then we can go. Also we must all clear British customs before we can take possession of the boat. We paid for two weeks, which is the time when the woman and sailor are due back here. We should stock some food and drink on the boat and all that can be done there in the marina in a short time." Mhiki could barely contain himself, outwardly he appeared relatively calm, but on the inside he was enraged, here he was, so close to the one who had ruined him, yet finding him on this patch of ocean would be like finding the proverbial needle in the haystack. "Ok," said Mhiki, "we leave for Tortola on the noon ferry, Stephan I need you to do some shopping, I want you to build me a bomb that can be attached to the hull of the sailboat, a simple timing device should do, but it must be waterproof for at least ten meters, if the opportunity presents itself we will blow up the sailor's boat with he and the woman onboard while they are at anchor."

"You mean after we get the stones?" said Viktor.

"Yes, yes," said Mhiki.

Stephan said, "I need to make three stops, any hardware store, a supermarket and Radio Shack for the timing device and wires, maybe a marine store for the adhesive, whatever I use will have to be detonated while the boat is stationary and before it moves or the device will fall off from the movement of the water across the hull, I can plant it at night after we know that they are aboard for the evening, then boom, they go to the bottom."

"I am tired and need a good drink," said Mhiki, "Leo, call Lexi and advise him of the situation and tell him we will contact him periodically." Leo tried all of the numbers that he could for Lexi and his bodyguards but all of them put out a busy signal, odd thought Leo, he would try later. Moments later the front desk called in to inform Viktor that a large package marked boat parts had arrived for him. "Ivan," said Mhiki, "I think it would be best for you to remain here with our package while the rest of us go to pick up the boat, I don't believe customs here will be much of a problem, but still, I would prefer not to transport our weapons and an explosive device on the ferry to British territory, you can call a cab to take you to the marina where the sailor keeps his boat and we can load the box there. We will return here to pick up you and the more volatile cargo, but we will take the diving equipment with us to keep up appearances while we load the boat."

Halston called White who relayed the information about to the Russians to Billy. Billy decided that he should move the boat to Crown

Bay Marina now since it was closer to the airport. He could pick up Dan and Will there in the morning and beat Mhiki and his group to Tortola and plant one of the tracking devices on their boat before they ever had a chance to board the vessel. With their speed advantage, they could wait for Valentnikov and company in Road Town and observe them from there, and be able to follow them when they departed Tortola. With the tracking device planted on the boat, they could track them throughout the Islands and use the speed advantage for an intercept if necessary.

Billy had Bill Reynolds contact the BVI police department who in turn contacted the boat rental office and informed them that a gentleman would board the boat that the Russians had rented prior to their arrival and that it was to be kept in the strictest confidence. Billy then called Dan Wilcox back in the States and let him know the plan. "You know Billy," said Dan, "this also gives a chance to narrow the odds a bit, we will have this Ivan character isolated, I think we should take him out while we have the chance."

"Yeah," said Billy, "I thought about that too, the only problem with that is that it may spook the rest of them."

"True enough, but what can they do if the guy just doesn't show up, freak out, I like it. They have no way of knowing that we are on to them, I think the loss of coms with home and the unexplained disappearance of one of their guys can only work to our advantage, plus, we get their weapons, which they may not be able to replace down there."

"Ok," said Billy, "as soon as you guys get here we haul ass for Road Town, plant the GPS transmitter on their boat, then haul ass back here. We take him at the hotel after his buddies leave."

Dan said, "Why don't you go shopping for a big trunk today, that and a spare anchor. "We don't need a trunk, I can use one of our equipment boxes, it's big enough and it's made out of aluminum" "Good, said Dan, we can be in and out of the marina before the Russians even get there so they never see our boat." Billy said, "Timing and Ivan's movements after the others leave could become an issue."

"We'll deal with it but Ivan and his box do not get on that boat, agreed."

"Agreed," said Billy, "we can't waste the opportunity, and you're right, it will shake them up a bit. Just take a cab to Crown Bay Marina when you get here, I'll have the boat ready to go as soon as you show up."

Alex was still lying on deck by the mast when Jack fired up the engine on the boat. When she felt the engine come to life, Alex went back to the cockpit and said, "Time to put the laundry away huh."

"Yep," said Jack, as he turned the boat into the wind. "Take that line there and wrap it around the starboard jib winch four times, it's the retriever line for the jib." Alex took the line and did as she was told, once she had done that, Jack sheeted the main in to centerline, then took the port jib sheet off the winch and hit the switch on the console and the jib began to roll itself up around the forestay. As soon as the jib was stowed, Jack hit another switch and the main sail rolled itself back down the mast and into the oversized main boom.

Alex noted how easy everything was and said, "Do you ever feel like you're cheating?" Jack laughed as he turned the boat towards the entrance to bight and said, "Nope, nobody ever said it had to be hard to be fun." Alex got a laugh out of that and without having to be told, got the boat hook out of the port laz and went forward with it.

Jack slowed the boat to about three knots as he entered the Bight. At first there did not appear to be any empty mooring balls. Jack drove the boat all the way to the far end of the bight almost to where Billy Bones, now known as Pirates Bar and Grill is, and then turned around to make another pass when Alex shouted, "Jack, over there," pointing to where a bareboat was getting ready to cast off from a ball. The angle worked to Jack's advantage as the wind was coming straight down through the harbor entrance. As Jack lined up on the ball, running into the wind, the skipper on the other boat saw his intentions and waved him in. Jack put the boat in neutral and watched as the other boat drifted back from the ball and started to move out toward open water.

Alex, who was wearing that little thong of hers, was leaning over the bow rail with the boat hook and had one foot up on the lower bow rail. *Damn*, thought Jack, *don't aim that thing at me.* Alex looked back and caught the grin on Jack's face and said, "What"

"Nothing," said Jack, "get ready." Alex gave Jack the stop signal and got the line on her first grab and ran the pendant through the eye on the mooring line and cleated it off and called, "Ok." Jack responded by saying, "Taking tension," as he shifted into reverse and gave the throttle a quick bump before shifting back into neutral. The boat backed down and took the slack out of the pendant and gently came to a stop. Jack walked up to the bow and noted that was all secure. Alex was smiling at him looking somewhat like a little girl waiting for praise or a treat of some sort. Jack smiled back at her and said, "Nicely done Madame, would Madame care for some lunch prior to exploring the caves?"

"Why yes, I think that would be in order," mocked Alex in her best British accent. As Jack and Alex made their way back aft, Jack said, "I'll go ahead and get the dingy in the water while you make lunch, by the way, what are you making?"

"How's turkey and Swiss on rye with hot mustard, chased with an ice cold Carib beer sound?"

"Perfect," said Jack, "couldn't have placed a better order." While Alex was fixing lunch, Jack rigged the swim ladder and got the dingy in the water and positioned on the starboard side by the ladder. Just as he was tying off the dingy, he heard Jimmy Buffet start singing through the boat's speakers. Jack also noted that Alex had taken time to open the hatches over the bow and aft cabins to allow for some airflow through the boat while at anchor. Jack was folding the cockpit dining table that was mounted to the steering pedestal into position as Alex emerged carrying a wicker basket with their lunch. Alex sat down opposite Jack and set a paper plate in front of him, then placed his sandwich on it and handed him a napkin and his beer. "Thank you very much," said Jack. Jack held up his beer and said, "Prost." Alex clicked the neck of her beer against his and said, "Prost, God this place is beautiful, I went to Hawaii once but it doesn't have anything on this place"

"I agree," said Jack "I've been there too and would much rather be here." They ate their sandwiches without conversation and when they were finished Alex said, "Well big fella, ready for a swim?"

"Sure, look in the aft laz there and get yourself a mask and fins that fit and we can get going. There's a black mesh bag in there with my stuff, if you would, grab it for me please. There should be some more bags in there, pick one and keep the stuff you want to use in it." As Alex was trying on different fins, Jack said, "Look in that blue bag, it's full of dive booties, find a pair of those that fit, then try on those grey split fins, I think those will fit you." Alex found a set of booties that fit her and then tried on the fins. She clipped the ankle buckle and adjusted the strap and extended her leg and shook the fin up and down. "Perfect," said Alex, "and here is your bag," as she handed it to Jack. "I like this mask," said Alex as she selected a clear frame wrap around mask with a clear snorkel attached to it.

Jack watched as Alex pressed the mask up against her face and breathed in through her nose to check the seal, satisfied Alex put her gear in her yellow mesh bag and said, "Ready."

"Ok, let me get in the dingy first, then climb in but wait till I have the engine started before you cast us off, it's a bitch draggin this thing behind you doing the sidestroke." Alex giggled as Jack hit the engine trim switch and lowered the lower end of the motor into the water. Jack squeezed the primer bulb on the fuel line then turned the key. The motor instantly came to life and Jack said, "You know what, I almost forgot, could you go back down below and get us a couple of towels."

"Oh, sure," said Alex, "anything else?"

"Nope that ought to do it." As Alex climbed back up the ladder, Jack wondered what he really wanted more, a towel, or to watch Alex climb the ladder wearing that thong. He found himself grinning again. Once Alex had climbed back into the dingy, Jack said, "Go ahead and cast off and give us a push. After they were clear of the boat, Alex moved back and sat next to Jack on the bench seat. "Care for a little history lesson?"

"Sure."

"Ok, you ever read *Treasure Island* by Robert Louis Stevenson?"

"Sure, didn't everyone in high school?"

"Right, well this is the island that Stevenson based that book loosely on. Back in the early nineteenth century, a fisherman from St. Thomas was out here checking his nets when a bad storm came up. He couldn't run from it so he took his little boat back into the largest cave seeking shelter and when he got to the back of the cave, he found this huge amount of treasure that had been stashed by some pirate. It took a couple of trips to haul it all out of there and as the story goes, his family today, is still among the richest in the islands."

"You're kidding right?"

"Absolutely not, true story." Jack was past the mooring field now and throttled up the engine on the dingy and brought it up on plane Alex was surprised at how fast it was. Jack sped out of the harbor entrance and turned left and then throttled back as they approached a line that ran the length of the cliff face in the water. There were a dozen or so dingys tied off to the line and a few larger boats as well. As they approached the tag line, Alex moved to the front of the dingy and tied the bow line off to the tag line next to one of the buoys. She took her mask out of her bag and rinsed it out in the sea water then spit into the mask then rubbed her saliva around the inner surface of the mask lens.

Jack watched with approval, he always carried some mask defogger in his bag for guests, not everyone was comfortable with the natural method. Jack readied himself and placed his mask on the top of his head and said, "We can start at the far end down there and work our way to the left, the caves get progressively larger as we move down the line. Keep your eyes on the bottom as we move from cave to cave. You never know what kind of critters you'll see down there."

"Ok, you take the lead and I'll follow." Jack lowered his mask over his face, put his snorkel in his mouth and took off toward the first cave with Alex in trail. The pair had looked at the first couple of caves and saw lots of fish but nothing really noteworthy. Alex was simply awestruck by the clarity of the water. As they were moving towards one of the larger caves, Jack stopped and waved Alex over to him and said, "Look straight down there." All Alex could see were rocks on the bottom about fifteen feet below. Jack said, "Dive down with me." Alex nodded her head in agreement and they both took a breath and headed for the bottom. Alex watched as Jack swam up to, and pointed to what looked to her like just another rock. Jack extended his arm and was about to touch the rock when it transformed itself into a mass of body and legs about three feet in length and scooted off across the bottom for about thirty feet or so and then wrapped itself around another rock. Within a second, its color and skin texture matched that of its new perch almost perfectly. After they had surfaced, Alex said, "That was so cool, an octopus, I couldn't even see it until it moved."

"The only reason I saw it is because it moved one of its legs right as I looked in that direction." Jack swam back to the caves and now they were getting large enough to swim in and out of. Alex was thoroughly enjoying herself, as they worked their way down and into to the last cave, Jack said, "Here it is, the treasure cave, you see how it curves back to the left and widens out. That flat area back there out of the water is, where legend has it, the treasure was found." As Jack looked at Alex, she was looking at the back of the cave with a detached sort of smile on her face, Alex was thinking, I know a little about treasure. Jack said, "Let's swim around out by the entrance, I want to look for something."

Alex followed Jack and soon he was pointing at something on the bottom again. Alex looked at him and Jack raised his hand to his forehead and extended two fingers and wiggled them and pointed again. Alex had no idea what he meant so Jack said, "Bugs."

"Bugs," said Alex questioningly. "Yeah bugs, sea roaches, you know, lobsters, there are a bunch of em under that rock ledge, follow me." Jack headed straight for the bottom but this was more like twenty-five feet deep and Alex had to stop and equalize the pressure in her ears by pinching her nose and blowing into it until she felt her ears pop. When she caught up with Jack, he was pointing under the rock ledge and there was a massive lobster sitting there backed into the space between the ledge and the bottom, and there were several other smaller lobsters crowded around the big one. Alex looked at them until she was ready for another breath of air. After Jack joined her on the surface she exclaimed, "That's the biggest lobster I have ever seen, how much you think that thing weighs." Jack thought about it for a moment and said must run ten pounds or more, "You're right, that is one big crustacean."

"I had no idea they even got that big. You ready to go back to the boat; I think I'm ready for another beer."

"Sure lead on." Jack followed Alex back to the dingy and climbed in ahead of her. Jack was ready to help her into the dingy but she used her fins to get a good push and hopped right up on the side of the dingy. Jack tried to be nonchalant about blowing the snot of his nostrils from the salt water and Alex just pushed one nostril closed with her finger and let her rip, then repeated the procedure with the other one. Jack looked at her and they both laughed. Alex smiled and said, "I know, not very ladylike but thoroughly effective." That brought another round of laughter and as Jack was removing his mask and fins; Alex reached both of her arms up to her head and grabbed her hair in her hands and drew it back behind her head squeezing the water out. Of course as she did this, her breasts and nipples now erect from the temperature change, strained at the sheer white bikini top. This time Jack was cold busted, he could not help looking at them any more than a cat could ignore a mouse running right past it. Alex saw the, oops, look on his face and smiled a big smile and looked away and thought to herself, about time you big oaf. Jack shook his head and said, "Alrighty then," and started the motor on the dingy.

After Alex untied them, Jack backed away from the tag line and started for the entrance to the Bight. Once they were clear of the other swimmers, Jack hit the throttle and zipped back into the harbor. As they started to enter the mooring field, Jack throttled back again and headed back towards the boat. Jack pulled the dingy up next to the boat and Alex tied the dingy off and climbed up the ladder back onto the boat. She didn't know if Jack was watching her, but she hoped he was.

He was. Back on the boat, Jack walked back to the stern and opened a little panel and pulled out a plastic nozzle and a hose from its storage spot and told Alex, "Go ahead and rinse off with this but be careful, it might be hot at first, after you're done, I'll rinse myself off, then rinse our gear. Jack went to the cockpit and made busy with something as Alex rinsed herself off. She looked at Jack who had his back to her and grinned. *Sissy*, she said to herself with a smile. When she was done, she looked at Jack and said, "All yours," and stood there holding the nozzle out for him to come take from her. Alex was well aware of the wet fabric perfectly forming itself to her shape and she found herself wanting to make sure that Jack was as well. Jack put on his best game face and walked over to her, smiled and while looking at her incredibly green eyes, said, "Thank you," as he took the hose from her.

As Jack was rinsing off Alex went down below and got two more beers and brought them up as Jack was finishing off the gear. He thanked Alex for the beer and said he was going down to get a dry shirt. As Jack was down below changing, Alex wondered why he didn't just take it off and hang it on the rail to dry, or for that matter, why had he worn it at all while they were snorkeling. She could tell that he was all muscle, and as yet, she had not seen him with his shirt off. Jack came back up wearing a mostly worn out Mickey Mouse shirt and Alex had to laugh at him. Jack just looked at her and said, "What."

"Nothing," said Alex. "Hey, I like this shirt," said Jack. Alex, smiling at him, said, "Did Mommy buy that for you at the park?"

"Man, what's a guy got to do to get a break around here." They both laughed and Alex said, "Well, you could start by getting me one of those big lobsters."

"For that, I am afraid we must go ashore, they're protected here unless you have a commercial fishing license."

"Can we get lobster at that Billy Bones place?"

"Sure can but with this many people here, I suggest we make it an early dinner and get there before the cook gets overwhelmed."

"Would five be ok?"

"Yeah, we'll hit the happy hour crowd but we'll beat the dinner rush."

"Ok then five it is then I think I'll go up forward and get some more rays," said Alex. Jack watched as Alex went to her sunning spot by the mast and laid out her towel and then took off her top and began rubbing suntan oil on herself. *Damn*, thought Jack. "Hey," said Jack, "I'm going down below for a bit, I want to run the generator for a few minutes and make sure everything is ok." Alex lifted herself up on her elbows and said, "Ok, wake me up at four if I fall asleep." Jack, trying not to appear to be staring said, "Sure," then retreated for the relative safety of his engine room. As Jack was fidgeting with the gen set, he was thinking to himself, *Ok, beautiful topless hardbody on deck, big deal, been lots of them on the boat before.* But, they were usually someone's wife or girlfriend, and his auto disconnect always worked, he saw them without really seeing them, as was his job as a charter Captain. So why was this one getting to him? Being alone on the boat with this woman for two weeks was going to be like playing soccer in a mine field.

VI returned to the command post at the airport and reported in to Nolan. Brady and Eggers listened as VI detailed Lexi's willingness to cooperate. Brady said, "I would be curious to know what you did or said to get this level of cooperation."

"Detective," said VI, "while you may find that tidbit of information interesting, possibly even entertaining, you must trust that it is in your best interest if you do not know." Nolan was the next to speak. "So this idiot actually believes that if they just shut down their criminal activities, we will just let them all walk and keep everything they earned illegally?"

"That is what I told him, and at the time he presented me with that CD, he would have believed or done anything I said, I left him in a most agreeable mood. With the information you now have on that disc, and the Federal Warrant you have, as each of those individuals reactivates their phones and email accounts you will have immediate access to all communications of every member of the organization. Also, as they scurry to shut everything down, if they actually do so, they will no doubt reveal details of many past unsolved or otherwise undetected crimes. At the very least you should be able to get most of them on RICO violations."

"VI," said Nolan, "I don't know how, and I probably don't ever want to know, what you did to shake this guy up so bad but thanks. You are sure he won't try to contact Valentnikov?"

"Positive, Lexi will make himself easy to arrest, and he will definitely not try to contact Mhiki, for two reasons. First, he is a greedy man, he believes he will inherit all of Mhiki's assets and second, he is too afraid. Not to mention the fact that you can track him and listen in on him at any time. I believe I forgot to mention to him that among the other features of his cell phone is the constant on microphone. I can stay until the day after Christmas, and then I will have to return to my job unless you know that you will require my services."

"Mr. Borden," said Nolan, "you have already done these people in, we will have these guys wrapped up in a week, I know you would like to go to St. Thomas, but the men who went there will handle it."

"Of course, you are correct, however, if I can be of help at any time please feel free to contact me."

"We have a suite for you at the Crowne Plaza hotel which is right here by the airport. We have your cell number, if we need you we will call."

"I would like to call Lexi before I go to the hotel, let him know I really care as it were." The three law enforcement officers shared a laugh and Eggers dialed the number and put it on the speaker phone. The phone was answered after the second ring. "Yes, Lexi here."

"Very good Lexi, you were paying attention, now I have other matters to attend to for a time, you are to follow the instructions of whoever calls you on this phone. If they have this number you should assume that they report to me, and do not forget the penalties for making me upset."

"Of course not, you were very clear."

"Good now have a nice holiday and remember, much like Santa Clause, I know who has been naughty, and who is nice, suddenly VI's voice took on a cold, chilling edge to it and he said, and you do not want to be on my naughty list." VI then hung up before Lexi could reply. VI smiled at the three men and said, "That should be all it takes for him, he will do whatever anyone who calls him on that line asks, and now gentlemen, I think I will retire to my room. You know how to reach me if you need me."

"Thank you again," said Nolan. After VI had left the room Eggers said, "He scared the fuck out of that guy. Whatever he said or did certainly made an impression." Just as Nolan was about to say something, one of his assistants walked over carrying an envelope addressed to Brady and Eggers, it was from the State Department.

Back at the conference table, Eggers dumped the contents of the file on the table and began to read the document. "It's the info on the old Kraut," said Eggers, "his real name was Klaus Von Stratton, after his third serious combat wound, and act of extraordinary heroism on the battlefield, the one that earned him the Diamonds on his knights cross, he was reassigned to work for one of his old college buddies who's name was Walter Shellenberg, General Walter Shellenberg. He was the SS General that was in charge of intelligence for the Reich, an organization known as the SD. After Hitler had Admiral Canaris, head of the principal spy agency for the Germans, executed for acts of treason, the SD took over the whole show. While he was in an operational status, Von Stratton ran around with Otto Skorzeny and his band of SS commandos until he ended up commanding a special ops unit of the SS paras. Skorzeny was the guy who founded and funded Odessa, the organization that had worldwide contacts, and relocated scores of SS officers after the war. Evidently though, Von Stratton hated Hitler. He had personally met with Allen Dulles, who at the time was a senior officer of the OSS, working under diplomatic cover in Sweden. Dulles and Shellenberg were up to something and Von Stratton was the go between. This doesn't say what the deal was but while they were working it out, Dulles convinced Von Stratton that he would enjoy life in America much more than he would running from the Soviets or the Jews after the war. Von Stratton was an old school Prussian aristocrat and professional soldier, not however a Nazi. According to this, Von Stratton, as an executive assistant to the head of the SD was privy to the best intelligence that the Germans had on the Russians at the time, and, getting him to come over played a big part in getting Dulles appointed as head of the CIA a few years later. What this doesn't say however, is what was in the damn safe deposit box."

"Well," said Brady, "if she lives long enough we can ask the girl. And by the way, what do we do about the contents of the box when this thing is all said and done?"

"If she lives, and we get this mess cleaned up I say who cares," said Eggers. "What we can assume is, whatever was in the box was something that is easily portable and convertible to cash, relatively small, and worth a shitload of money. Von Stratton was supposed to use it to help finance the upper crust of SS leadership going into hiding after the war. Instead, he cut a deal with Dulles, got himself and his wife an apartment in Manhattan and only used enough of the loot to live comfortably and not draw undue attention to himself."

Nolan looked at Eggers and Brady and said, "No wonder the State Department is willing to bend all the rules to clean this up, it's their mess from the beginning, starting with Von Stratton and all the other scumbags that they cut deals with over the years just to get a leg up on the Soviets. Some of it worked out good, some of it didn't, like Valentnikov, he gave them lots of good info but then turned into something of a festering sore. This thing, now that it involves one of their own being in danger, has them wanting to make that sore go away, and you know what, I don't mind helping. My principal mission in life in my official capacity is counter terrorism, and we do not always operate above board, can't and expect positive results. Sometimes it takes bad, nasty men doing nasty things to worse men, to be able to get the right thing done. It's just the way it works in the real world. What we do now, is use the wire taps and other surveillance to get the goods on these guys and shut them down. We carefully edit all the tapes as not to implicate or reveal any complicity on our parts to illegal methods. Even if they hire good lawyers, the evidence against them will be overwhelming and any claims and or complaints will appear to be nothing more than a desperate attempt to turn attention away from their own numerous criminal acts."

"So the good guys get to win a few rounds," said Eggers.

"Jewels," said Brady, "has to be jewels, small, easily convertible to cash and totally untraceable, that is what was in the box, I'd bet my badge on it."

Eggers said, "Yeah, that would explain why Valentnikov went through so much trouble to track the McTeal woman, she must have the stash now, or at least Valentnikov thinks she does. Then she turns up being photographed with Saunders and that sweetened the pot for him. Mike, these guys that went to the island, the ones that Matthews sent, what do you think they will do?"

"Personally, I don't think that any of them, the Russians that is, will be coming back from their island vacation, and I don't have a problem with that. Do you guys?" said Nolan addressing the two detectives. Brady and Eggers looked at each other for a moment and then Eggers said, "Why should we care what happens in the Caribbean, not our jurisdiction, besides, we are in the middle of an ongoing investigation into organized crime right here in New York."

"Very well," said Nolan, "we are all on the same page, we will continue to provide Intel and logistic support to the island team and when this is all over, none of it ever happened."

"Look you guys," said Nolan, "it's Christmas Eve, go home and spend some time with your families and get back here the day after tomorrow, anything happens before then I'll let you know." Sam Brady said, "Look, if it's all the same to you, I'll stay here so I can keep tabs on things, I've got nobody waiting for me at home, not even a cat. Anything comes up; I can get in touch with one of you two. Dave, go spend Christmas with your wife and kids and I'll let you know if anything significant develops."

"Yeah," said Brady, "Chloe would be pissed if I didn't show, again, you sure you don't mind?"

"No man, really, it's fine, I'll stay here in the bunkroom, I already brought a couple of changes of clothes and a shaving kit, had it planned all along."

"Ok," said Nolan, "I'll see you in a couple of days; use my cell any time, day or night. I'll check in from time to time to check on things."

"Get out of here, both of you," said Brady, "don't worry, anything big breaks I'll call you both ok."

Mhiki and Stephan had just finished making their bomb and Stephan had shown Mhiki how to set the timer. Mhiki insisted that he was to be the one to plant the device if and when the time came. Mhiki was also sure that he could easily reproduce the device if need be. He was amazed at the simplicity of the concoction and the ease with which Stephan had acquired the ingredients, in separate stores as not to alarm anyone or raise suspicion. Nothing but harmless ingredients sold over the counter, harmless as long as they were not mixed in a manner that turned the ingredients into a violently fast burning, self oxidizing compound needing only a small electrical current for an initiator. The three pound charge would burn so fast that the explosive properties would nearly rival a similar weight of C-4. Mhiki was pleased enough with this development that the five men shared a bottle of Stolichnaya vodka while watching TV before turning for the night.

Jack was napping in the cockpit when Alex got up from her designated sunning spot. She put her top back on and went back to the cockpit. As she was stepping in, Jack opened one eye and said, "Greetings, it's three thirty now, you want a real shower or perhaps a bath before we go ashore?"

"Trust me, I will check out that hot tub before this trip is done," said Alex, "but for now, yeah, I would like to take a shower before we go in, I need to wash the salt out of my hair, how about you?"

"Yeah," said Jack, "I'll use the forward head and we can both get ready at the same time. We can leave as soon as we're done and we can do a booze cruise in the dingy."

"Booze cruise?" queried Alex.

"Yeah," said Jack, "we can mix a couple of cocktails to go, and cruise around the mooring field in the dingy and check out the other boats before we head in to eat."

"Ok, sounds great I'll meet you up here when I'm ready. The two retreated to the opposite ends of the boat to get ready. Alex was still amazed at the luxurious appointment of the aft cabin, well, the whole boat for that matter. She had never been in the shower of a sailboat that had this much room. Alex was surprised to find a blow drier plugged into an outlet next to the bathroom sink. When she was done, Alex put on a pair of snug fitting blue deck shorts, her blue bikini top and her thin white blouse, the tail of which she tied around her waist in a knot. As she came forward into the main salon Jack was getting a couple of thermos type mugs out of the cabinet. Alex was pleased that he had changed into a different shirt. She said, "Here, let me, what's your poison skipper?"

"Pussers Rum and some of that milky yellowish looking stuff in that plastic jug in the fridge for me please."

"What is it?" asked Alex.

"If you like drinks with fruit juice, you'll love that, give it a try, you'll need two shots each in that size mug. After you get it mixed, put three good shakes of that Nutmeg in there and stir it up." After she had finished mixing the drinks, Alex tried a sip and said, "Wow, what do you call this stuff, it's delicious?"

"That, Madame is a Pussers Painkiller, invented right here in the BVI on the Island of Jost Van Dyke."

"This is tasty, I put two full shots in each one and I can't even taste the rum."

"I know said Jack, that's why they call it a painkiller. After a couple of those you are pretty much anesthetized, you ready to go?"

"Sure," said Alex, "let's hit it." They got in the dingy and Alex cast them off after handing the drinks to Jack. They took a slow leisurely lap around the harbor and chatted about some of the nicer boats, some of the big power yachts Jack referred to as battleships. Jack had pretty much timed it so that as they were finishing their drinks, they were on approach for the dingy dock in front of Billy Bones.

They had arrived at Billy Bones, actually, now Pirates, at about two minutes till five and Jack was smiling to himself, looking at his watch as Alex was cleating off the dingy. Just as she had finished and stood up, there came a deafening blast that made Alex nearly jump out of her sandals. "What the hell was that?" she exclaimed.

"Oh," said Jack, "guess I forgot to tell you about the happy hour cannon, they fire it off every day at five to announce the start of happy hour." Alex was giving Jack that mischievous smile of hers when she said, "You shit, you knew that was coming didn't you? That's ok, but remember that's gonna cost you somewhere down the line." Alex was totally at ease now; she had to credit the scenery with much of that but there was more to it than that.

The bar/restaurant was open air, and right by the water. Jack and Alex placed their dinner orders and got another round of painkillers, then walked down by the water and grabbed a couple of chairs and sat with their feet in the ocean sipping their drinks. Alex was envying Jack's lifestyle; he actually did this for a living, sailing around in one of the most beautiful places on the planet with very little in the way of worries except routine maintenance on his boat. She could do this thought Alex. And do it without the working part of it, just sail around diving and playing in the sun, bar hopping on a yacht.

Jack noticed the look of concentration on Alex's face and mistook it for melancholy or concern and said, "Is everything ok?" Alex smiled at him and said, "Oh yeah, I was just thinking about how much your life and job suck, I've been busting my butt in a Manhattan office for years, don't get me wrong, I have made a bunch of money, but this is the first time I have ever really done anything about having fun with it. I sit here on this beautiful beach, on this beautiful island, drink in hand, cooling my feet in the sea and realize that no matter how much I love this, it has a beginning and an end to it. You sir, on the other hand, sit here on this same beach, drink in hand, yet you, are, in your office. Therefore, I have come to the conclusion that you suck." Jack wasn't sure quite how to react to that and before he could, Alex playfully leaned forward and scooped up a handful of water and splashed Jack in the face with it. Jack jumped back and almost fell over in his chair and Alex let out a shrill laugh and jumped out of her chair and ran for the safety of the bar. She was there before Jack could catch her. Jack caught up to her as she was ordering another round of painkillers. "I think I may have created a monster," said Jack. Alex gave him a serious look and said, "No, I have always been a monster, I just never really get a chance to be myself, I guess this place has that effect on people."

"Yeah," said Jack with a big smile, "that and the painkillers." Alex looked at him, then raised her cup in a toast and said, "When in Rome." The waitress who had taken their order got Jack's attention and directed them to a table toward the back of the seating area and said, "You're less likely to get something spilled on you back here, the happy hour crowd is piling in." Alex looked at the dingy dock and it was full, in fact the incoming dingys already had to tie off to other dingys and climb across them to get to the dock.

The music was a mix of rock and reggae and it was getting louder. People were dancing everywhere and then Alex saw a topless college girl lying on her back on the bar while the bartender squeezed lime juice on, and then salted one of her nipples, and then poured a shot of tequila into her navel. Alex watched in awe as one of her male companions licked the lime and salt off of her nipple and then sucked the tequila out of her belly button. Alex said, "Holy shit, did you see that?"

Jack shook his head, smiled at her and said, "Yep, every day, give this place two hours and it will be a sociologist's heaven, people come here to cut loose and rather than frown on it, it's actually encouraged as long as things don't get to unruly. They don't call it happy hour here for nothing."

"Ok doky," said Alex as the waitress appeared with two huge spiny lobsters. The lobsters had been sawed in two lengthwise down the middle and covered in a rich, creamy seafood sauce. Alex tore into hers and after a few bites said, "This is truly excellent, it tastes much better than Maine lobster, but where are the claws." Jack laughed and explained that the spiny lobster doesn't have claws, but the flavor is unsurpassed. Alex had to agree with that. After they had finished eating Alex said, "I think I can do without another painkiller for a while, what do you want to do?"

Jack said, "Hey it's your nickel, whatever you want."

"What do you say we just go tool around in the dingy for a bit, I want to go by the Willie T and have a look."

"Sure thing," said Jack. After finally getting the waitress's attention, Alex paid the tab and told Jack, "Look, I'm supposed to be cooking on this little adventure so let's get this straight, when we go out for dinner, lunch, or drinks, I get the check, I like being able to do that for a change."

"Whatever Madame wishes," replied Jack. When they got to the dingy, Jack handed Alex the key and said, "Venture forth and explore."

"Really?" said Alex. "Cool, let's do a long lap around the harbor then we can go by the Willie T." Jack untied the dingy that was tied off to the grab line on the side of their dingy and tied it off to the dock in their place and Alex backed out and headed into the Bight. The two cruised around the harbor with Jack pointing out the different types of boats, showing Alex how she could spot the bareboat charters. As they approached the Willie T, Alex asked Jack if he wanted to stop there for a drink. "Madame, as I have said, I am but your humble servant, do as you wish."

Alex gave Jack her mischievous smile again and said, "I could get used to this boss stuff, sure, let's stop for a cocktail, I want to check this place out." Alex drove the dingy around until she found a spot to tie off. After they boarded the Willie T, Jack took Alex up the ladder and back aft to where there was a fairly spacious bar with plenty of seating and a small dance floor. All the way at the stern was a massive sort of sofa where several people could lie back and relax.

As they got to the bar, Alex decided on rum and Coke and Jack had the same. They sat at one of the tables closest to the stern. Alex was looking around and could see that everyone was just having fun. Why was it she had never come down here before? Well she was here now and she was going to enjoy herself. The events that had driven her to come here, though only a few days ago, seemed as though they had taken place years ago. Alex still had plenty of time before she needed to check in with Janet, so she would just concentrate on not concentrating for a while.

The two made some idle chat and then Alex heard a girl's scream come from above them on the roof and then saw two half naked women plunge right past where they were sitting into the water below. That was followed by a loud chorus of whistling, clapping, and cheering. As the two women popped to the surface they were howling triumphantly and raising their fists in the air. Alex got up and watched them swim around to the dingy dock and climb out of the water where their friends met them with their tops. After a round of high fives, the two women put their tops back on and came up to the bar deck and got a couple of drinks. When the bartender gave them their drinks, he also gave each of them a Willie T, tee shirt. "What was all that about?" asked Alex.

"It's bar policy for women, if you jump off the roof topless; you get a free tee shirt."

"Is it like this everywhere in the islands?"

"No, not really," said Jack, "something about this island just has a no-holds-barred party atmosphere. There is one place on Tortola that gets pretty wild every month on the night of the full moon. It's called the Bomba Shack, every full moon they block off the street for a whole block and have this big party. You see, magic mushrooms are legal in the BVI and they actually sell mushroom saturated rum drinks at the bar. And, if it has rained lately, they have a big pizza tray full of mushrooms sitting on the bar next to the cash register and people can just help themselves as they're waiting to get served."

"You're kidding right," said Alex.

"Nope, serious as a heart attack, you end up with a bunch of tourists tripping on mushrooms, howling at the moon, and dancing on tables and such. I avoid the mushrooms myself, but it is quite a party. The mushroom facet is downplayed somewhat, but, they always seem to be there nonetheless." Alex digested that info for a bit then said, "And so, when is the next full moon?"

Jack laughed and said, "I believe that it's on the 29th, five days away."

"Well," said Alex, "let's see how that fits into the schedule, maybe we can check it out. Sounds like something worth seeing while I'm here in the islands."

"If were going diving in the morning, we should probably get back to the boat and get some rest, you haven't been diving in a while and this is a deep dive, so you should be fresh of mind when we do it."

"Oui, oui, Mon Capitan, on matters such as these, I shall defer my boss role to your judgment."

"If you wish," said Jack, "we can watch the movie, *The Deep*, I just happen to have it on DVD on the boat. I can point out some of the things we'll be seeing tomorrow on the dive."

"Cool," said Alex, "it's been years since I saw the movie, I don't really remember most of the plot or who else is in it."

"Ok, we're all done here, let's shove off." Jack and Alex went down to the dingy and Jack once again had Alex drive, this time he wanted her to put the dingy alongside the boarding ladder. Jack explained that during the duration of the trip, he would be having her do more of the routine things so she could sharpen up her boat skills. That prospect actually excited Alex, she was eager to be part of the crew and not just a passenger.

Back on the boat, Jack put in the movie and as he and Alex watched, Jack pointed out parts of the wreck they would see the next day and Alex pointed out Jacqueline Bissett's wet tee shirt. Alex said, "This is really neat, sitting here watching a movie made on a wreck I get to dive on tomorrow."

"And," said Jack, "it's been really calm for about a week now so the visibility should be about as good as it gets." After the movie was over Jack asked Alex, "Do you want me to close the hatches and fire up the air conditioners, or you just want to use the fans." Alex thought for a second and said, "No, fans will do, I want to be able to listen to the night sounds through the aft hatch."

"Fine, open air it is, well, I'm headed up forward to hit the rack, you know where everything is, so I'll see ya in the am. We should get an early start so I'll wake you when I get up, good night." Before Jack could retreat, Alex grabbed him and gave him a close and remarkably strong hug that lasted for a few seconds, then disengaged and said, "Thank you so much, I haven't had this much fun in years, good night Mon Capitan." Jack, slightly startled, smiled and said, "I aim to please Madame, see you in the morning."

That said, Jack went to the forward cabin and hit the rack. As he lay in his bunk, he kept seeing Alex in that wet white bikini and had difficulty shaking the image. As he lay back to sleep, Jack began reciting the no-decompression dive tables to himself.

Alone in the huge bed in the aft cabin, Alex was thinking that Jack was the most complete, self-assured and genuine man she had ever met. He was polite and proper to a fault though. He was also ruggedly good looking and although she correctly placed him near fifty, he was hard as a rock, and could easily pass for just over forty. As Alex lay on top of the sheets she said to herself, "Sailor boy, you are in trouble." She would see if she could make him break, if not, she would have to do something about it.

Chapter Eighteen

Mhiki and his crew awakened and had coffee. Mhiki was yelling at Leo. "What do you mean you can't get through to anybody, why not, you are the communications expert and you are of no fucking use to me if you can not communicate with anyone, am I communicating clearly here, or do I need to do something to ensure that you understand me?"

Leo was shaking with fear now, he had seen Mhiki kill a man who had displeased him, killed him with his bare hands, beaten him to death, slowly and methodically, prolonging the man's agony while savoring it. Not a scene easily forgotten, nor was it how he wanted to die, especially today, here in this place. When he spoke, Leo's voice was shaken. "Boss, it's not my fault, I have tried every number, none of them work, and there is nothing I can do. Our phones work fine, we can call each other, or we can call outside, but none of our numbers in New York work." Mhiki stared hard at Leo for a moment, then growled like an angry animal and grabbed Leo by his face and viciously rammed the back of his head into the wall of the hotel knocking him unconscious.

Viktor ran to his side to make sure he was still breathing as Mhiki stormed out of the room onto the patio. "This is not a good development," said Stephan, "and it will not help if the boss loses control." Viktor looked at Stephan with a hard look and said, "You are an enforcer, not a policy maker, you work for me, and I work for Mhiki; do not forget your place." Stephan looked away from Viktor's eyes and said, "Of course, I mean no disrespect, but clearly, this is not good."

Ivan had the advantage of not being very bright, physically imposing and as brave and loyal as any man could be, but not really a thinker. He had nearly been denied selection for Spetznaz training but his regimental commander had personally vouched for him, saying that anything he lacked in intellect, he made up for in his innate ability to learn anything he was taught, he simply required direction, and with that, he was remarkably efficient.

Viktor looked at Ivan who was still drinking his coffee and reading the morning's *New York Times*, and said, "Do you have anything to add Ivan?"

A simple, "No boss," was his reply. Leo was coming around now but his eyes refused to cage up in the same direction. *Damn*, thought Viktor, *we need him and he is going to have a concussion at the very least*. Stephan helped Viktor move Leo over to a chair at the table and set him down. Ivan began to look at the back of his head surveying for any obvious signs of a fracture. Satisfied that Leo's skull was relatively intact, Ivan said to Viktor, "He will have a bad headache for a while but he will be ok." Leo had said nothing since regaining consciousness and was looking at Viktor like a scared puppy that had just been smacked with a rolled up newspaper.

Outside, on the patio, Mhiki was fuming at the gills; he could not figure what was going on back at home, was Lexi making some kind of move? Ordinarily, Mhiki would have been on the next plane back to New York, but he would not let anything stop him from finding and killing the sailor, nothing. Viktor thought about going out onto the patio and decided to let Mhiki cool off a bit. After a few minutes, Mhiki came back in and walked over to Leo who immediately began trembling with fear and said, "Continue attempting to contact our people, if you can not, we will deal with that issue when we return." All of this was recorded and reported to Billy who was waiting on the boat for Dan and Will who should be arriving any time. Billy thought about how much more rattled Mhiki would be when Ivan disappeared and smiled to himself.

Jack woke as soon as the sun came up and crawled straight out of the top bow hatch over the bed and jumped into the water and swam three laps around the boat. As he was climbing the boarding ladder he smelled coffee brewing on the stove. Jack called, "Good morning and Merry Ho Ho day Madame," as he walked aft to rinse off with the deck shower. "Coffees up in a minute and Merry Christmas to you too Mon Capitan," was Alex's response. Jack was at the aft laz in the cockpit putting dive gear together for Alex when she emerged with two cups of coffee and some Danish rolls. "If you're ready," said Jack, "we can get underway as soon as we finish this."

"Works for me," said Alex, "how long will it take us to get there?"

"Half an hour or so once we clear the entrance of the Bight. We'll anchor on the south side of the island then dingy around and tie off to one of the buoys. It's pretty flat so we'll just tow the dingy there. I have your gear ready so we can go over some of that safety stuff before we get ready to dive. How'd you sleep?" asked Jack.

"Like a baby, best night sleep I've had in a long time." After finishing their meager breakfast, Jack said, "You ready to shove off?"

Alex said, "Light this thing up and let's get going." Jack started the engine and watched as the oil pressure and charging system gages came up into operational range and signaled Alex to cast off. Alex came back into the cockpit and said, "No wind at all huh?"

"Nope," said Jack, "that's ok though, we'll still make good time motoring. Some people are purists, they won't use the engine unless they absolutely have to, me, if I want to get somewhere, and there is no, or not enough wind to make five knots, I light off the engine."

"You have my full support skipper, I want to get there and get into the water. That was so cool to be able to watch the movie last night and then dive on Christmas morning. I still can't get over how clear the water is here." Alex went down below and put on some music and when she came back topside, went forward to the bow rail and sat with her legs dangling over the bow and took in the scenery.

Billy had just finished doing a full systems check on the sleek Donzi when he heard a knocking on the hull of the boat. Billy went topside and Dan and Will were standing on the dock with their bags. "Permission to come aboard?" said Dan. Billy smiled at the two men and said, "Sure, hop onboard and stow your gear, and I'll give you the latest sitrep. Make sure your stuff is secure because once we get underway, we are going to be hauling ass."

The two men stowed their belongings and changed into their boating clothes and joined Billy in the cockpit for their in brief. "Ok," said Billy, "that is the latest info, before we split I'll make another call. The van is here in the parking lot and ready, I already put the equipment box in there. I also have two FedEx shirts for me and Dan, Will, you wait in the van while we take out Ivan. We go to the room and knock on the door and tell him we have a box for his boss Mhiki. We carry the box inside the room so no one sees me pop him. Dan, you hold out the clipboard as if for him to sign for the box, and while you have him distracted, I'll put two in his pump with the Glock. We stuff him into the box and get him back here on the boat and run about ten miles out and have a quick funeral at sea, merry fucking Christmas Ivan."

All of these men had killed in the service of their country before and the demise of Ivan meant nothing more to them than part of a strategy to deal with an adversary force. "What about blood at the scene?" asked Will.

"Shouldn't be any," said Billy, "I'm loaded with subsonics so the rounds will stay in the body, we just have to get his big ass in the box before he has a chance to leak all over the place. Dan, as soon as I hit him, you help me lower the body down on his back so we don't get any blood on the rug."

"Sounds good to me," said Dan. "So, Valentnikov already started smacking his boys around, finding Ivan gone should really improve his mood." The three men smiled at each other and Billy said, "I need to make a call."

Agent Wilson informed Billy that the Russian Mhiki had assaulted wasn't feeling all that well and still could not establish any communications with home, and, that it would be an hour before the Russians boarded the ferry for Tortola. That was all Billy and his team needed to know. Billy told Halston that he was to discontinue surveillance of Ivan on his signal after the team returned from Tortola. No sense having the FBI record Ivan getting taken out. Billy fired up the twin V-8 engines and the team started off for Road Harbor.

Christmas morning, Detective Brady received a phone call from the surveillance team watching Lexi's place. "Yes sir, the cleaners were in there for about an hour and they carried out three rolled up carpets. We have a vehicle following the cleaners, looks like they're headed to Jersey; I'll let you know what happens with that when I get word. Then our subject went to a pay phone and made several phone calls and then a car came for him and took him to another location in Brighton Beach. After the principals' arrival, seven vehicles carrying a total of thirty individuals arrived at said location. Their conversation was monitored and recorded and the tape is being sent to you via courier as we speak. As per previous instructions, no transcript of, or copies were made of the tape, the original and only copy is being delivered to you. After the meeting adjourned, the principal was driven to his home of record and is currently with his wife and daughter. The device is functioning flawlessly, GPS track and microphone functioning at peak. We get every word he says."

"Outstanding," said Brady, "stay on him, and report anything significant to me immediately."

"Got your sorry Russian ass now," said Brady.

As Jack approached Salt Island, Alex came back to the cockpit with Jack and said, "I forgot to ask, are we going to anchor here?"

"Yep," said Jack, "right over there around the point on the north east side of the island."

"Anything I need to do?" asked Alex.

"Nope," said Jack, "just kick back for a minute." Jack approached the beach at an angle and when he was about thirty yards out, he turned the boat into the wind and shifted first into neutral, then reverse to stop the forward momentum of the boat. When the boat had stopped, Jack hit a switch and the anchor and chain began to pay out. Alex noted that the anchor chain was painted in red and white lengths, roughly a boat length each as a means of keeping track of how much chain was being paid out. When Jack was satisfied, he let off the switch and walked up to the bow to check the anchor. Alex followed him and was surprised that she could see the anchor on the bottom in thirty-five feet of water. "That should do it," said Jack, "let's go get ready, do me a favor and pull in the dingy and tie it off by the ladder."

"Aye aye skipper," said Alex as she went to secure the dingy. Jack went to the aft laz and dug out the gear as Alex was finishing the dingy. Jack gave Alex a run through of her equipment and was pleased to note that she seemed familiar with all of the gear except the air integrated dive computer. "This is way cool technology," explained Jack, "it gives you tank pressure, depth, water temperature, no decompression time adjusting for current depth, and air time remaining based on your rate of consumption. All of that is on these two displays, if, during the dive, you see me point two fingers at my eyes and then my console, I want you to show me your console. Remember this is a deep dive, eighty feet in one spot. You haven't dived in a long time and we have never been diving together. I want you to stay close to me throughout the dive, I'll be like the mother goose on this dive, then after I see what your skill and comfort level is, I'll slack off on subsequent dives ok."

"Fair enough," said Alex, "we ready?"

"Yep," said Jack, "I put twelve pounds of weights in your vest, it's probably too much but I'd rather have you too heavy than light, we can adjust as required for the second dive. Go ahead and get into the dingy and I'll hand the gear down to you." Alex did as she was told and as Jack was watching her secure the gear, he noted that she was sporting a blue thong today. That made Jack think of something else. "Do you get cold easy?" asked Jack.

"No, why?" asked Alex.

"Well, the water temp at eighty feet today should be in the upper seventies at its coolest, you want a dive skin?"

"No way," said Alex. *Good*, thought Jack.

"Ok, let's get going." Jack climbed into the dingy and Alex cast them off after Jack started the engine. As they rounded the point and turned left, Alex saw several small boats, a few of them with dive flags on them tied off to different buoys. Jack approached one and told Alex too tie off to it. After securing the dingy to the dingy, Jack and Alex put on their gear. After Alex was done, Jack checked to make sure that her air supply and her dive computer were turned on, then Jack said, "Ok, inflate your BC, then roll out into the water and grab that buoy line, we're going to follow it to the bottom and I want you to maintain contact with it at all times on the way down, if you need both hands to clear your ears, hook your leg around the line alright."

Alex nodded her head, then Jack said, "Mask down, snorkel in your mouth, regulator in your right hand." After Alex had complied Jack said, "Now, over the side with you." Alex rolled straight backwards out of the dingy and immediately rolled over on her stomach and cleared the water from her snorkel by exhaling sharply and gave Jack the OK signal before swimming to the buoy line and grabbing it. Satisfied, Jack did the same. Jack moved next to Alex and said, "First things first, put your face in the water and look down." When Alex looked she couldn't believe it, the bow of the wreck was in nearly eighty feet of water, and she could see it plainly, that and the dozen or so divers swimming around the wreck. She was still looking when Jack tapped her on the shoulder and said, "Let's go join them, put your regulator in your mouth and raise your inflator hose above your head with your right hand and deflate your vest when you're ready." Even with the regulator in her mouth, Jack could see that Alex was all smiles as she began to deflate her buoyancy compensator and began her descent to the wreck site.

At about thirty feet Alex had to stop and equalize the pressure in her ears, but after that it was a smooth descent to the bottom. Once on the bottom, Jack adjusted his buoyancy with his inflator valve and Alex did the same. Jack gave Alex a chance to get comfortable and both gave the other an OK signal and Jack motioned Alex to follow him. They had begun their descent directly in front of the bow of the ship and Jack swam just over the surface of the hull until he reached the hatch opening that Nick Nolte's character had entered the wreck. Jack had attached powerful dive lights to both of their BCs on a self retracting reel so they could not get lost if dropped. Jack took his light and shined it into the hatch and communicated that he would enter first, and then Alex would follow.

Alex nodded her head in agreement and Jack swam head first into the opening. Once inside and clear, Jack shined his light up and motioned Alex to follow. Alex did not hesitate a bit and swam through the opening and came to a stop next to Jack. The two shined their lights around the large space inside the wreck and Alex took note of what Jack had said earlier about the inside being unrecognizable as a shipwreck, just rotting rusty iron. Jack motioned for Alex to follow him and began to swim toward the other end of the wreck. After a little ways, Jack switched off his dive light and Alex did the same. Then she saw how the ambient light began to light the interior of the wreck as they approached the point where the vessel had been blown in half when the sea water had hit its boiler.

As the opening came into view, Alex was mesmerized by what appeared to be thousands of brightly colored fish playing in the rays of sunlight at the broken section of the hull. As they swam through the opening, Alex followed Jack and he showed her the mast and crows nest and then the old signal cannon. For a time, the two swam around the large debris field and then Jack signaled that he wanted to see her console. Satisfied, Jack made a circling motion with his index finger raised above his head and began swimming back to the buoy line that they had followed down from the surface. When they reached the buoy line, Jack indicated to Alex to hold on to the line for the ascent. Satisfied she was ready, Jack started toward the surface ahead of Alex. Again, at about thirty feet, Alex had to stop to adjust the pressure in her ears. After a few seconds, she gave Jack the OK sign and the pair started back on their way slowly to the surface.

Alex was showing twelve feet on her depth gage when Jack signaled for her to stop. The pair hung out at that depth for ten minutes in order for the excess nitrogen, forced out of solution into their surrounding tissues by the increased pressure at depth, to diffuse back into their blood stream. Once the pair had surfaced and was back in the dingy, Alex said, "That was incredible, I have never seen so many different colorful types of fish on all my dives put together."

"Yeah," said Jack, "it's easy to get spoiled diving around here, if you want, we can do some reef diving later and really see some color. You ready for some lunch?"

"Sure," said Alex, "let's head back to the boat." Alex untied the dingy after Jack had started the engine. After they were back onboard the boat, Alex asked Jack, "Do we have to do the second dive?"

"No," said Jack, "what do you want to do?"

"I think I'd just like to head over to Cooper and relax, besides, I'm having trouble with my left ear, can't quite equalize yet." Jack thought for a second and then said, "Not a problem we can get going after I clean the gear. As for your ear, look in the top drawer next to the stove, there's a pack of gum in there, chew a couple of pieces of that, the motion of your jaw chewing the gum should relieve the pressure, it helps open the passages."

"I've never heard that one before, but I'll take your word for it skipper." As Alex was getting her gum, Jack got busy rinsing off the dive gear. Alex came up and helped him finish cleaning and stow the gear. Alex went below and selected a Bing Crosby Christmas CD and put that on as Jack was getting the engine started. Alex sat next to Jack as he hit the switch and raised the anchor. Once the anchor was seated at its stop, Jack shifted into gear and swung around and headed east for Cooper island.

After Billy, Dan, and Will had cleared water island, Billy hit the throttles on the big Donzi. It took about seven seconds for the boat to plane out, but once it did, the acceleration was impressive. In no time they were doing fifty knots and Billy had a lot of throttle left. The surface was like glass and the group made Road Harbor in short order.

After they had tied off the boat, Will went to the rental office and was taken to the boat that Mhiki and his crew were to rent. Will looked around for the best place to install the device and decided to mount it in plain sight next to the helm and tie it into the boats twelve volt system using a voltage regulator that he had in his installation kit. After he had installed and checked the device, Will told the rental office manager that if anyone asked, the device was a backup GPS antenna. Satisfied, Will returned to the Donzi and said, "As long as they use that boat, we will know their position to within ten feet."

"Technology, ain't it wonderful," said Dan. Dan placed a call to Agent Halston who informed him that three of the Russians were just climbing into a cab for their trip to catch the ferry to Tortola and that he would sit on Ivan until the team was back in St. Thomas. Dan looked at his companions and said, "Ok, let's get going, Mhiki and company have left the hotel and Ivan is there by himself, Halston is going to keep an eye on him until we get there, then I tell Halston to have a nice day. Let's go.

At the hotel, Ivan sat alone in the room pondering the current situation and came to the conclusion that it sucked. He did not like the fact that they were unable to contact anyone in New York, and was even more concerned about Mhiki, everyone else was as well. Leo did not look so good, his eyes still did not point in the same direction and he had thrown up his breakfast, Ivan knew the symptoms of a brain injury when he saw one, he had seen plenty of them caused by various means in

Afghanistan. Well, he thought, it did no good to worry, like he had done for all of his life, he would follow orders and leave the heavy mental lifting to those in charge.

Billy pulled all the stops for the return trip from Tortola, on the flat calm water, the Donzi was cruising at sixty-five knots, slowing and maneuvering only to avoid collisions and finally at the entrance into Charlotte Amalie. The moment the boat was secure; the three men leapt out and got into the van. On the way there, Dan and Billy put on their FedEx shirts and ball caps. Billy called Halston as the hotel came into sight. "Yeah, he's still in the room," said Halston, "their box is in the room with him."

"Ok," said Billy, "disengage, I repeat, break off surveillance at this time, go get some lunch. See to it that Agent White is ready to take up surveillance at the marina when I call and not before. When the Russians get back, watch them and report back to me, there will be no need to follow them. After I call you back, resume surveillance of the room and report to me if the Russians return there, it is a possibility, understood."

"Yes sir," said Halston, "anything else?"

"Nope, that should do it for now, call me when you're clear. Ok Dan, as soon as Halston calls clear, were on, any questions?"

"Nope, let's bag this fucker and split." Billy took out his Glock and screwed the suppressor onto the threads of the specially extended barrel of the weapon. Then he checked to ensure he had the correct magazine with the subsonic loads and chambered a round.

Halston thought about sticking around to see what was going to happen, but decided it was best if he did not know, he was being called off for a reason, he could never have to testify about something he knew nothing about, so he decided on a sandwich and left the area and called Billy to inform them that he was clear. Billy acknowledged Halston's call and said, "Will, back the van right up in front of the door, let's go." Will did as told and Billy and Dan got out of the side door and opened the double doors at the back of the van and removed the empty equipment box. It was about four feet square and four feet deep, certainly big enough for the task at hand. The open van doors were only a few feet from the hotel room door. Dan had his clipboard with some useless papers attached to it and Billy was ready with his Glock stuck in his waistband at the small of his back.

Dan knocked on the door. Inside, Ivan was startled by the knocking at the door; he was expecting no one so he hesitated. Billy and Dan looked at each other and shrugged. Dan knocked again and said, "Hello in there, Federal Express, we have a big box for a Mhikiail Valentnikov and it's marked urgent." Now Ivan was confused, he knew of no other equipment for Mhiki, but no one outside of their people knew he was here. Ivan looked through the peephole and saw two men in FedEx uniforms so he opened the door and said, "Bring box in, I sign for it." Billy and Dan exchanged a quick look; Billy's heart began to pump faster in anticipation of the upcoming action. As soon as the box was in the room, Dan came to a stop with his right leg and foot within range of the front door and held out his clipboard and said, "Just sign here." As Ivan had his head turned away from him, Billy swung his Glock up and jammed the muzzle of the suppressor into Ivan's solar plexus upwards at a forty-five degree angle and pulled the trigger as soon as the weapon made contact with the Russian's body.

The round misfired; there was insufficient powder in the casing to propel the round much over three inches into Ivan's chest cavity, far short of reaching his heart. Worse yet, there was insufficient recoil from the round to fully extract the spent casing from the Glock, causing a classic stove pipe malfunction of the weapon. This occurs as the detonation of the powder in the shell casing is insufficient to drive the slide on the pistol back far enough to fully extract the spent casing, and also not far enough back for the slide to pick up the next round in the magazine. The result is that the spent casing ends up pinched between the extractor and the firing chamber with the open end of the casing sticking straight up like a stove pipe. An easy malfunction to clear when you have a free hand, you just turn the weapon on its right side and rack the slide back again, this allows the spent casing to fall away and the weapon chambers another round as the slide moves forward. However, when your other hand is hanging on to a two hundred twenty-five pound former commando that is scared, surprised, and suddenly quite pissed off, it is not so easy.

Dan instantly knew something had gone to shit and shoved the edge of the clipboard into Ivan's Adam's apple with all the force he could muster and immediately kicked the hotel room door shut. At the same time, Billy kicked down just above Ivan's left ankle bone as hard as he could, shattering his leg just above the ankle and then swept his good leg out from under him. Ivan went down hard on his back making a horrible gurgling sound as both of his hands clutched at his crushed larynx. Within a second and a half after Ivan hit the floor, Billy had cleared the malfunction and chambered another round. The last thing Ivan ever saw was Billy pressing the suppressor into his sternum before he pulled the trigger twice. Ivan's body went slack and the two men looked at each other, Dan was the first to speak and said, "Well, that certainly went smooth eh."

"Fuck me," said Billy, breathing hard as he picked up the three spent shell casings, "goddamn short load, didn't do more than piss him off, good work with the clipboard. Let's get this big bastard in the box." As Dan was opening the fasteners on the box, Billy went to the bathroom and grabbed a couple of towels and placed them on Ivan's chest and face, he had bled some through his mouth, no doubt from his crushed larynx. Billy wanted to ensure no blood stains would be visible on the rug if Mhiki came back to the hotel. Something he was almost certain to do once Ivan failed to show up at Crown Bay Marina as planned.

The two men wrestled Ivan's lifeless body into the equipment box, sealed it, and dragged it out to the van where Will helped load it into the back. Dan went back into the room and picked up the smaller box that contained the Russians' weapons and explosive device. He also checked to make sure there were no blood stains on the rug. Dan called the front desk to inform them that the entire party was checking out and that the keys would be left in the room, and to bill any charges to the credit card of record, then locked and closed the door on his way out.

Billy, had blood on his arm, chest, and some splatters on his face from the blowback caused by the increased pressure in Ivan's chest cavity from the muzzle of the Glock He used the uniform shirt and some bottled water to clean himself off. Contact shots are always a little messy. As they were headed back to the marina Dan powered up his laptop and noted that Mhiki's boat was still in its slip. Will said, "What do we do after the funeral Billy?"

"We can go to Soapers Hole, maybe try and get a slip, whichever direction they head from there, it's an easy intercept or we can follow if need be. I would feel a lot better if Jake would call so I can let him know what's goin on here, I'll call the booking agent again after we drop off Ivan. Also, I want to be stationary for a while so Halston and White can call and let us know what's going on with the Russians.

As Billy's team was headed for deep water south of St. Thomas, Mhiki and company were boarding their rental boat. Stephan was about to start the engines when Mhiki said, "Wait, Viktor, call Ivan and make sure he is on his way to the marina." After trying twice, Viktor looked at the still glassy and cross eyed Leo and thought hard about his next remarks to Mhiki. "Uh, Mhiki, he does not answer his phone or the room phone." Much to everyone's surprise, Mhiki just said, "He will be at the marina when we get there, let's get moving, I want to pick up Ivan and get back here and check around the jewelry stores in town. I want to know if the woman can sell the stones here." That said, the group departed for St. Thomas.

Twelve miles south of St. Thomas, Billy brought the boat to a stop and put the dingy that was mounted on the swim platform in the water and tied it off to the stern cleat. Will broke out one of the three MP-5K, 9 millimeter submachine guns and attached a suppressor to the end of the barrel. Billy had attached a forty pound anchor and fifteen feet of chain to the box. After Billy and Dan had pushed the box off the stern, Billy threw the anchor over the side. When the slack came out of the chain and the box was bobbing on the surface, Dan asked if anyone wanted to say anything and Will said, "Yeah, adios you murdering communist piece of shit," as he opened fire at the waterline of the box. Will expended a full thirty round magazine into the box filling it, and Ivan with holes, thusly ensuring that it would sink to the bottom forever in a few thousand feet of water. The men made sure that they had disposed of all of the spent shell casings over the side as well and Billy said, "How's lunch in Tortola sound, as I recall, there's a great restaurant right by the Moorings docks."

Dan said, "Yeah, I could use some lunch, maybe a beer too." Will simply nodded in agreement. With that decision made, the men headed for the Moorings at the West end after calling Agent Halston and telling

THE GREEN FLASH

him to resume surveillance at the marina. Once the Russians arrived, another agent would resume surveillance at the hotel.

It only took Jack and Alex about ten minutes to motor over to Cooper Island. As they were approaching the island, Jack called the resort on the radio using the call sign Captain Jack and was told which mooring ball to use for the night. Actually, he would have had a fifty fifty shot at it as there were only two that were not in use. Alex went up to the bow and secured the pendant to the ball and then came back to the cockpit. "Hey, that chewing gum trick worked, my ear popped a minute ago, thanks. Jack, why didn't you use the boat name on the radio?"

"Well, I have had some problems in the past with people bugging me about trying to arrange charters while I have guests aboard. So, when I use the radio, I use a different call sign and rarely answer my cell phone. I have a system set up with my charter broker so anyone that I might actually want to talk to, can leave a message with her, she gets it to me, and I can call them."

"Pretty slick, want to have a Pain Killer and hang out a bit before we go ashore."

"Why certainly Madame."

Stephan pulled the boat up to the service dock at Crown Bay marina. Now that Ivan was not waiting there for them, and could not be raised on his cell phone, Mhiki was furious and having a hard time not making a scene. "Stephan, get a cab and go to the hotel and find Ivan and get back here, if he shows up while you are gone, we will call you. He had better have a good fucking excuse for not being here, go, now goddamnit." Stephan wisely said nothing and went to get a cab. Viktor looked at Leo and was concerned, Leo had thrown up twice on the way over and Mhiki had written it off to sea sickness but Viktor was not so sure. Leo was pale and having a hard time focusing his eyes and seemed to get less coherent by the hour.

Stephan arrived at the hotel just as the cleaning lady was leaving the room that he and Ivan had shared. Stephan asked the woman if she had seen his friend, all she could tell him was that the party had checked out about an hour ago. Stephan talked the woman into letting him into the room. Inside, Stephan noted that everything was gone, not a trace that they had ever been there.

155

Outside the room, Stephan phoned Viktor to ask if Ivan had shown up at the marina yet. "What do you mean he is not there, he is not here either and he isn't answering his cell phone, fuck, where could he be?"

"Viktor, do you think he would just leave? Be careful what you say if Mhiki is next to you, but if he is not there and he checked out of the rooms an hour ago, what else could it mean?" Viktor looked at the glaring face of Mhiki and said, "I see what you mean, get back here as fast as you can."

"What the fuck is going on Viktor, where is Ivan?"

"I don't know Mhiki," said Viktor, "he checked out of the rooms an hour ago."

"Give me that goddamn phone," screamed Mhiki.

"Stephan, go straight to the airport and see if that piece of shit is there, look everywhere do you understand, if he is, I don't care how you have to do it but you fucking kill him, do you hear me, if you don't see him, check all outgoing flights within the last hour and the time you get there, now go." Mhiki hung up the phone, gave it back to Viktor and walked away down the dock. "This is no good my friend," said Leo. It was the first he had spoken since they had left Tortola. Viktor looked at Leo and said, "How are you doing Leo?"

"I am dizzy, nauseous, my head hurts, and I can't focus my eyes. Other than that, I feel fine. There is something Mhiki is not telling us, I have a bad feeling about this Viktor, where could Ivan have gone; do you believe he would try to run?"

"No my friend, he is not very bright, but he is no coward either. I just don't know. Quiet, Mhiki is coming back."

"Ok, let's go to the bar and eat, Ivan will either show up or he won't, if he went to the airport, Stephan will find him." Leo said, "Mhiki, I am not up to going to the bar just yet, Viktor, would you please bring me a cheeseburger when you come back, I just want to rest for now." Mhiki just looked at him with disgust, Viktor said, "Of course Leo, with everything I assume?"

"Fine," said Leo. Leo had already taken half a bottle of aspirin and it had done nothing to ease his discomfort so he went to his cabin to lie down for a few minutes, if he could just get some rest, maybe the nausea would pass.

White, who had been sitting at the bar at Tickles and watching the Russians since they had arrived, was amused, it was obvious that the Russians were distraught over their friend not showing up, White wondered what they had done with Ivan and decided it was not productive to ponder such things. White called Billy, who was sitting at the bar at the moorings landing.

"Yeah, they're here and their boss is pissed, he sent one of them presumably to look for Ivan, the one he smacked around earlier is on the boat, and the other two are walking over here now, call you back." Billy looked at Dan and Will and said, "Uh oh, our Russian friends have figured out that something is rotten in Denmark. That was White; we'll talk at the boat."

The three men finished their lunch and went to the slip they had rented for their boat. Back onboard the boat Will said, "Wonder what they'll do now?"

"Hard to say, said Billy, it looks like Valentnikov sent Stephan out looking for Ivan, we'll just have to wait and see. I guess we hang out here until White tells us that they're on the move. I don't know how long they'll stay there trying to find him, but it gives us more time to try and figure out where Jake is, I'll call the charter broker and have her try Jake's phone again. In the meantime, let's get the shore power and cable TV plugged in and op check that plasma TV." Will called the broker and was told Jack had as yet to return her call; she would try again and contact Billy as soon as Jack called her. Billy hoped Jake would get the Muller reference. Steve Muller had been their supervising agent when he and Jake worked together in D.C.

Stephan had looked all over the small airport, and checked all possible flights Ivan could have departed on and he was sure he had not been here. Stephan had a very uneasy feeling, something was going on here that he could not figure out and it was unsettling to say the least. He had never seen Mhiki act without a solid plan before, it would make sense to just watch the marina and wait for the sailor and woman to come back and take them then, but Mhiki was determined to go running around the Caribbean Sea looking for them. For that matter, why had he come here himself, this sort of thing was what Viktor, along with himself and Ivan took care of, what was so important about this woman that Mhiki had never met, that he had to come here and get personally involved. No, Stephan did not like this at all.

Stephan took his cell phone and tried I van's cell number several times and got no answer. *Where could he be?* wondered Stephan, he was not at the hotel, and had not tried to escape on a plane, and he had four pistols, four hundred rounds of ammunition, and a bomb. If the police had been involved, they would have been all over the hotel, at the very least; the cleaning woman would have said something. He could not have simply gotten lost; he was supposed to take a cab to the marina.

Stephan called Viktor and told him that there was no sign of Ivan and that he was returning to the marina. Mhiki looked at Viktor and said, "What did he say?" Viktor felt very uneasy and said, "He was not, and has not been to the airport, of that Stephan is sure, he is on his way back here now." Mhiki was about to say something but stopped short. Mhiki also could not figure out what was going here. Ivan was as reliable as any man could be; he was totally ruthless and did not even understand fear as a concept. Mhiki had heard of tourists disappearing here through foul play on occasion, but could not believe that any common thug could get the best of Ivan. Mhiki was disturbed about the fact that their weapons were gone, another bomb could be manufactured anywhere, but the small arms were another matter. Mhiki took out his phone and tried to call Lexi again and became even more upset by the recording that told him that he had reached a number that had been disconnected.

Halston phoned Billy and reported that he had observed Stephan looking for Ivan at the hotel, about his phone call that he had been unable to hear, and about following him to the airport. Billy thanked him for the information and told Halston to contact White and arrange shifts for keeping tabs on the Russians at the marina. Billy said, "They don't appear to know what to do just yet, Mhiki sent Stephan to the airport to look for Ivan and I would assume it's to see if he skipped out. They may be afraid to stay there much longer, hard to say for now. We sit here till White calls and let's us know they are on the move."

Stephan returned to the marina to find Mhiki in a very foul mood. After Stephan had given Mhiki an accounting of his search of the hotel and airport, Mhiki remained silent for a moment and said, "We leave here now, we will go back to Road Harbor in Tortola and anchor out and use the dingy to get to town. If Ivan is able, he will call us. I do not like this; I want to get off this island now." No one had anything else to say so the group boarded the boat and left for Tortola. As they were disappearing around the seawall, White called Billy and repeated what he had been able to hear of the conversation. He was sure however that they were going to Road Harbor. Billy thanked White for his and his coworker's assistance and told him that their assistance may or not be required in the upcoming days.

White said, "We don't know what is really going on here and I don't think that's a bad thing, let me know if we can be of any more help." Billy thanked him again and said he would be in touch. White was thinking that they would never see the Russians again, just a feeling really.

As their boat was clearing Water Island, Viktor went below to give Leo his cheeseburger and saw that he was sleeping on his stomach with his head turned to its right side. Viktor shook Leo to wake him but got no response. Viktor, immediately concerned, checked Leo's pulse, there was none. When Viktor moved Leo's head, there was a watery bloody stain on his pillow and Viktor could see where it had been leaking out of Leo's right ear. Cerebral spinal fluid, obviously the impact had been sufficient to rupture the lining around Leo's brain. The subsequent swelling and increased pressure inside his skull had forced the fluid out through his ear. It was most likely that same swelling or a hemorrhage that killed him. Viktor sat with him for a moment, and then went up into the cockpit. "Mhiki, Leo is dead."

Mhiki looked at Viktor with a stunned look for a moment then said, "Are you sure?"

"Of course I'm sure, he has no pulse and he is getting cold, yes he is dead, a brain hemorrhage probably, you hit him too hard." Mhiki scowled at Viktor momentarily, then grabbed the chart from the console and looked at it for a moment. "Stephan," said Mhiki, "turn south now for open water, we can go out until no one can see us then dump his body, is there a spare anchor on the boat?"

Stephan thought for a moment and said, "Yes, there is a second anchor in the aft chain locker."

"Good, I will drive the boat; you and Viktor go get the body and bring it up here and get it ready, as soon as we can do it without being observed, we will dump him." Viktor and Stephan looked at each other for just a moment and Viktor said, "Of course Mhiki." Below, in Leo's cabin, Stephan quickly checked Leo's pulse and confirmed what Viktor had told Mhiki. Stephan said, "All he said were the facts and Mhiki killed him for it, now we are abandoning Ivan to who knows what, this is not good Viktor, I do not like any of this."

"And just would you have me do about it, we can't contact Lexi, or anyone else for that matter, we just have to let this play out, we find the woman, get the stones and go home, we have no choice. Do you want to go tell Mhiki that you want to quit and go home, how do you think he would react to that? No my friend we are stuck here until this thing is finished. Now help me get Leo up on deck." Viktor and Stephan carried Leo up into the cockpit and laid his body on the deck behind the helm. Mhiki looked back at the corpse of Leo and spit on him and said, "You miserable worthless piece of shit, I always said you were weak, I have hit women harder than that and they were fine."

Viktor and Stephan said nothing and avoided looking directly at Mhiki. After a while, Stephan looked at the GPS display and noted that they had traveled about ten miles into open water and decided they had gone far enough. He looked all around and saw no other vessels close by and said to Mhiki, "This is as good a place as any." Mhiki stopped the boat and Viktor tied the anchor line around Leo's waist, and without fanfare, he and Stephan rolled his body into the sea. What they could not know, was that Leo's body would come to rest less than a mile and a half from Ivan.

Dan had been watching the Russians boat on his computer since it had departed St. Thomas and had been wondering where they were going. Billy said, "Damn, looks like they went almost to the spot where we dropped off their buddy, what do you think they were doing there?"

Will said, "We know one of them had a bad head injury, maybe he croaked, or Valentnikov just didn't want him around anymore, not like they could just take him to the local hospital. Look at their track, they turned south as soon as they cleared Water Island, went roughly to the same spot we did, were only there for a couple of minutes, now they are headed for Tortola."

"Too bad we don't have an asset on Tortola to check it out for us, but I bet next time we see the Russians, there's only three of em, said Dan. Well, we'll wait here and see what they do, Goddamnit, I wish Jake would call. It would be a big help to know where he is right now."

Jack and Alex had a couple of painkillers and were hanging out in the cockpit listening to Christmas music. "What time are we going in for dinner?" asked Alex.

"Our reservations are for six and it's two now, why you getting hungry?"

"Yeah, a little," said Alex. "Look in the fridge for a yellow plastic bowl, bring that and two forks." Alex went below and got the bowl and forks and when she got back topside, Jack had setup the cockpit table so Alex sat down next to Jack and said, "Ok, so what's in the bowl?"

"How's fresh octopus salad in a vinaigrette sound for a snack, I made it three days ago so it should be just right by now."

"Yummy," said Alex. After a few bites, Alex said, "This is delicious, you actually made this yourself?"

"Merely one of my many talents Madame, more shall be revealed as we continue our journey." Alex thought, *I certainly hope so.* What was with this guy, most of the time, especially when she was wearing a bikini, men were staring at her tits and or her ass, now that she was trying to get one to do it, he was being the perfect gentleman. *Huh, we'll just have to see about that.* "So, what are you wearing in to dinner Jack?"

"Haven't given it much thought really, probably a polo shirt and a good pair of shorts, why?"

Alex thought for a minute and said, "I was just wondering what I should wear, I have one dress with me, I guess I'll wear that. I'm getting hot, time for a dip in the pool." Alex climbed out of the cockpit and jumped over the side and swam a ways underwater from the boat. When she surfaced, she said, "Come on in, it feels great."

Jack said, "On my way," and did a cannonball landing right in front of Alex. When Jack surfaced, Alex grabbed him by the head and pushed him underwater. Jack simply pushed upwards with his palms up and his arms extended, forcing himself deeper underwater and stopped with his head level with Alex's feet. Then he grabbed her by the right ankle and tickled the bottom of her right foot. Good guess, the most ticklish spot on her body was the bottom of her feet. Judging by the way she screamed and struggled, Jack figured he had found a weak spot. Jack decided to let her get one in so when he surfaced, he had his back to her and she immediately pounced on his back trying to push him under again. In about a second, Jack had spun her around and had her left arm pinned between her back and his stomach, and his right arm was around her rib cage just below her breasts, and his right hand clutched her left shoulder and Jack was swimming backwards as casual as could be and he was laughing.

Alex tried to struggle for a second and knew that it would be useless, besides, this was the most physical contact that they had had so far and she didn't want it to stop. As Jack felt her relax, he let her go and as soon as she turned around, she splashed water in his face. "Where did you learn how to do that?" asked Alex.

"Just an old lifesaving move I learned, never know when you might really want someone off your back while you're trying to swim."

"Ok," said Alex, "let's go back to the boat, I don't know about you big fella, but I'm ready for another cocktail." They swam around to the ladder and Jack let Alex climb up first. As she was climbing the ladder, Jack was looking at that little blue thong. Jack climbed up next and walked straight aft to rinse off. Alex was standing right next to him and he noticed that like the white one, when wet, her bikini top clung to her breasts like it was painted on. Damn, he thought to himself, think about the fuel lift pump old boy. Alex smiled at him as he handed her the hose. This time Jack watched her as she rinsed off with the hose. Alex noticed that he was watching and smiled inwardly. He's finally starting to notice, she thought.

After Stephan had anchored the boat in the harbor, the three men boarded the dingy and went ashore. Mhiki was further disappointed to find that all of the high end shops were closed. Now, thoroughly frustrated, Mhiki and company returned to their boat. Back on the boat Mhiki had Stephan call the marina on the VHF radio and arrange for a slip for the night. After making the arrangements, Stephan piloted the boat into the marina, and their assigned slip. Mhiki said very little, but told Viktor and Stephan that they were free to roam around a bit if they wanted to. Both men decided to walk around some just to have something to do. Mhiki sat in the salon of the boat and took out the photographs of Jack and stared hard at them. *Where are you?*

In Soapers Hole, Dan was periodically checking his computer to check the Russians' position. He noted that they had moved to a slip, presumably for the night. "Looks like our friends have decided to stay for the night, they moved to a slip in Road Town. Billy said, "Will, they haven't seen any of us, I want you to catch a cab and do a recon, see if you can get close enough to see if Leo is with them or not, be very careful that you don't get made though. Right now, they're confused and they have no way of knowing what's going on, it is imperative that we keep it that way."

Dan said, "You want me to go too?"

"No, less a chance of getting spotted with just Will, just do the tourist thing, walk around the docks and check out the boats, maybe you will be able to spot and watch the boat from the bar."

"Ok," said Will, "I'm outta here; I'll call if I see anything noteworthy." Once Will had left, Dan said, "Let's see if there's anything worth watching on HBO."

Jack had showered and was relaxing in the cockpit when Alex came up from below wearing a semi sheer white sundress, tantalizing yet tasteful and she looked absolutely radiant, Jack appreciated for the first time how beautiful this woman was. "Ready to head in?" she asked.

Jack said "Why certainly, let's go." It was a short dingy ride and the walkway from the dingy dock led straight to the restaurant and as they approached the restaurant, a jovial woman in her early fifties approached Jack and gave him a big hug and said, "Merry Christmas Jack, this is your guest I assume?"

"Call me Alex."

"Alex, I am Jane, let's get you two to your table and get a drink in you while you look at the menu." They followed Jane to their table and ordered drinks. After looking at the menu, both selected the grilled Mahi with Cajun mango sauce. The two finished eating shortly before sunset and Jack had Alex walk down to the dingy dock to watch the sunset. As the sun set down the Francis Drake passage, Alex stood transfixed by the beauty of the scene. After the sun had dipped below the surface of the Caribbean Sea, Alex looked at Jack and said, "Have you ever seen anything more beautiful than that?"

Jack matter of factly said, "Yep, looks even better from the north side of Virgin Gorda. But even that pales in comparison to the first time you see the Green Flash."

"I've heard of it," said Alex, "but I've never seen one."

"You have to be further south, and conditions have to be just right but when you see it, it's an oooh, aaah moment."

"What causes it?" asked Alex.

"Well, it has to do with atmospheric conditions and light refraction off the surface and so on, I'm no physicist, but I know this much. When the sun dips below the horizon, and conditions are just right, right at that moment, and only for a moment, the horizon lights up a brilliant green, and then, poof, it's done."

"What color green," asked Alex.

Jack was looking directly into Alex's eyes, lingering on them for a moment and said, "Just like those," pointing his middle and index fingers at her eyes.

Alex positively beamed, then said, "No, you're kidding."

"No, no I'm not, I'd say something about your eyes right now but it would just sound like a line of crap."

Alex looked at Jack and smiled, then, taking him by the arm, said, "Come on skipper let's go have us a brandy before we go back to the boat." Alex hung on to Jack all the way back to the bar and ordered both of them a brandy and then excused herself to hit the ladies' room. When she was gone, Jane came up to Jack and said, "Its about damn time, I'm so happy for you Jack."

Jack, confused for a moment said, "Huh, oh, no, no, it isn't like that, she's a paying customer." Jane looked at Jack, smiled a broad smile and said, "Jack, you really are dumber than I thought, I've been watching you two since you got here, she is smitten and you know what, if you don't do something about it, you are a fool." Jane reached up and kissed Jack on the cheek and walked back to the kitchen just as Alex was walking back over. Jane shot Alex a wink when Jack wasn't looking that almost made her laugh.

After they had finished their brandy, Alex said she wanted to go back to the boat and watch a movie. "Sure," said Jack, "anything in particular you want to see?"

"No, not really I'll just have a look if that's ok with you."

"Sure," said Jack, "whatever you want." Back at the boat, Alex was looking through Jack's DVD collection and suddenly giggled and said, "How about this one." The movie she had selected was one of Jack's favorite comedies, *Operation Petticoat*, with Cary Grant and Tony Curtis. It is the story of a WW-II submarine whose Commander is forced by events, to take on a bunch of Army nurses who have been stranded on a Pacific island. As one could imagine, madness and mayhem ensue. As Jack was setting up the movie on the DVD player, Alex went back aft to change. Jack had the movie ready to go when Alex came back into the salon wearing a pair of tight white nylon shorts and a white half tee shirt. To make matters worse, since Jack was already sitting on the end of the settee, Alex came and sat right next to him and leaned up against his side and said, "Hit it." Jack hit the play button on the remote and they were about halfway through the movie when Alex said, "Pause it please, I want to fix us some popcorn, want a Gatorade with that?"

"Sure," said Jack. It was just a few minutes before Alex sat back down and told Jack to start the movie. They laughed and chatted their way through the rest of the movie and when it was over, Jack said, "Have you given any thought as to where you want to go tomorrow?"

"Not really," said Alex, "what do you say we decide after breakfast." Jack said, "Sure, that works for me. Look I'm going up forward and hit the rack, stay up for a while if you want, but I'm turning in." Jack thought he saw a moment of disappointment on her face but then she gave him a bear hug and thanked him for a wonderful Christmas and said goodnight.

Jack had been up in the V-birth for about ten minutes when he heard Alex calling his name. Jack quickly went to the salon where he heard Alex call his name again. This time he went to the aft cabin and Alex was sitting up on the bed with her arms folded around her knees. "What's wrong," said Jack in a concerned voice. Alex looked at him for a moment and said,

"I'll tell you what's wrong, me sleeping back here in this great big bed all alone while you spend the nights alone in that small cabin up forward. This is your boat and you should be sleeping back here in your own bed. Jack looked at her and wasn't sure what to say, and before he could say anything Alex said, "Jack, you should be sleeping back here, with me." Jack was about to say something when Alex said, "Jack, don't think, don't say anything just come here, this is what I want. If it's too much for you, you can take me back to St. Thomas in the morning." Jack looked at her for a moment and said, "Oh boy," as he entered the cabin.

Will walked the piers at the Moorings marina in Road Town until he spotted the boat the Russians had rented. He would be able to sit at the Marina Bar and watch the boat, not bad duty for surveillance; there were a bunch of attractive women around as well. Will had ordered a beer and was casually scanning the area when he recognized Viktor and Stephan walking up to the bar. They ordered drinks and sat at a table about thirty feet from where he was sitting at the bar. They did not appear to be in a very good mood but were too far away for him to make out any of their conversation. After about ten minutes, Mhiki joined them. Mhiki appeared to be more frazzled than the other two, and kept looking around. Mhiki appeared to be talking at, not to, the other two men, and he was visibly upset. Viktor and Stephan were avoiding looking directly at Mhiki.

After a few minutes, Mhiki got up and kicked his chair then walked off to the boat, then Viktor and Stephan came up to the bar and stood almost right next to Will, trying to get the bartender's attention to pay for their drinks, their waitress was nowhere to be seen. While they were standing there, Will heard Stephan say, "First Ivan, now Leo, which of us will be next my friend?"

Viktor looked solemnly at Stephan and said, "Shut up." Stephan paid the bill and then the two joined Mhiki, who was sitting on the boat drinking straight out of a liquor bottle. Will had ordered his second beer when the group left for the boat where they sat on deck and had another drink before going below. After that, Will called Billy and let him know what he had observed. Billy said, "Good, I'm glad they look spooked, uncertainty breeds fear, fear breeds sloppiness, and sloppiness breeds mistakes. Come on back and we'll get some sleep, I want to be up at six and continue to monitor their position via the GPS link, too bad we couldn't bug the boat but oh well."

"Yeah," said Will, "see ya in a bit." Back at Soapers Hole, the men discussed what to do next. Dan said, "So, it appears we were correct about Leo. We shouldn't do anything else to them until we contact Jake, I wouldn't mind an assault, just overtake em at sea and fill their sorry asses with holes and split, but we were told to be low key. We do remain at a disadvantage though by not knowing Jake's location. We won't know if they find, or just happen upon Jake by just tracking their movements. The only thing we can do for now, is move when they do and arrive wherever they do shortly thereafter and try not to be observed ourselves, which will be difficult to do driving this rig around. It does kinda standout, even here," said Will.

Dan said, "Ok, tomorrow we follow the Russians, get a fix on their position, then pick another spot for a quick rendezvous or intercept, it's all we can do until we can contact Jake." The men were all in agreement and turned in for the night.

Brady was on his third run through of the recording of the meeting Lexi had hosted. Everyone would have phone service restored the day after Christmas, new email accounts would be set up and most of them were pissed. Lexi had boldly told them that Mhiki was gone and that he was in charge now and that they were going legit. The three men, who had made the most noises of dissent, were the three men who ran gambling and loan sharking, which certainly go together, prostitution, and narcotics respectively. They had told Lexi to basically go fuck himself, and that if he wanted out, fine but who was he to make decisions for them.

With those three, and the others identified, their new phone connections would be bugged at the trunk before they even got to use them. Lexi had warned them about penalties for not following their orders but the meeting ended without resolution. About the time that Brady was finally finished with the tapes; another agent showed up and said, "Detective Brady, I'm Frank Hall, FBI, I was told to get these to you right away, as he held up a portable USB drive. You got a computer I can plug this gizmo into?"

"Yeah, sure," said Brady. As the agent opened up the pictures he explained what had happened after he had followed the cleaners from Lexis' place to New Jersey. "They went straight to this land fill, which by the way is owned by Yoskov, once there, they dumped three rugs and a bunch of garbage bags. After they split, we opened up the bags and rugs and found this." Hall opened up a series of photos that showed, in graphic detail, the bodies of Lexi's former body guards, also the bloody rags and tablecloths that had been used to help clean up the blood.

So, thought Brady, *that is how VI was able to make Lexi so cooperative*, no one else would ever know that though. Hall said, "The bodies were taken out of his place, while he was there, then dumped across state lines, on a property that he owns, you've got him by the balls. Whatever else you have on him, or still want to get on him, this will nail him. The bodies have been moved to the morgue in Newark for the time being. Merry Christmas Detective, we'll have more tapes and photos for you tomorrow."

Brady said, "Yeah, merry Christmas to you too, looks like it's going to be a whole different kind of New Year for these guys." Hall smiled and said, "Be seeing ya." *Nothing much to do for now*, thought Brady. He would wait until Nolan and Eggers showed up in the morning to brief them in, but he was thinking about something, something not so very nice, but still, it brought a smile to his face.

When Nolan and Eggers showed up at the command center in the morning, Brady wasted no time in filling them in on the events of the previous day. Nolan said, "So, you figure VI took out the three dead guys at the land fill to make an impression on Yoskov."

"Either that or he had to," said Brady, "doesn't matter, either way, his move whatever it was, has the ball rolling."

It was Eggers turn to speak. "Hall was right, we can nail Yoskov for the three stiffs, but it would not work to our advantage to nab him just yet, we still need more on the rest of them."

Brady said, "I've had a while to think about this, and I want to run a scenario by you guys. The Galliano's hate the Russians, and the Russians hate the Galliano's, we all know that, also it was members of the Galliano family who killed Saunders' wife and child. What if, we could convince

Yoskov that VI was actually working for the Galliano family, and that the whole thing at his place was really about the Italians trying a power play? We get the two sides to go after each other, if it looks like things are cooling off; we throw some more gas on the fire. Lexi doesn't know anything about Saunders or why Mhiki really went to the islands. It wouldn't be too hard, with the right persuasion, to convince him that Mhiki knew it was coming and left him to hold the bag and take the hit, sold him out as it were. We have the tools and assets in place to totally fuck over both organizations. It could mean a bunch of killings, but who the fuck cares as long as it's the right people getting killed. We would have to be very careful, we carefully select and edit video and wiretap information to take down the ones that don't kill each other off."

Nolan and Eggers both sat in silence pondering Brady's proposal, Eggers was the first to speak, "Ok, how do we get Yoskov to believe that VI was working for the Galliano's?"

"Well. I've thought about that too," said Brady, "Mike, we need to talk to the guy that took credit for Saunders' phony hit, get him to drop a dime with Yoskov, tell him that for the right money, he'll rat on the crew that is getting ready to try and whack him, then we get VI to contact Galliano and tell him that Lexi is running the show now and wants to take him out. If VI is willing to play ball, we use him to do the initial stirring, on both sides, then he can go back to his job and life and never hear from us again."

"Are you suggesting," asked Nolan, "that we use the three stiffs as leverage against VI to get him to play ball?"

"Absolutely not, I actually like the guy, I hate to ask him to do this, but it will, get both sides going after each other. Don't you see, these fucks have been committing major crimes in our city for years, and us, restrained by legalities and proper procedure, have had to sit by and do nothing or very little of effect about it. Don't you guys see, we can shut down the most ruthless bunch of thugs in the city, think of all the otherwise decent and law abiding citizens that have had and are having their lives poisoned by these guys. If we can do this and stop just that much, isn't that alone, all the justification we need to do this, we all took an oath to serve and protect, so let's serve up some genuine justice for a change."

Nolan looked at Eggers, Eggers sat silent for a moment and then said, "You know, I always thought about something like this, but, I just as quickly dismissed the idea because of my sense of morality and what is right, you know, play the game by the established rules and hope that through perseverance, the good guys will eventually win, well guess what, it don't work. Sam, count me in, what do you say Mike?"

Nolan looked at the two detectives and said, "You guys know that if any of this gets out, we will go to jail, most likely for a very long time, or until somebody shanks us in the shower. Looking the other way while something happens in the Caribbean, or ignoring what happened at Lexi's place the other day, is completely different from deliberately starting a major gang war right here in New York." After a pause, Nolan said, "Ok, let's hurt these guys. I'll have Frankie Minetti, AKA Frankie Fingers brought here, I know his handler, we'll talk to him tomorrow at the latest. If Frankie says no, we let him know that he is a dead man unless he comes on board, if he plays, we take care of him when the smoke clears. If not, we send Niko Galliano J.R. photos of Saunders alive on his boat. He's semi retired now, owns an upscale club in Manhattan. Supposedly killing the guy that killed a Boss, set him up for life, he owes us. Sam, get VI over here now and see if he's willing to help us out with this, I also think it's time for me to call Rick and the other guy Matthews sent." Brady asked, "One question, why do they call him Frankie Fingers?"

Nolan said, "It goes back to a long time ago when he started out as an enforcer for the loan sharking boys, if people didn't pay up enough or on time, our boy Frankie would smash all of the fingers on their weak hand with a ball peen hammer, he would leave their dominant hand intact so they could still earn. Nice guy huh?"

Mhiki woke up with a hangover and couldn't get the coffee maker on the boat to work; his cursing and stomping around woke up Viktor and Lexi who both came up into the salon. "Let's go get some food and some coffee, I need to think about what to do today, I want to look around at the jewelry stores and see if the woman can sell the stones or not." Mhiki couldn't have cared less about the stones any more; finding them only meant finding Jake.

Mhiki had always been a sociopath, but now, he was nearly completely mad, what sanity or reason he had once possessed was rapidly being consumed by his lust to kill Saunders. At the marina bar/restaurant, the Russians ordered breakfast and ate and drank their coffee mostly in silence. Viktor and Stephan could see that Mhiki was unraveling and it was beginning to affect them as well. After they had paid their bill, the men walked into town. The largest jewelry store on Tortola is called, Columbian Emeralds, and Mhiki guessed that they would be the best place to start. Inside the store, there were several display cases with very high end items. The atmosphere was opulent and the place reeked of money. Mhiki got the attention of a sales person and asked if he could speak to the manager. The manager was an older English gentleman wearing a finely tailored suit who declined to introduce himself by name. Mhiki said, "Sir, if I were to possess a large flawless emerald, would you be interested in purchasing the stone?"

"Sir," said the manager, "we only purchase our inventory through recognized reputable brokers."

"I see," said Mhiki, "Hypothetically, if I were to have a gem of such quality, is there anyplace here in the islands that it could be sold for fair market value?" The manager gave the trio a smug look and said, "No, I do not believe so, gems of such quality as you describe are rare indeed, and no retail outlet that I am aware of anywhere in the islands would touch such an item, unless, as I said, the item were being made available by a known reputable broker." Mhiki was fuming; it was all he could do to not lose his composure. Mhiki smiled and said, "Thank you for your time, as I said it was a hypothetical question." Mhiki turned around and started for the door without another word as Stephan and Viktor followed. Outside, Mhiki was visibly shaking. He looked at Viktor and said, "Let's get back to the boat, I need to think."

Jack woke up and wasn't sure if he was dreaming or not, Alex was curled up against him like a cat and he could smell her strawberry scented shampoo, appropriate he thought, for a woman with strawberry blond hair. Jack was looking at her when she awakened. Alex looked up at him and smiled as she was stretching. "Good morning Mon Capitan, how'd you sleep?"

Jack smiled at her and said, "Wonderful, you?"

"Great," said Alex as she smiled and slid her hand under the sheet. Some time later, they went topside and Jack dove over the side and started swimming his customary three laps around the boat. Alex had noticed the puckered scars on Jack's chest and back, and the apparent surgical scars that accompanied them. No wonder he never took his shirt off in front of guests, it was obviously a gunshot wound.

Alex had guessed that Jack was former military, the way he carried himself, the self assurance and confidence without arrogance, were trademarks of the professional soldier. Jack climbed back up the ladder and went aft to rinse the salt water off. As he stepped into the cockpit, Alex was smiling at him. "How you doing?" asked Jack.

"The only thing that could make this better would be a servant fanning us with palm fronds, while another fed us grapes." Jack laughed and said, "That, Madame, costs extra." Alex laughed and said, "How's omelets with bacon sound?"

"Simply marvelous," replied Jack. Alex moved over and kissed Jack on the forehead and said, "Coming up, I'll be just a bit." Alex went below to cook breakfast and Jack sat in the cockpit thinking. In moments, Jimmy Buffet was once again singing through the cockpit speakers and the smell of bacon wafted up through the companionway. *What the fuck am I doing*, thought Jack. He was trying to reason that what he had done was wrong; his personal code of ethics told him that it was, but his heart was raising the bullshit flag on those thoughts.

What to do, how much could, or should he tell her, the questions were certain to start now, he had seen her looking at the bullet hole on his chest, Jack figured that there wasn't much use trying to hide it now. He knew one thing, he would not lie to this woman, he wouldn't give up more than he had to, but he would not lie.

Alex came up with the plates of breakfast, then went back down to retrieve the coffee and orange juice. After they had finished eating, Alex looked at Jack and said, "I like seeing you without your shirt on." Jack looked at her and said, "Even with this?" as he looked at the scars on his chest. Alex cocked her head to one side and said, "Makes you look even sexier." Jack smiled as he shook his head and waited for the questions that never came. Alex had already decided not to pry, whatever his story was, it would come out in due time.

She wished her mother was still alive; she would take Jack to her and ask, "Can I keep him." Her mother would laugh and give Jack a big hug. She had found the right man. Somehow, Alex was sure. One could argue that it was just the recent events, or something to do with the boat and sailing around with the ruggedly good looking sailor, but that was not it. She had found the one; she knew it in the very depths of her soul, now she had to tell him the truth, the danger, the gems, Bob, and what happened to him, all of it. Bob had told her to find someone to share her life with and be happy and she had. If Jack would have her, she would stay with him as long as possible and play in the sun for the rest of their time together, doing just this. They would have more money than they could ever spend, this life truly could last as long as they wished. "Jack, I have something I need to tell you."

Jack looked at her and thought, *here it comes.* "You're married." Alex sat with a stunned look for a moment then laughed. "No, no that's not it, really."

"Well then," said Jack, "it can wait. I want to take you somewhere today and show you something, there's no wind at all today so we'll have to motor again, should only take about an hour or so but I think Madame will approve."

Alex said, "Let's get going then, fire this thing up, I want to be lazy, I'll do the dishes later, I'll just put them in the sink for now, and I already made the bed."

"Ok, let's do it," said Jack. He started the engine and Alex went forward and waited for the signal to cast off from the mooring ball. As soon as they were underway, Alex came back to the cockpit and took off her bikini top and began seductively rubbing suntan lotion on her breasts. This time, Jack took pleasure in watching and Alex smiled coyly as she reclined back on the cockpit cushion next to Jack.

Mhiki sat on deck on the boat trying to figure out just exactly what to do, he could still not make contact with anyone in New York and he was now short two people. Where had Ivan gone? There was no explanation that made any sense. He felt no remorse over the death of Leo; it was simply an inconvenience, nothing more. What concerned Mhiki now was the way Viktor and Stephan were acting, questioning orders and daring to speak back to him. Mhiki thought that the untimely demise of Leo should have been enough to set them straight.

"What do you want to do?" asked Viktor. Mhiki gave Viktor a nasty look and thought, *I want to kill the sailor and go home and find out what the hell is going on.* Mhiki looked at the chart and decided to go to the Bitter End Yacht club on Virgin Gorda, the woman was used to finer things and it made sense to Mhiki that she would want to be around other people with money, and the Bitter End was all about catering to people with money. Mhiki looked up and said, "We go to Virgin Gorda, the Bitter End Yacht club and look for them there, she is a woman of means and would be comfortable there. Stephan, get this thing underway." Without comment, Viktor and Stephan cast off the dock lines and the trio departed for Virgin Gorda.

Dan had been periodically checking the Russians location on his laptop when he saw movement. "They're underway," he said to Billy.

"Ok," said Billy, "let's see which way they go. Let's get ready to get underway." The men disconnected the TV and shore power cables and Billy fired up the engines to let them warm up. After a few minutes, they left Soapers Hole and headed northeast. Billy kept the speed to about twenty-five knots so they would not overtake the Russians and after a while, it looked they were heading to the far end of Virgin Gorda. Billy said, "Look, I want to top off the fuel tanks, let's go to American Yacht Harbor on Virgin Gorda, it's about half way to where it looks like where they're going, I don't like following them out of visual range, but we can't risk being made. Goddamnit, I wish Jake would check his messages."

Jack wanted to surprise Alex as to their exact destination so he didn't call the Marina at Virgin Gorda on the radio prior to pulling in to the harbor entrance, when he did; he used a different call sign to reserve a slip. The harbor master told Jack he was lucky to get something without notice. Alex readied the dock lines and fenders on the starboard side of the boat and Jack expertly docked the big Gulfstar in the narrow slip. There was a marina employee there ready to catch the dock lines. After the boat was secure, Jack said, "Let's go for a walk, I need to stretch out a bit. Why don't you make up a picnic basket and we can get going." Alex knew that Jack wanted to show her something special so she didn't ask any questions and did as she was asked. It only took her five minutes and she emerged from the boat carrying a wicker basket and said, "Very well Mon Capitan, I'm ready, lead away. Jake smiled and took Alex by her free hand and led off down the road away from the marina complex.

As soon as Jack and Alex rounded the corner walking away from the marina, Billy was pulling up to the service dock.

After about a ten minute walk, Jack and Alex arrived at a touristy looking combination beach bar, souvenir shop, and restaurant built right on the rocky surroundings. "This is cute," said Alex.

"You ain't seen nothing yet," said Jack. He led the way down a rocky trail and then over, through, under, and around a bunch of boulders and rock formations. When they came out into the clear, Alex was stunned by the beauty of the place. "Welcome to the Baths at Virgin Gorda," said Jack. They had emerged into the most unspoiled, pristine looking beach Alex had ever seen. There was a smallish main cove surrounded with sugar white sand that led up to the various rock formations. Alex said, "You know, this place looks familiar."

"Well, it should, that is if you ever saw a high end swimsuit catalog, a lot of them are shot here. Let's pick out a rock and have some lunch." Alex was beaming as she and Jack sat down to eat their picnic lunch.

Billy was just handing the fuel hose back to the helper when Dan walked up to him with a big grin and said, "Guess what I found in slip 23." Billy looked at him and said, "No fucking way."

"Way," said Dan.

Will said, "Yep, it's him alright, they aren't onboard though, and, there's an open slip right next to theirs, I suggest you have a chat with the harbor master." Billy made the arrangements and the team moved next door to PRIVATEER. Billy said, "When they get here, I'll approach Jack, he should recognize me but I need to find a way to let him know what is going on without alarming the girl, we'll play it by ear."

Will said, "At least we don't have to track them both anymore, now we have to figure out what to do with Mhiki and company."

As Stephan rounded the corner and followed the channel markers into the Bitter End, Mhiki said, "There must be hundreds of boats here."

"At least that," said Stephan, "we can get as close as we can and tie off to a mooring ball. We can't really drive this thing all around looking for them, we should use the dingy." Mhiki nodded in agreement. He was beginning to think that it would have been better to just watch the Marina in St. Thomas; this seemed an impossible task, to find one boat in these islands among thousands of boats. Stephan and Viktor secured the boat to a mooring ball and readied the dingy.

Jack and Alex had finished lunch and were playing in the water, swimming and generally just enjoying the day. Jack walked back up to where they had laid out their things and toweled off. Alex joined him and said, "Painkillers sound good to you?"

"Yeah, sounds good to me, we have to walk back to the entrance though." They made their way back to the bar and Alex bought a tank top after they got their drinks. She walked out onto the deck overlooking the crystal clear waters and stood looking at the beauty of the Caribbean. Jack walked over to her and said, "This sure sucks don't it." Alex laughed and said, "No, no Jack, it doesn't," as she slid an arm around his waist and snuggled up against him.

As much as he thought he wanted to feel otherwise, Jack was also smitten, she could handle a boat, she could cook, and she could dive. Also, Jack could not recall her bitching about anything. All this and she was drop dead gorgeous as well. "Jack," said Alex, "as nice as all of this is, let's sit, I need to tell you some things." Jack was about to protest but Alex cut him off before he could even begin. "You have to listen because you need to know about this, about me, I have to talk to you then it will be your turn. You may not still want to be around me after I finish, but you have to let me talk." Jack rubbed his face with both hands, then blew out a big breath and said, "Ok, let's hear your story. But know this, you ain't scaring me off."

"God, I hope not, but here it goes."

Alex told Jack the whole story, everything, Bob, the Russians, the jewels, the money, everything. "Well, what do you think now?" asked Alex.

Jack smiled at her and said, "That's interesting; let me tell you a story." Jack told Alex about his career, starting with the SEALs, his time in

Afghanistan, how he got shot, the gunfight with the Mafiosos, the killing of his wife and child, his savage vengeance, and his second shot at life arranged by the State Department. When he was done, Jack looked at Alex and said, "So, you still want to hang out with a known murderer, a man with no past and damn little future?"

"Jane was right, you are a lot dumber than you look, we have millions of dollars worth of precious gems, a shitload of cash and not a lot to spend it on. And guess what you idiot; I want to share it all with you, if you'll have me." They stood there for a few moments looking into each other's eyes, expressionless, then Jack began to smile and he said, "What the hell, I was going to fire the mate when she came back anyway." Alex positively beamed and threw both arms around Jack and gave him a big hug and said, "What do we do now." Jack said, "We can start by going back to the boat, I need to check my messages and you need to check with your secretary to see what's going on back in New York."

When Jack and Alex returned to the marina, Jack immediately noticed the big Donzi that had tied up next to him. From a distance, he noted three men sitting in the cockpit each drinking a beer. As they got closer, Billy stood up and said, "Ahoy there sailor, long time no see." Alex tensed for a moment and Jack smiled at her and said, "It's ok." Billy started with some kind of cover story and Jack waved a hand and said, "Good to see you Billy but don't bother, she knows all about me, and I know about her." Billy had a somewhat puzzled look on his face and then said, "Well, be that as it may, there is a wrinkle that I'm sure you don't know about."

"Tell you what," said Jack, "help me get my shore power hooked up and we can all go below on my boat and talk." The men made quick introductions with Alex and got the power cable hooked up and went down into the salon on PRIVATEER. Jack fired up all three AC units and once everyone was seated, Billy began. "We were sent here to protect you and the girl; evidently she has something that the Russians want." "I know," said Jack, "it's a shitload of precious stones, they killed her friend for them but he had arranged for her to get them if anything happened to him."

"Yeah, well, guess who their boss is, Mhikiail Valentnikov." Jack sat for a moment saying nothing then said, "No shit." Alex asked, "Who is this Valentnikov?"

"He's the guy that gave me the sexy scars on my chest and back, I shot off part of his face."

"Yeah," said Billy, "he had Ms. McTeal here followed to St. Thomas and some of his goons photographed you and her together and now, he is after your ass old buddy. He thought he killed you that day in Afghanistan and evidently, when he saw pictures of you alive, he went ape shit. He's at the Bitter End as we speak, he and his boys have rented a power cat and they have been trolling around trying to find you and the girl."

"Alex, my name is Alex." Everyone smiled and Alex said, "See Jack, we were meant to be together, the same guy wants to kill both of us." Jack shook his head and said, "Oh boy, what next." That made everyone laugh and then Billy filled Jack and Alex in on everything, when he was done, Jack said, "God, Borokovsky is in on this as well huh, good man, very dangerous though, I for one, would not want to be on his bad side. What do we do now?"

"I don't know about the other two," said Will, "but Valentnikov will never stop as long as he knows you are alive, we have to take him out."

"He's right you know," said Dan, "it ends here if you two ever want peace." Jack looked over at Alex and said, "Do you understand what this means, it means I may have to kill again."

Alex thought for a moment and then said, "Those animals killed Bob, I wasn't in love with him, but he was my friend, and he is the one that gave me the jewels, as far as I'm concerned they need to be killed. He came here to kill us both so, no, I won't lose any sleep over it Jack, do whatever you need to do to get rid of them, it won't change the way I feel about you. What about me Billy," asked Alex, "is NYPD looking for me, am I in any trouble because of this?"

Billy smiled and said, "No Alex, they know you have something that the Russians want, but they don't care about it one way or the other, as far as anyone is concerned, whatever it is belongs to you now, they just want to be sure that these assholes don't kill you and that they shut down the operation in New York, and they are not playing by the rules in doing it either." Alex said, "We don't have enough makings in the fridge, so I suggest that we go get a round of cocktails and get some dinner, my treat, then we can come back here and you boys can scheme into the wee hours of the night. I refuse to let the fact that a homicidal maniac is after me to ruin my vacation." Everyone got a laugh out of that and the group padded off to the bar. Dan used his laptop to confirm that the Russians were stationary at the Bitter End.

Stephan had been driving around for over an hour in the dingy and Mhiki was visibly irritated. "Let's go to the dock," said Mhiki.

"What are we going to do now?" asked Viktor. Mhiki gave him a hard stare and said, "I don't know yet, I just want to go ashore and look around." After Viktor and Stephan had secured the dingy, the three men walked around the marina for a while and checked the boats that were in the slips, not finding the sailor's boat. They went to one of the several restaurants and sat down. "Stephan," said Mhiki, "call the marina in St. Thomas and see if the sailor has returned." After placing his call, Stephan informed Mhiki that PRIVATEER was still out on charter. Mhiki was beginning to think that they would have been better off just staying on St. Thomas and waiting for the woman and sailor to return. Mhiki was worried about spending too much time there considering the disappearance of Ivan. He believed something bad had happened to him. Perhaps, somehow he had been caught with the weapons and explosives or maybe he got hit by a car crossing the street, it made no sense that he had just vanished. Mhiki decided that they would stay put for the night, maybe the sailor would come to them, it seemed reasonable that a woman such as the McTeal woman would want to visit a place such as this. Mhiki decided that as long as they were ashore, he should send Stephan shopping again, Mhiki wanted to have the explosive device as an option should the opportunity present itself.

Chapter Nineteen

Frankie Fingers sat outside the situation room at JFK waiting to talk to the Feds. He had no idea why they had picked him up this time. When they came for him, he had hoped it was with a warrant, it would be less dangerous than doing more business with them; Frankie thought he was done with that. In a sense thought Frankie, the Feds were no different than the Mob, once you did business with them; you weren't done until they said so. Inside the situation room, the two detectives and Nolan were laying out their plan to VI. "So, let me make sure I have this right," said VI, "you want me to contact the head of this Mafia family and convince him that Yoskov has already killed Mhiki, and is going to try to kill him next?"

"That's right," said Eggers, "we are going to send our little Mafia rat to Yoskov and tell him that you're an outside contractor working for the Italians, and that your real game is to weaken their organization for the Mafia to take control. Frankie will tell Yoskov that he can help setup Niko Galliano Jr. for a hit. At the same time, you tell Niko that Yoskov is sending people to kill him. Once we know where both sides are, we direct the opposition to the other's locations and watch the fireworks, if this works, all we need you to do is make your house call to Galliano and that's it." VI thought about the plan for a bit and began to smile. "You know gentlemen, if anyone were to find out about this, it would not go well for your careers." The three law enforcement officers looked at VI, and Brady said, "We are aware of that, but, this will do more real damage to these guys than we could inflict in years going by the book, not only that, we really just don't like em."

VI said, "In that case, when am I to pay my visit?"

"Soon," said Nolan, "would you mind waiting in the other room for a minute while we explain the situation to Mr. Fingers." VI smiled and said, "Of course," and went through the door to the adjoining room. Nolan pressed the intercom and the agent sitting with Frankie told him to go in. When Frankie walked into the room, he had already decided to be indignant. "What the fuck is this about goddamnit, I done everything you guys ever asked, it's over, got it." The three cops looked at each other and laughed, then Nolan said, "Frankie, sit down and shut your fucking hole. I'll tell you when you're finished, and that won't be until we don't need your sorry pasta eatin ass anymore, do not fuck with me, not now, not ever. I have some pictures I want to show you." Nolan handed the photos of Saunders taken a few days ago to Frankie. At first it didn't register, and then he said, "Oh shit."

"That's right Frankie," said Eggers, "you don't have to play ball with us, but if you don't, I send a set of eight by tens of these to Niko, how do you think that would go over with the Boss?" Frankie knew real fear then, Nolan watched as the tough guy's hands began to tremble and his color began to drain. Frankie looked up and said, "This ain't right man, why are you doin this to me?"

"Well," said Brady, "actually were doing it to Niko, we have decided to break it off in his ass once and for all, the Galliano family is soon to be finished, how you come out of it is up to you. Play your part and you come out a survivor, you get to keep your restaurant and life goes on, fuck with us, just a little, one fuck up, and you are toast, got it?"

Now it was Nolan's turn, "Ok Frankie, here's the deal." After explaining what he was to do, Brady gave Frankie the basic script. "So, when do I do this?" asked Frankie.

"Soon," said Nolan, "go back into the other room for a minute." Frankie did as told; he had lost all of his bravado when he saw the pictures of Saunders alive. Nolan called VI back into the room. "Ok," said Nolan, "call this number and ask for Niko, it will be one of his soldiers who answers the phone, don't take any shit from him, just tell him to put his boss on the line, and use a Russian accent."

"A pity," said VI, "I worked so hard to lose it." Eggers placed a call to

Rick and told him that he had a surveillance job for him and his associate, separate locations. One would require video equipment and a laptop with wireless connectivity, the equipment would be provided.

When VI placed his call, the phone was answered with a simple, "Hello." In a heavily accented voice, VI said, "I need to speak to Niko Galliano immediately."

"Oh yeah, and just who are you?" the voice answered back.

"I am the only thing that stands between your boss and a bullet in his brain, I suggest that you waste no more of my time and put him on the phone, he will want to hear what I have to say."

"Hold on," said the voice. After roughly one minute, another voice came on the line. "Who is this," demanded the voice of Niko Galliano Jr.

"Who I am is not nearly as important as what I have to say, you are in danger and if you want to stay alive you will listen to me. Lexi Yoskov has already killed Mhiki and his closest associates; he has told his people that Mhiki left for the islands, but in reality, he is in a landfill in New Jersey. He is ambitious this one, you and your people are next on his list."

After a pause, Niko said, "And you are telling me this out of the kindness of your heart right." VI laughed and said, "Of course not, I am doing this for money, money you will pay me to warn you of where and when Yoskov's men will come for you. Lexi has shut me out; I should be helping make the decisions now that Mhiki is gone. I advised against this but Lexi believes he can get away with it, he is mad. Because I have disagreed with him, I am somewhat uncertain as to my own future. You will pay me to warn you, and if you wish, tell you and your men where and when the best time to rid yourself of this problem would be. Once our business is concluded, I am leaving for a place with a better climate."

"How do I know that you're not just full of shit and this isn't some kind of shakedown?"

"You will be certain, when the last thing you see is muzzle flashes all around you and you die. Remember, your men are street thugs, Lexi's men are highly trained professional killers, mostly ex Soviet Special Forces, do you really think you can protect yourself from that if Lexi wants you dead?"

Niko thought for a moment and then said, "Give me a number, I'll call you back." VI laughed and said, "Sure, I do not think so, I'll give you one hour to think it over and then I will call you back, and by the way, put together two million in cash, large bills, I will be traveling with it and I will need to move quickly." Having said his piece, VI hung up on Niko.

"He called me at my fucking home, screamed Niko, how the fuck did he get my home number." Niko's consigliari, Paul, listened while Niko told him the details of the phone call. When Niko was done, Paul said, "Mhiki was a ruthless man, if Lexi whacked him, he must be crazy, and if he is crazy, he may just attempt to annex our assets in the area, a hit on you and a couple of key Captains, he could consolidate power. And the guy on the phone is right, the reason your father worked a deal with Mhiki, was because he knew there was no way to defend against his kind of men, if they decide to take something by force, they will get it. It makes much more sense to cut a deal, he didn't like it, but he was pragmatic."

"So you're saying I should pay this Russian bastard two million dollars?"

"Niko think about it, two mil to be rid of these Russian bastards once and for all, and, with the expanded business, we'll make it back in six months, and you will stay alive my friend. I am your council, and I have given you my advice, if this guy can set Yoskov up, we have some guys that are ex military that can pull this off. With Mhiki and Yoskov out of the way, we will be able to return to the status quo, I'm afraid the Russians are here to stay, but we need to ensure that the ones in charge will continue to do things as they have been. The advantage will however shift to our favor." Niko mulled over what Paul had said for a bit and then said, "Goddamnit, get the cash together, we do the deal with this guy, no tricks, but so help me God, if this is a scam, I'll go to the commission and we will collectively take these bastards apart."

Nolan and Eggers along with Brady complimented VI on his performance. Nolan said, "Now VI, if you would be so kind as to wait in the other room again, we will have Frankie call Lexi."

VI said, "You are devious wicked men, I like you." VI flashed a big smile and went to the next room. When Frankie came back into the room, he was in a much more cooperative mood. "Alright Frankie, it's show time, call Yoskov, remember what to say." "Yeah, I got it, you guys sure this is gonna work?"

"You had better hope it does," said Nolan, "you better hope." Frankie called the cell phone that VI had given Lexi and it was answered on the second ring. "Yes," was all Lexi said when he answered the phone. Frankie said, "I ain't the guy that gave you that phone but I know who did, and guess who I got this number from." Lexi was confused now and said, "You know the man who gave me this phone?"

"No," said Frankie, "I don't know him but I do know who he works for, I got this number from Niko Galliano." Now Lexi was really confused. What could the Italians have to do with this? "You see Mr. Yoskov, they want you to think it's the feds or some fuckin thing like that but it ain't, Niko wants all of your action, everything, and Mhiki knew it was coming, that's why he split. The same guy that whacked your three guys the other day paid Mhiki a visit before he came to see you, I don't know what he told Mhiki, but he split right after the European came to visit him. The guy is an outsider, some euro type, very dangerous, works mostly overseas. Whatever bullshit this guy gave you, you're fuckin dead no matter what. I was supposed to get bumped up, I worked for Niko's old man for a long time and I'm getting crumbs, well fuck this, you want to live you give me two million bucks and I'll tell you where you can get Niko and his boy first."

Lexi said, "How do I know what you say is true, what assurances do I have that this is not connected to my visitor?"

"Listen up comrade, I will give you an account number that you can transfer the money into once you have proof that your visitor is working for Niko. Niko is about to pay him off soon, I have some good camera stuff, I can send you video of this guy meeting Niko himself and getting paid, you see that I'm on the level, you make the transfer, as soon as I confirm it, I tell you where Niko and his top guys are going to be, then your boys can settle this thing and I disappear, New York ain't gonna be too good for my health after this. I'll call back in one hour, if we got a deal, I'll give you more instructions, if not, good fucking luck."

Frankie hung up the phone and said, "What if he don't bite?"

Nolan said, "I think he will, he's scared shitless already, now he sees a possible way out. You see he's just like you and all the other worthless fucks like you. He will sell out anyone or do anything to keep what he has, or get more if he sees a way to do it, it's just in your nature. It makes you predictable; you always have been and always will be, that's why we are going to win."

"Yeah, maybe, but you had to break your own rules to do it."

"True enough," said Brady, "that's because we, are unpredictable."

The more Lexi thought about it, the more enraged he became. The Italians were behind this all, if it were not for a single greedy wise guy, he would be killed in the near future. Lexi decided he would have to pay the Italian, and then if he was provided with proof that his visitor was in fact working for Niko, he would kill them both. The money was a large sum but it could easily be covered, Lexi was a rich man and he could make the money back, he could not, he reasoned, rise from the dead.

Dan had kept his laptop close to hand, keeping track of Mhiki and his men. Alex asked how Dan was able to track the Russians in real time. Dan said, "For the most part this is your standard laptop computer with wireless capability, however, instead of using a commercial wireless provider, this one links up to a government satellite constellation. We planted a GPS transmitter on Mhiki's boat before they rented it. The transmitter sends signals to the satellites, and their real-time position is then transmitted out from the satellites and a program in the computer translates that data into an incredibly accurate nautical chart. It will also work with detailed land maps."

"Very cool," said Alex. "Well Jake, what do we do with the Russians now? I am turning command of this little op over to you."

"Well, for starters, call me Jack, Jake Saunders has been dead for several years now, and as far as the Russians are concerned, we have to take them out, but we also have to be careful not to stir up the locals, you guys have a pretty thin cover and I have none, not only that, I'm pretty well known around here. Right now my first and foremost concern is for your safety Alex. I think we should go to the bitter end and take care of this somehow, but I don't want Alex there, it's too dangerous."

Will said, "Jack, how's this sound, I know how to sail and Alex is already familiar with your boat, you, Billy, and Dan take the Donzi and go after the bad guys, and I'll watch Alex and your boat. Also, Viktor and Stephan have seen me. We can go moor at Cooper until we hear from you, the boat will be in plain sight, but you guys will be able to cover us if they make it this way, when it's done you meet us there. If needed, we can always relocate, and we do have secure coms now."

Alex said, "I don't like it, I want to stay with you Jack." Jack was about to say something when Billy cut him off, "Alex, Jack is right, we have all done this sort of thing before, it's what we were all trained for, not only is it dangerous for you to be with us, it adds an extra element of risk for us as well. We need to be able to focus on the task at hand, not worry about you."

"He's right," said Jack, "besides, I don't want you to get to know that part of me, I thought I was burying it with Jake Saunders. This has to be done and I can't just sit back and expect these guys to do my dirty work while you and I sit back and have cocktails, this is my mess and I need to help clean it up."

Alex thought about it for a while and then said, "I guess you guys are right, but I still don't like it, and don't forget I lost somebody I cared about too, and I'm pissed about it. Do you have to leave today?"

Dan said, "Well, they haven't moved yet, we could leave in the morning and get eyes on and then play it by ear."

"Works for me," said Jack. After checking the laptop again, Jack and company decided that Mhiki would be staying at the Bitter End, at least for the night. After some more discussion, Jack and Alex returned to PRIVATEER. Onboard, Alex immediately threw her arms around Jack and started to weep softly. "Hey," said Jack, "what's wrong?" Alex pulled back from him and looked into his eyes and said, "For an educated man of the world, you're sure not that bright sometimes. I am upset because I don't want you to go and I'm afraid something bad could happen to you. It's my fault this Valentnikov character is after you, if it wasn't for me, you would still be living your carefree life, just doing your thing."

Jack brushed a stray strand of hair from one of her puffy eyes and said, "Look, Alex, for starters, it is my life and the things I did earlier on in it that brought this on me, not you. I could have been spotted any time and the result would have been the same, it's because of you that I got a warning, and some help dealing with it, if not, somebody would have just come up behind me and either knifed or shot me and that would have been it. Your coming into my life was not by any means a bad thing, I am really alive again, not just going through the motions, and I want to spend the rest of my life with you. I know it is nuts, I mean we really just met but there it is."

Alex looked at Jack and said, "Don't you dare get yourself killed goddamnit, do you hear me, you be careful." The two said no more about the days to come and went back to the aft cabin for the night.

Billy was sitting in the cockpit of the Donzi drinking a beer when Will came out of the salon and joined him. "Well, ain't this some shit my friend." Billy laughed and said, "Yep, that it is, we have to figure a way to get all three of those guys without making a scene, night time would be best, pop em all, tow the boat out into deep water and scuttle it."

"Sounds good in theory," said Will, "but you know it won't be that easy."

"No, of course not," said Billy.

"Look, I'll keep the girl safe, they can't get near us without your being able to warn me, just get those fuckers." With that said, Will went back down below and left Billy with his thoughts.

After exactly one hour, VI called Niko back. "What is your decision," said VI.

Niko did not respond for a moment and then said, "You get your money, and how do you propose we complete our transaction?"

"We will meet in person, tomorrow; I will call you in the morning with details of where and when. As soon as I have the money, I will tell you where and when you will be able to get Lexi and our business will be complete."

"I don't need to tell you not to fuck around with me do I," said Niko.

"No, and I do not need to tell you not to miss when you get your chance do I," said VI who then hung up the phone. Brady looked at VI and said, "You sure about this, meeting him alone? We'll have you covered and the surveillance team will be armed, but if it goes south, we won't be able to help you until it's too late."

"I will be fine, he won't do anything to me, he wants Lexi, which will be enough."

"I hope you're right," said Nolan, "you don't have to do any of this."

"Nonsense," said VI, "I'm having fun, that is enough reason for me. Now, isn't it time for your Gangster to make his call."

"Yes it is," said Nolan, "would you please go next door again."

"Of course," said VI, who then departed the room. When Frankie came back he was more relaxed having accepted his fate and realizing that his future depended on his performance. "Well Frankie," said Nolan, "ready for this?"

"Yeah," said the Gangster, "let's get this done." Frankie picked up the phone and called Lexi. The phone was answered on the third ring. "We got a deal," asked Frankie.

Lexi allowed a pause and then said, "Yes, we do. How is this to be done?"

Frankie said, "Ok, tomorrow after lunch, you need to be somewhere that you and your boys can watch some video on the internet, you got a place like that? I can email you the video of Niko paying the European off."

"Yes, at my club, it will be closed then, we only open for dinner, and I have a computer with internet access there."

"Good," said Frankie. "Have your boys that are going to do the job ready to go, as soon as I confirm the wire transfer, I'll tell you where Niko is headed, I can tell you this much, it will be in Manhattan. Give me the email address." Lexi gave Frankie the email address and said, "As soon as I see the European, as you call him, taking money from Galliano, I will transfer the money to your account, no proof, no transfer."

Frankie said, "Listen up comrade, you better be fucking ready to roll right after I call, or that guy is going to punch your ticket, understand. He won't do anything until he gets paid, but after that he is going to make his move. I'll call you tomorrow." Lexi hung up and then made four phone calls to members of the organization whose specialties were in direct action. Lexi told them to be ready for a fast hard hit, possibly in public and to prepare accordingly, they were instructed to assemble and be ready and waiting in the van near central park at noon tomorrow.

Nolan looked at Frankie and said, "Good boy, I want you to be at your restaurant tomorrow, one of my people will take and transmit the video to Lexi. I'll call you when the video is sent and then when the transfer is made."

"Where is Niko going after the deal?

"He's going to have lunch at your place, be sure and put him at a table in the back, don't want any paying customers getting shot." Frankie suddenly went very pale and found it difficult to control his bowels. "No fucking way, you can't do this, this is bullshit," screamed Frankie. Eggers got up and slapped Frankie Fingers so hard that it almost knocked him out. "Listen to me you piece of shit, think about it, there is no way anyone will suspect you, he is just going to show up, this leaves you in the clear. Nobody will think you had anything to do with it because you couldn't know he was coming, get it." Frankie was wishing he had followed his uncle's advice so many years ago and joined the Navy and left all of this far behind. Now, these men had him by the balls and there was no way out. Frankie was pretty sure that if these guys would set up something like this, they would not hesitate in killing him themselves.

Chapter Twenty

Alex cooked breakfast for everyone onboard PRIVATEER, Jack asked if he needed to bring any weapons. "What have you got?" asked Billy.

"I have the Scorpion Borokovsky gave me, and I still have my trusty 1911 with a spare barrel fitted for a suppressor, which is also in the box," replied Jack.

Billy said, "Bring the forty-five, as I recall that Scorpion has a short barrel and is quite loud."

"True enough," said Jack.

"We brought MP-5K's with suppressors, same with our Glocks, don't want to wake up any of the neighbors." Jack smiled and looked over at Will and said, "Keep Alex safe, it would be nice to get her and the boat back, but, I'll settle for her." Alex moved to Jack and hugged him around his neck then pushed him back and said, "I see, you'll settle for me huh." Jack smiled at her and said, "Well, you know, a guy like me can't be too picky, so I guess you'll have to do."

Alex smiled and said, "Get out of here before I change my mind and just go back to New York."

Jack said, "Will, I think it would be best to just stay here for the time being. I'm parked in the back from the entrance and the Russians would have to get right up on the boat to ID it. Not only that, it's a good defensive position, your back is to the sea wall, they could only come at you from one direction."

When Jack was done, Will said, "You just don't want me playing with your boat." Jack smiled at him and said, "I guess that about covers it guys, be sure to keep that radio on Will, we'll call if it looks like the bad guys are coming here." Billy said, "Let's go fire up the Donzi guys, time to get it on."

Alex and Jack embraced and then shared a look; they had said all that needed saying before the other men came onboard for breakfast. The three men went over to the other boat. As they were stepping ashore, Will said, "Good hunting and don't forget to bring us a tee shirt or something."

Sitting in the cockpit of the Donzi, Dan checked Mhiki's position and determined that they were still at the same spot at the Bitter End. Jack said, "Ok Billy, let's see how fast this thing really is, I want to get there and get eyes on target, if we can, we pick up a mooring far enough away not to attract their attention but close enough to keep tabs on them."

"You wanna drive?" asked Billy.

"Nah, it's your boat," said Jack. "Dan, can you keep an eye on them while we head that way?"

"Sure, it's still pretty flat out there and this beast rides pretty well," said Dan. Will and Alex walked over and helped with the dock lines and Jack and Alex gave one last wave good bye as the Donzi exited the slip and headed out of the marina.

Mhiki woke up and went up into the cockpit and found Viktor and Stephan sitting back listening to the Caribbean news and weather report. The forecast was for continued light winds and sunny skies, there had been no mention of any major arrests in St. Thomas. Stephan was getting antsy sitting around on the boat and asked Mhiki, "Do you want to go and get something to eat? We can also get a newspaper and see if anything of interest has occurred lately." Mhiki looked at Viktor and said, "Yes, let's go, I don't want to just sit out here either. I have been thinking, we may stay here for a couple of days and see if the sailor brings the woman here. They would have to moor as well and if they do, we could board and search his boat. If we find the jewels, then we can dispatch the two of them and go home."

Home, Viktor had been thinking of home a lot lately, what was going on there. It made no sense to Viktor or Stephan that no contact could be established with any of their people, and it made even less sense that no one was trying to contact them, Lexi had all of their cell numbers but no one had called. Viktor wanted to sit at the outdoor lounge at the marina and watch the large screen TV that was perpetually tuned into CNN. If some action was taken against their organization by law enforcement authorities, it made sense that there would be some mention of it on the news. The three men got into the dingy and headed into the marina.

Nolan, Brady, Eggers, and VI were sitting in the situation room discussing the plan for today's action. Nolan said, "Ok VI, tell Niko to meet you in the parking lot of the New York Library at fifth and forty-second, we'll have surveillance in place to shoot video of the meet and cash transfer. Be sure that you open the bag to look at the money and make sure that you can be seen from the library where the camera crew is. After that you tell Niko that you want to go to Frankie's place at 50th and 7th for lunch and you'll get a phone call there letting you know where Yoskov is. When our surveillance team sees that Yoskov's group is about to show up, we'll page you, be sure the pager is set on vibrate. That's when you get away from the table, leave or go to the men's room or something because the shit is gonna hit the fan."

VI said, "It seems simple enough, how can I be sure Galliano will go to Frankie's place with me?"

"Two reasons, first you won't tell him where Yoskov is until you get your call, and second, the place is owned by none other than Frankie Fingers, and we know he likes the place. He has no reason to be suspicious, it's a familiar place."

"Very well, I will make my call." VI dialed Niko's number and the phone was answered by Paul, Niko's under boss and counsel. "I wish to speak to your employer," said VI.

"I take it you are the gentleman Mr. Galliano spoke with yesterday," said Paul.

"Your assumption is correct sir; again, may I speak with your employer." Paul gave the phone to Niko. "What do you have for me?" said Niko.

"Directions, I have directions for you. You are to meet me at 5th and 42nd across from the New York Library in one hour with the money; I will be driving a black Lincoln and wearing a charcoal grey suit. Once I am satisfied that the money is all there, I will tell you where Yoskov will be, I will say this much, it will be in or near Brighton Beach. Have your men stage near there."

Niko said, "I would rather pick the spot for the meet."

"I'm sure you would," said VI, "however that is not acceptable. Be there in one hour if you wish to remain alive." VI hung up the phone and looked at Nolan. "You're all set VI, we'll be watching your back and I'll call your cell once I know the video has been transmitted to Yoskov."

"Very well, I'll be going now, I want to park and wait for Galliano, and make sure there will be an adjacent parking spot for him."

"Good luck," said Eggers and Brady as VI departed.

"You know, that guy has ice water in his veins, he doesn't seem at all concerned," said Eggers. "Yeah," said Brady, "I'm glad he's on our side now."

"Alrighty then," said Nolan, "let's get Frankie in here." Frankie was ushered into the room and sat down; he looked like a condemned man. "C'mon Frankie," said Nolan, "don't look so glum, once this is done, you'll be done with us and Galliano, you run your restaurant, keep your nose clean and all is well."

"Don't bullshit me Nolan, I'm fucked and I know it. Why should I believe that I get to stay alive after this, I mean, I know what you guys are doing, you have to take me out, it's what I would do."

Brady said, "You see Frankie, there you go again being the predictable wise guy, we don't have to kill you. Nobody would believe you for one thing, and second, now that we have you firmly by the balls, we are not going to waste your potential. After the smoke clears, we'll need somebody on the inside to fill us in on who is going to take over and what they're going to do. No my little dirt bag, we own your ass from now on, you will hardly notice though. We need some info, you tell us, we need a favor, you do it, you fuck with us, we drop a dime on you and you end up in the river, got it?"

Frankie sat looking at the three law enforcement officers and realized that his worst fears had come true, he was squarely screwed, he had no choice anymore, his life was no longer his own. He was on the hook with these guys until they said otherwise, his only chance at being able to enjoy life at all, was to keep them happy. *Fuck it*, he thought, *a man's gotta do what he's gotta do*. "So," said Frankie, "when do I make my call."

"Good boy," said Eggers, call him now and make sure he's going to be ready, then tell him you'll call him back after you send the video. You leave for your place right after you call, the money transfer should be complete before Niko shows up at your place, I'll call you, and you call Yoskov right after, and remember," said Eggers as he slid a pen into Frankie's pocket, "we will be listening in."

Frankie had a shocked look on his face as he looked at his shirt pocket. "That's right," said Nolan, "we got you bugged." Frankie dialed Yoskov's number and it was answered before the second ring. "Yes," answered Yoskov.

"Good morning comrade," said Frankie, "you got my money ready to transfer." Lexi was irritated, he did not like this Italian, but he knew that if what he said was true, he had to deal with him. "Yes," said Lexi, "I am ready to have the money transferred as soon as I see the video."

"Good," said Frankie, "have a Vodka and some borscht or something, I'll be callin ya soon." Frankie left for Manhattan followed by one of Nolan's men. As he was on his way, VI pulled into a parking space in front of the library and got out of the Bureau owned Lincoln and leaned against the trunk. It was bitter cold but VI hardly noticed. After about five minutes, a minivan tried to take the spot behind VI's car. VI waved the guy off but he tried to park there anyway. VI walked up to the driver's side door and as the man tried to open the door, VI shoved it back closed and said, "This spot is taken." The minivan driver rolled his window down a bit and said, "Hey, I can park where I want." VI smiled a cold, humorless smile and said, "Yes you can, in most instances, but if you park here, now, I will burn this van with you in it, I said this spot is taken." The minivan driver took a better look at VI, noticed the Lincoln with the engine running, VI's build and the expensive suit he was wearing and decided to fight another day. The man sped away from the curb muttering something and just as he was driving off, a black stretched Sedan Deville slowed and then pulled into the spot. VI stood where he was and one of Niko's bodyguards got out of the front of the Caddy and opened the door for Niko Galliano Jr.

Niko walked up to VI and said, "I take it you are the one that called." "And I take it you are Mr. Galliano."

"Yeah, let's get this done, it's freezing out here, and your money is in two gym bags in my trunk."

"Very well," said VI, "have your man bring it here to me, I will check the contents of the bags and we can conclude our business." Niko motioned to his bodyguard and the trunk popped open as the man approached it. The man sat the two bags down next to VI. VI first opened the trunk on the Lincoln with his remote and then opened both bags and took out a bundle of hundreds from each and leafed through both of them. "Goddamnit, do you have to do that here in the street," cried Niko.

"Who is to see?" said VI, as he tossed the bags into the trunk and closed the lid.

"Now," said Niko, "I believe you have something for me."

"Yes I do," said VI, "an invitation to lunch." Niko looked hard at VI and said, "What, lunch, what is this?"

"Mr. Galliano," said VI, "I must wait for a call to tell me exactly where Lexi and his men are, as soon as I get that call, you can dispatch your men, I need to be certain Yoskov is going where I think he is." Niko thought for a moment and decided that made sense and said, "And just where do you suggest we have lunch?"

"Actually," said VI, "I know a place near here, excellent Italian food, it's called Frankie's." Niko looked at VI and smiled, "Sure, why not," the food was good and he had a piece of the joint, Niko wondered if this Russian knew he was about to have lunch in a connected restaurant. Most likely not, or he would never have suggested it. Damn, thought Niko, these Russian bastards are stupid, ruthless but stupid. "I know the place, I'll follow you."

VI said nothing else and got into his car and drove towards Frankie's restaurant. As soon as he had pulled away, his cell phone rang; VI answered and spoke to the bullet mike on the visor. "Yes." The call was from Rick who said, "Green light, video captured and transmitted, Frankie should be making his first call now."

"Excellent," said VI, "call me three minutes after we go inside the restaurant."

"Got it," said the other voice. At the same time, Frankie was talking to Lexi. "Ok," said Frankie, "you got the video yet?"

"Yes," said Lexi, "it just came through; call me back in a few minutes." Lexi watched in horror as he saw his visitor leafing through the cash from the gym bags and stow it in the trunk of his car. Even more disconcerting was the warm smile Niko had on his face after the European put the money away. The Italian was right; it had been Galliano all the time.

Lexi had five men with him; they would constitute the core of leadership when this thing was done, and he wanted them to see the video for themselves. Lexi made a call to the leader of four men that were sitting in a plumbing repair van near Central Park. Two were armed with folding stock Kalashnikov assault rifles, and two had semi automatic shotguns loaded with buck shot. Each was dressed in black fatigues with body armor and black ski masks rolled up on top of their heads. "Be ready to go soon," was all Lexi said, the man on the phone acknowledged and hung up and told the other men to get ready to move.

The phone rang and Lexi answered, "You were telling the truth, where is Galliano going?"

"Not so fast," said Frankie, "there is the matter of my money."

"Yes," said Lexi, "I will initiate the transfer, as soon as you confirm it; tell me where Galliano is going."

"Sure thing comrade, one thing at a time," said Frankie. "I'll call you as soon as I know my money is there," then he hung up.

Just as VI, followed by Niko and his men were pulling up in front of Frankie's, Nolan got the confirmation that the money had been transferred. Nolan called Frankie and told him to wait five minutes before he called Lexi.

VI, Niko Galliano, his number two Paul, and his three top Captains walked into Frankie's restaurant and the hostess immediately recognized Niko and made a fuss. VI did a good job of looking surprised and looked at Niko, who smiled at him and said, "Excellent choice for lunch, I guess you didn't know, I own a piece of this place. As they were talking, Frankie walked up to the group and shook hands with Niko and Paul and said, "Niko, you should have told me you were coming, I could have had the cook fix you something special."

"It's ok Frankie," said Niko, "we were just in the area and decided to stop in." Frankie moved the group to a table near the back of the restaurant, ostensibly for privacy, and the group sat down. Just as the waitress was showing up, VI's cell phone rang. VI answered the phone and said, "Yes, ok, thank you," and hung up. Niko looked at VI and said, "Well."

VI said, "Lexi and his top men are at the Little Armenia Restaurant in Brighton Beach as we speak." Paul immediately took out his cell phone and dialed a number. It was answered by one of four men in a stolen Cadillac Escalade. The men in this group were all mob associates with military experience, and were all armed with pump shotguns and handguns for back up. The group leader told Paul that they would be at the target in less than ten minutes and wanted to know if this call was the go signal. Paul looked at Niko who nodded his head. Paul said, "Go," and hung up.

At the same time this was happening, Frankie had stepped into his office and called Lexi. Lexi answered the phone after the first ring and said, "Well."

"Ok, I got my money," said Frankie. "They all went to a place called Frankie's in Manhattan."

"I know where it is," said Lexi, "I take it we will not speak again."

"Of that, I can assure you, I'm outta here," said Frankie who then hung up. Lexi called the men in the van and gave them the address for Frankie's, the leader said five minutes, no more, and that he would call when the job was done. The waitress had just brought the drinks when VI's pager began to vibrate. VI looked over at Niko and excused himself saying he needed to go to the men's room. VI got up and walked past the rest rooms which were out of view from the table, through the kitchen, and out into the back alley just as the four Russians were parking their van. In Brooklyn, the four mob guys had just stopped across from the Little Armenia.

As Billy approached the channel leading to the Bitter End, Dan checked the Russians' position on his laptop and said, "They haven't moved as of yet." Dan pointed to the west side of the mooring field and said they should be right over there. "Hey Jack, you should get out of sight till we see if they are on the boat or not." Jack moved down into the companionway and waited for an all clear. Billy looked around and said, "There it is Dan, right where your little gizmo says it should be, let's make a close pass and see if anybody is home."

Billy drove the Donzi right past the Power Cat and it appeared that all were gone in the dingy. Billy said, "Ok Jack, looks like nobody's home but stay outta sight until we tie off to the ball and make sure, we're going to tie up about seventy-five yards away." After the Donzi was secure on the mooring ball, Dan and Billy broke out their binoculars and confirmed that nobody was on the boat. Jack came up into the cockpit and looked at his two friends and said, "What now?"

Billy said, "To be honest, I really don't know, I know how I'd like to do it, swim over there and stick on of our mines on the bottom of the boat and when we see them board, boom, no mo bad guys."

"Yeah," said Jack, "effective but not exactly discreet." Dan appeared deep in thought and then said, "Well for the time being, we can't board their boat, we don't know when they are coming back, and their dingy looks like every other one around here so we have to wait until they come back out and then watch to see what they do next, if we get an opportunity to get any of them alone, we should take him out if possible, narrow the field at each opportunity."

"I agree," said Billy. The men sat in the cockpit and caught up with each other, talking about what they had been doing since they had last seen each other. Billy and Dan were careful not to ask about Jack's murdered family. Jack, in no time had the others howling with laughter as he recounted stories about past charters and the misadventures associated with them. After a bit, the mood had become a bit more somber and Jack asked Billy, "So, what have you been doing with yourself these last few years?"

"Something noble and of great benefit my fellow man, I bought a little shit hole surfer bar in Cocoa Beach and turned it into a biker bar. Tripled the revenue in less than two months, we sell burgers and sandwiches and such, and we get local bands to play on the weekends. All in all, it's a good gig, then this came up and I came running."

"What about you Dan?" asked Jack.

"Nothing so noble for me, I stayed in the D.C. area, opened up a lawn furniture shop in Indian Head, make the stuff out of wood in my garage and sell it for a hideous profit. Between that and my retirement checks, I do pretty well. You, my friend, appear to have done quite well for a dead guy, this charter thing looks like a dream life."

"Yeah," said Jack, "mostly, it doesn't suck." The men shared a laugh over that and then Billy asked, "What about after this?"

Jack thought that over for a minute and said, "I just don't know. Before Alex came along, I was really just going through the motions you know, I was content, but I was just rolling along. Then Alex showed up, and for the first time since Sue was killed, I was really enjoying being with someone, hell, finally enjoying being alive again, just to find out somebody wants to kill both of us. Well guess what, that ain't gonna happen, first, I am going to kill that asshole, and then I'll play it by ear. I think she wants to be with me, and I know I want to be with her, so, we'll see how it goes."

Dan smiled at Jack and said, "You know, when this is all over and you guys are done with the honeymoon, you owe us a free charter on that boat of yours."

Just as VI had made the safety of the alley, Niko suddenly became concerned about his abrupt departure; right as the four Russians in combat gear stormed into Frankie's place. The five wise guys knew they were in trouble. Niko did not even have time to react, he knew he was about to die and all he could do was watch it happen. Unlike in the movies where the assassins spray bullets everywhere, each man took quick and careful aim, the two men with the AK-47s, individually fired three round bursts into Niko and Paul's heads almost simultaneously, and the two shotgun men took out the other three, one firing once and the other firing twice. All five mobsters were down and dead with no one hit but the targets. After the initial volley, there was no need for any more shooting and the Russians were out the door in under twenty-five seconds from the time they entered the restaurant.

Immediately after they left, Frankie was on the phone calling 911. VI walked back in and cried, "Oh my God, someone call an ambulance," and casually walked out the front door, got in his car and drove away just as the sound of sirens could be heard in the distance.

At the Little Armenia, Lexi was on the phone with his team leader who was reporting that the job had been done on the Italians when he heard the door slam open. Lexi's men were just getting their weapons out when the room erupted with the thunderous roar of the four twelve gauge shotguns blasting away. The leader of Lexi's hit team heard the gunfire and held the phone away from his ear. The man looked at his accomplices and said, "We may encounter some difficulty getting paid for this morning's work," and put his phone away. One of Lexi's men actually got a shot off, but all he hit was a wall. Lexi was trying to figure out what had gone so horribly wrong, when he saw the muzzle flash of the shotgun. A millisecond later, the load of buckshot tore through the center of his chest cavity killing him instantly. The four Mafiosos were in and out in less than 35 seconds. Surveillance at both locations reported to Nolan that each party had received their gifts. Nolan told the two men to disengage and return their hotel. Nolan looked at Eggers and Brady and said, "Well, I guess we can call this taking a bite out of crime, we will debrief as soon as everyone is back in from the field. Gee boss, we sure didn't see this one coming. You guys practice that line, now we put the remaining members under surveillance and as they try to re-organize, we get everything on audio tape and video, then we hit em with warrants under the RICO act, and the live ones go to jail."

Eggers smiled and said, "I do love happy endings." Brady just sat on the edge of his desk with a big grin on his face.

Mhiki, Stephan, and Viktor had just finished having lunch and were sitting in the outdoor lounge area at the marina watching CNN when the newscaster announced a major breaking story. The screen first showed the outside of the Little Armenia Restaurant in Brighton Beach Brooklyn, and then, an upscale Italian restaurant in Manhattan called Frankie's. All three men were mesmerized as the reporter described how at least five suspected senior members of the Italian and Russian Mafia had been killed at each location almost simultaneously. The attacks, said the reporter, had been carried out with military precision at both locations, with no bystanders injured. Names of those killed were not available for release at the present time but were expected to be known later in the day.

An NYPD spokesman being interviewed, said that apparently a turf war between the Russians and Italians had escalated to the point that each had gone after the leadership of the other. He further stated that the police department would not rest until the killers and those who had ordered the killings were brought to justice. He went on to state that it was possible, that the individuals who had ordered the killings were themselves among the dead, they would have to wait and see what the investigation turned up.

"Well," said Stephan, "now we know why we have not been able to contact Lexi, it appears he was more ambitious than you thought Mhiki." Mhiki gave Stephan a look that would have made a lesser man soil himself, but Stephan merely shrugged and said, "What now?"

Viktor said, "We should return to the boat, we can speak more freely there." Mhiki said nothing and started walking for the dingy dock. Viktor looked at Stephan and said, "I would advise that you choose your words carefully at this point my friend." Stephan said nothing and followed Mhiki to where their dingy was tied off at the dock. The men cast off and headed back out to their boat.

Billy's cell phone rang and he was given the report on what had happened in New York, he couldn't help smiling at the news. The caller also informed him that the news was being covered by every major media outlet, so if Mhiki did not already know, he would soon. Billy hung up and turned to Jack and said, "It appears that there are several management openings in both the Italian and Russian Mafia. Niko Galliano Jr, his number two, and several others were shot to death early this afternoon. It also appears, that at the same time that was happening, Mhiki's number two and several others were killed in a similar attack, Mhiki is good and fucked now. Even if he were to survive us, which I fully intend to see he does not, the Italians will leave no stone unturned looking for him. They will never believe he wasn't behind the hit on Galliano."

"You know," said Jack, "that's the last branch on the Galliano family tree, Niko Jr. had two daughters, no more male children to carry on the family name, they're finished." Will, who had been looking around with his binoculars said, "Aargh, there be Russians," pointing to the dingy approaching the Power Cat, "Jack, get below and stay out of sight." Jack moved into the companionway as not to be seen, but was still able to see the three Russians getting out of their dingy and boarding the boat. Jack was able to rule out one of the men immediately by looking at Viktor's shoulder length pony tail. The first, and last time Jack had seen Mhiki, had been a long time ago, and their eye contact had lasted only a second before the lights had gone out as Mhiki's slug had bored through his chest.

Unlike Mhiki, Jack had felt no ill will towards Mhiki for having shot and nearly killed him. It was after all, an occupational hazard, and Mhiki had simply been doing his job. However, now that Mhiki was after not only him, but Alex as well, Jack decided it would be ok to take it personal. After the Russians had boarded their boat, Dan could hear yelling across the distance, obviously, there was quite an animated conversation taking place aboard the Power Cat. Billy smiled and said, "Looks like they caught the news on CNN, I'll bet Valentnikov is as about as pissed as he's ever been."

Dan said, "Most likely so, now we have to see what he does, but we need to get him soon."

"Agreed," said Jack, "let's watch for now and see what they do."

Mhiki was trying to make sense of all this, what had Lexi done, whatever it had been had cost him his life, of greater concern now, was the fact that business as usual had come to an abrupt end. All the time, money and work setting up his little empire was fairly down the toilet now, Mhiki knew that he could not go back to New York, that was finished. Viktor and Stephan sat in silence, each afraid to say anything to further anger Mhiki. Mhiki went below for a minute and emerged with four fingers of Vodka in a tumbler which he downed in one big gulp. After a moment, he said, "Stephan, take me back ashore, I need to use a computer, Viktor, you will stay with me, Stephan, you are to return to the boat and construct another device for the sailor's boat. I will call you when I am ready to return."

Stephan said, "Very well Mhiki, but I still need to purchase the components." "Do it then, and get to work as soon as you get back to the boat, I will call you when I am ready."

As the Russians were getting back into the dingy, Dan ran down into the salon and came back up with a handful of sugar packets. "What are you doing with those," asked Jack. Dan smiled ruefully and said, "I'm going to follow them in and spike the gas tank on their dingy, give em something else to be pissed off about, they should make it about halfway back out before the motor on their dingy croaks. Let em row for a while."

Jack smiled and said, "You're mean."

"I know," said Dan, "hey Billy, be sure to keep that two way close, I may be in a hurry if I get caught." Billy shook his head and said, "Sure thing, we'll be ready." Dan jumped into the dingy any followed the Russians into the dingy dock. Dan tooled around and made note of where the Russians had tied off and waited until they had all walked out of sight before moving in. Dan did not even tie off, but just grabbed the grab line on the side of the Russians' dingy. After a quick look around to ensure no one was paying any attention to him, Dan quickly unscrewed the cap off the dingy's fuel tank and dumped eight packets of sugar into the fuel, then secured the cap and headed back out to the Donzi.

On his way back, Dan called Billy on the secure walkie talkie and told him all was well. Back on the Donzi, Dan laughed and said, "I would hate to be stuck in that dingy with Mhiki when that motor craps out, he may just blow a gasket right there." The three men all laughed and Jack asked, "So, you guys have any beer on this tub or what?"

Billy said, "Right you are sir, three beers coming up," as he went down to the galley. Billy turned on the radio while he was below and emerged with the beers smiling broadly. As the men were drinking their beers, Jack said, "I want to put a scuba rig together. I may decide to swim over there and poke a hole in their dingy after they row it back; I want that asshole as rattled as I can get him."

"Ooh, I like it, not only will it really piss them off, it may keep them here longer if they have to get it fixed." Jack drained his beer and went below and returned with a set of dive gear and his old Navy issue dive knife. After Jack had the rig set up, the men sat around for about a half an hour making small talk when Dan said, "Look over there, it looks like one of them is coming back alone."

The men could see a dingy a little over halfway back to the Russians' boat with only one person aboard. Through the binoculars, Dan could see that it was Stephan, and he was standing up yanking away at the pull start on the dingy motor. They watched as Stephan tried the primer bulb, and then tried the pull start again. After about three more tries, Stephan gave up and took to the oars. "Man, he looks pissed," said Dan,

They watched as Stephan rowed back to the boat and tied off the dingy and unloaded a shopping bag and then went below. After a few minutes, Stephan got back into the dingy and removed the engine cover and started doing something to the engine.

Suddenly, Jack sat straight up and shouted to Billy, "Get me all the weights you have, belts too, now, and load the weights on the belts." Billy wasn't sure what Jack was up to but he wasted no time in retrieving the dive belts and weights. As soon as he came back with them, Jack, who was putting on his dive gear, told Dan, "Get me some wire ties or some rope, whatever you can find, do it now."

As Billy was finishing with the weights, Dan came back with a handful of large black plastic wire ties from the boat's tool box and gave them to Jack, who stuck them in his pocket. Billy looked at Jack and realized what he was up to. "What are you going to do with him Jack," asked Dan. Jack looked at him and said, "I'm going to strap that asshole to the bottom of that mooring line, another unexplained disappearance in the Caribbean. Dan, keep an eye on him while I swim over there, as long as he keeps sitting where he is on the back of the dingy, I can come up and snatch him over the side and take him down. If it looks like anyone is watching, make some noise, I only need a couple of seconds to make him disappear."

Billy looked at Jack and said, "Don't let him get loose, all hell's gonna break loose if you do." Jack took a compass bearing at the Russians' boat and smiled at Dan and Billy and said, "Ready or not, here it goes," and slipped into the water.

Stephan was busy removing the screws that held the small outboard motors carburetor onto the cylinder head. Stephan correctly assumed that something had clogged the main jet on the carb, what he did not know, is that the blockage had been caused by hardened sugar. As Stephan was working on the engine, Jack was steadily closing the distance to the Russians boat.

Jack had learned long ago during his time as a SEAL, how to measure distance underwater by counting his kicks with his fins. Every person, based on their strokes, will travel a certain distance underwater per kick of the fins. Once an individual knows their personal kick to distance ratio, they can calculate their rate of travel with remarkable accuracy. In the crystal clear water, Jack could actually see the dingy when he was within forty feet. Jack decreased his depth to about ten feet and continued to close the distance to his target. When he was directly below Stephan's dingy, Jack slowly surfaced. Jack had to kick constantly to move closer to the surface, he was wearing three weight belts with a combined weight of nearly fifty pounds. Jack broke the surface right next to the dingy and grabbed onto the grab line on the side of the dingy, then spit out his regulator and exhaled loudly. Stephan, startled, looked at Jack in surprise. Before Stephan could react or say anything, Jack, in a panicked voice said, "Oh god have you seen another diver, I can't find my wife." The dive mask sufficiently concealed Jack's facial features so that Stephan never suspected treachery until it was too late. Jack, acting as though he was looking for his missing wife, did a quick scan in all directions, and not seeing anyone nearby watching, reached up and grabbed Stephan, who was looking away, by the shoulder with his left hand and stuck his regulator back in his mouth with his right.

Stephan was caught completely off guard, he never even saw Jack reaching up to grab him and as soon as he hit the water, Jack rolled back into an inverted dive while pulling Stephan's back against his chest putting a vice like grip around the Russians throat with his left forearm. The combination of Jack kicking for the bottom and the extra lead weights propelled the pair downward like an underwater rocket. Stephan was in a state of total panic, he had been unprepared for the sudden attack. The vise like grip around his throat, coupled with his awareness of the increasing water pressure had him terrified. He struggled with all of his strength but could not break this madman's grip. Panic turned to horror as Stephan felt the long blade of Jack's dive knife penetrate first his right, then left lung. Stephan died not understanding why this stranger was killing him, he had imagined his own death in many scenarios, but this certainly had never been one of them.

Jack hit the bottom head first and only then realized that Stephan was no longer among the living. Jack swam the big Russian's body to the base of the mooring line which was in about seventy feet of water, and used the plastic wire ties to strap Stephan's wrists, then ankles securely around the mooring line. After Jack was satisfied with that task, he took off two of the weight belts and fastened them around Stephan's body. Jack took a moment to look into Stephan's lifeless eyes and shot him the finger before turning around and swimming back to the Donzi.

Jack returned to the Donzi and took off his SCUBA rig underwater and tied it to a line that he had left trailing behind the boat. Once his gear was secure, Jack climbed up on the swim platform and then took a seat in the cockpit. Billy and Dan said nothing for a moment then Dan said, "I don't think anyone noticed his departure, hell, I was watching and I barely noticed, well done Jack."

Jack held his right hand out and spread his fingers wide apart and looked at them; steady as a rock, not even a hint of shaking. Jack felt neither grief nor remorse for the death of Stephan, and that fact bothered him little, the soldier turned thug was simply not worth pity or remorse reasoned Jack.

"Whew, anybody else want a beer," asked Jack. "Sure," said Dan, "I'll grab em." After Dan had passed out the beers and sat down, Billy took a pull from his beer and asked Jack, "How long before someone finds the body?"

"Don't know," said Jack, "maybe never, he won't float up, I punctured both lungs and his abdominal cavity so there won't be any internal gasses building up creating buoyancy, and he has enough weights on him to keep a horse down. Critters will likely get most of him before anyone finds him, if anyone ever does. Mhiki will certainly never know what happened." Billy smiled at Jack, then raised his beer bottle in toast and said, "And then there were two." The three men clicked the necks of their bottles together and each took a long pull of the ice cold beer.

Mhiki had gone into the internet café at the marina and began checking on his various offshore and overseas bank accounts. Satisfied that those were all in order, he made a major decision, it was time to go. He would find the sailor and the woman, kill them and leave for Europe, maybe France and buy a nice villa somewhere in wine country and take it easy for a while. Mhiki had millions salted away in various accounts, more than enough to live very well. Mhiki also had a Polish passport and spoke the language fluently; he could easily establish himself as a wealthy retired Pole, just wanting to relax in the country for a bit. As for Viktor and Stephan, they would just have to take care of themselves.

Mhiki told Viktor to call Stephan and have him pick them up. Viktor's heart began beating faster and he became worried as he tried Stephan's phone a second, then third time. Mhiki looked at Viktor and said, "Well, what is going on?"

Viktor genuinely did not want to speak at all, but said, "He does not answer his phone, I tried three times, he does not answer." Mhiki was about to explode with rage, what else had gone wrong. Mhiki thought for a second and said, "Find a ride out to the boat and see what Stephan's problem is, maybe he lost his phone or something, whatever the problem is, call me, I need to get back on the computer and check on something else, now go." Viktor stood for a moment looking at Mhiki not knowing what to say or do, wisely, Viktor turned around and walked to the dingy dock to try and find a ride out to the boat.

Mhiki went back online and transferred all of the money from his Bahamian and Cayman accounts to his bank in Paris. When he finished that, Mhiki went to where the ferry ran and checked the schedule. There was a boat leaving for Tortola in thirty minutes, enough time for Mhiki to have a stiff Vodka at the bar and wait for Viktor to call.

Viktor was standing at the dingy dock when a young couple walked up and started climbing into one of the dingys. "Excuse me," said Viktor, "could I trouble you for a ride out to my boat, I can not seem to reach my friend on his phone." The couple looked at each other then the young man in his early twenties said, "Sure, hop in, where you at man." Viktor pointed to the Power Cat in the distance. As they approached the boat, Viktor saw that the dingy was tied off to the back of the boat but he saw no sign of Stephan. Viktor thanked the young couple for the ride and apprehensively boarded the Cat.

Jack saw the couple dropping Viktor off and said as much to the other men.

Viktor looked around the boat and seeing no sign of Stephan, looked closer at the dingy and noticed that the engine was partially disassembled.

Viktor was very frightened now, if Stephan had flagged down a ride to get to the island for a part or something, he would certainly have called Mhiki or himself. No, Viktor did not like this at all.

Jack, Billy, and Dan watched in amusement as Viktor used his cell phone to call Mhiki. Jack wished he could be listening in on this conversation. Mhiki was in a rage, "Listen to me Viktor, you will keep trying to call him, wait there for him to show up and call me when he does do you hear me?"

"Yes, of course Mhiki," said Viktor who was getting ready to say something else when Mhiki hung up his phone. Viktor had a giant knot in his stomach now and did not like the thought of being alone on the boat. Too many people were disappearing.

As soon as Mhiki hung up his phone, he walked to the nearest trash can and threw his phone into it, then proceeded to the ferry landing and purchased a ticket to Tortola. He had both of his passports on him and enough cash, if he needed more he could hit an ATM.

Viktor, thought Mhiki, *you are on your own.* The sudden disappearance of one man was a concern, possibly an anomaly; the disappearance of two was foul play. Mhiki needed to get clear of Viktor and the boat, they were being hunted, he was sure of that now. Mhiki had no idea who, how or why, but nonetheless, he needed to work independently now. Mhiki, who was sitting on the top deck seats of the ferry, took a last look at Viktor as the ferry passed the Cat. Viktor had no idea, or reason to suspect, that Mhiki would abandon him like this.

On the Donzi, Jack and his friends had no idea that Mhiki had left either. Billy said, "What do we do now Jack." Jack thought for a moment and looked at Dan. Dan smiled and said. "Let's pay him a visit, I'll go alone, give him some bullshit story and pop him with the Glock if I can get him inside out of sight. Then I'll come back here and we wait for Mhiki, or better yet, let's go ashore and find him, follow him back out here and finish it."

"What about Viktor's body?" asked Billy. Jack looked at Billy and said, "Fire, tragic boat fire, if there is anything left of his body, or his and Mhiki's I doubt they would do an autopsy as long as the fire looked accidental. Didn't you say that thing had an alcohol stove on it Dan?

Those things cause fires and explosions all the time. Ok, you go take care of Viktor, come back and get us, and then we all go look for Mhiki."

"No Jack, I don't think so, me and Dan will go look for Mhiki, you need to stay here and watch the boat, Mhiki may show back up here and find Viktor. We need somebody here to radio us if we miss him." Jack thought about it and had to agree, he didn't like it, but it made sense. Jack said, "All right, you have a point, when you go over to the boat, leave here and approach from seaward, you can tell him you came from one of the big sail boats out there further out."

"Sounds good," said Dan as he screwed the suppressor onto the barrel of his Glock and chambered a round. Dan stuck the pistol into his waistband and got into the dingy.

Billy went below and came back up with a can of carburetor cleaner and said, "Tell him his buddy asked you for this." Dan smiled and nodded his head and said, "That ought to work." Before he left, Jack tossed him one of the secure radios and said, "Let us know when it's done, we'll keep an eye out for Mhiki." Dan took the radio, then left in the dingy and made a wide loop out to seaward before turning in to the Russians' boat.

When Dan got to the Cat, Viktor was in the cockpit and looked nervous as Dan approached the vessel. "Ahoy there, where is your friend, I brought him this carb cleaner." Viktor wasn't sure what to do.

"You talked to my friend," asked Viktor.

"Well, yeah, I was on my way out to that big blue sail boat over there and I picked your friend up drifting and towed him over here, motor conked out on him. I told him I'd go get this carburetor cleaner, and maybe have a look at the motor for him, got one just like it on our other dingy, damn thing quits on me all the time." Viktor thought about it and then said, "Tie off and come aboard." Viktor had no idea where Stephan was, but he did need to get the dingy motor running again and for Viktor, outboard motor repair may as well have been particle physics.

Dan climbed up on the Cat and looked around and said, "Ok, where's the carb." Viktor looked at him with a blank look and Dan smiled and said, "Let me look in the dingy." Dan pulled in the painter line securing the dingy to the boat and said, "There it is, looks like your buddy got it off the motor, that's a good start, I'll climb in there and get it, here hold this line." Dan had Viktor hold the dingy as he climbed in and retrieved the carburetor. "Oh man, this thing has salt water all over it, why don't you take it into the galley and rinse it off real good for me and get me a couple of napkins while you're at it." Viktor, oblivious to the danger, did as Dan requested and went into the galley with the carb and turned on the water in the sink; that was his last conscious thought. As he turned the water on, Dan held the end of the suppressor about a foot from the back of Viktor's head and pulled the trigger twice. Viktor went straight down and did not so much as twitch, he was dead before he hit the deck in the galley. Dan grabbed a towel and wrapped it around Viktor's head so he wouldn't bleed all over the place and then picked up the two spent casings. Then Dan grabbed his radio and transmitted a simple, "Done," to Jack.

Jack keyed the microphone twice, making a click, click noise in acknowledgement of Dan's transmission. Dan took the time to look around and not seeing anything of interest, left the boat and took a circuitous route back to the Donzi so no one would remember seeing a dingy going back and forth from the two boats. Dan boarded the Donzi and said, "Billy, grab a weapon and let's go, Jack, you just wait here end keep an eye on the boat, call me on the cell if you see anything."

"Will do," said Jack, there was no reason to ask how things had gone on the Russians' boat. As Billy and Dan headed in to the island, Jack took off his shirt to get some sun while he watched for Mhiki.

Nolan, Eggers, Brady and VI were in the command center discussing the day's events. VI said, "I realize that it really is none of my business, but what about that," pointing to the two gym bags containing a million dollars each. Nolan looked at the two detectives and said, "Why don't you take a few bundles and buy something nice for the wife."

"For one thing sir, I am not married, at least not yet, and I did not do this for money."

"Easy," said Eggers," we know you didn't, that's why we want you to have a piece. We decided we're going to give it to a priest that runs a couple of youth centers, get it flowing back in the community where it will do a lot of good for some kids, maybe keep them from ending up like those other scumbags."

VI walked over and opened both bags and held up some of the money and smiled and said, "Easy come, easy go, and put the money back into the bags. I appreciate your offer gentlemen but no, I have all that I need, do as you say and put this to good use, you are doing what is best with it, in the right hands; it could make a world of difference. I will take my leave now if you have nothing else for me to do."

The three law enforcement officers shook hands with VI and Nolan told him that the government Lear could take him back to Virginia today, or he could go tomorrow. VI said, "I think I will go see a Broadway show tonight, I have never done that." Nolan smiled and made a quick phone call and handed VI a piece of paper with the theatre address and the name of the manager and said, "I got you two tickets to see *Cats*, the manager will have them at the door for you, call me in the morning and let me know when you want to leave, I'll have the plane on standby for you. In the meantime feel free to use the Lincoln."

After VI had left Brady asked Nolan about the other two million. Nolan said, "How's the American Red Cross sound." The others nodded in agreement.

VI left JFK and returned to his hotel, after settling on the sofa in his room, he allowed himself a rare glass of good Russian Vodka and then called Liesel, his significant other of the last three years and told her that his consulting gig was done and that he would be home sometime tomorrow. Then he called the training officer at DEVGRU and informed him that he would be at work the following Monday. As VI watched the evening news and the reports of the killings in Manhattan and Brooklyn, he felt nothing in the way of remorse or regret, what he had done, had been for the right reasons and ordinary people's lives would be the better for it. VI did not really condone these types of operations, and had Saunders not been involved, he would not have participated. Funny, thought VI, when something becomes personal, one's perception of where the line is between right and wrong, become somewhat blurred, legally, what he had done was a capital offense, morally; he knew in his heart he had done, and helped do the right thing. VI would go and see the play tonight and then sleep fitfully, undisturbed by any moral demons.

Mhiki was getting off the ferry in Tortola even before Billy and Dan had returned ashore. Mhiki needed another boat and he needed to purchase some more dive gear, he was annoyed that he had lost his rebreather rig but he would have to make do with whatever he could get. Mhiki looked at the available boats and decided to rent a 44' trawler, it was large, but not too large for him to handle alone. Mhiki endured the safety brief and the rest of the ordeal associated with the rental process and did some shopping. Among the articles Mhiki purchased were the components to manufacture another bomb with a waterproof timer, a full set of dive gear, food for four days, some new clothes, a long black wig, and some basic necessities, and a bunch of Vodka.

Mhiki was having dinner at the marina restaurant when he saw a couple wearing I KNOW JACK SCHMIDT tee-shirts. Mhiki put on his most affable face and approached the couple. "Excuse me, said Mhiki, I see you too know Jack Schmidt." The couple both laughed and the wife said, "Yeah, best charter in the islands, have you sailed with him before?"

"No," said Mhiki, "I always seem to catch his booked periods when my vacation rolls around. Which islands did he take you to," asked Mhiki.

"Well, we hit most of them, but we did hit Norman twice, I get the impression he goes there a lot, he knows the owners of the Willie-T really well and the diving and snorkeling are really good, if he's on a week charter you can count on seeing him there at least twice."

Interesting thought Mhiki; he could just go to this island and wait for the sailor, blow his boat out from under him and then take the next available flight to Paris. Mhiki made some more small talk with the couple, excused himself and then returned to his boat. He would leave for Norman Island in the morning. Mhiki was of a single minded purpose; he believed that Viktor would be disappearing any time now. He also believed that he knew who was hunting him; it must have something to do with the Goddamn Italians. Lexi had done something to anger the Pasta Bosses, as he called them, and sold him out, that was why he could not contact Lexi before.

His old friend Lexi had tried to set him up, well, the Italians had robbed him of his chance to settle that score, but at least now that he had changed boats, the wise guys that were after him would not know where to look anymore. That would be the only reasonable explanation; Lexi had sold him out to the Mafia and told them exactly where to find him, which hotel; that would explain Ivan, and the type boat, which would explain Stephan. Too bad about Viktor, thought Mhiki, he had invested a lot of time and money in the young man and he had progressed well, but he did stand out in a crowd and would make it easy for his hunters, Mhiki, felt no sense of betrayal or any true feelings at all, leaving Viktor for the wolves was nothing more than an evasion tactic, and it left Mhiki free to continue his own hunt.

Billy and Dan looked everywhere around the resort and saw no sign of Mhiki. They went to the bar that was in view of the dingy dock and sat down. Billy called Jack and asked if he had seen anything. "Nada," said Jack, "what do you think?"

"I don't know," said Billy, "but I don't like this, we're on our way back out, see ya in a few." Jack was beginning to think Mhiki had bolted, maybe Stephan's departure and news of the events in New York had him spooked and he split. Hard to know, but they would continue to watch the Power Cat. Besides, they still had a little chore to take care of before they could leave.

Jack caught the painter line for Dan and cleated off the dingy. After all we're aboard the Donzi, Billy said, "I guess we should wait for dark before we start our little weenie roast huh."

Dan said, "How do you want to do this Jack?" Jack had been thinking about it for a while and said, "Look around in the galley and see if there is anything greasy in the fridge, you know, bacon or something like that, and leave it in the skillet with the burner turned up on high. Also, look around and see if there are any jerry cans of gas for the dingy, if so, put them right outside the salon door. Once the grease in the skillet catches fire, it won't take long for the fiberglass above the stove to light off, after that begins to melt, it'll drip flaming strands of fiberglass onto the counter top and within ten minutes, the whole salon will be engulfed in flames. Put the body right in front of the stove, that's where the fire will burn the hottest and longest. There is no provision for fighting a boat fire here, so once it gets going, it'll burn to the water line until there is nothing left to burn. Where he's at, even if the mooring pendant burns through, the wind will take him out into open water." Everyone agreed it would be best to burn the boat tonight but the larger question was; where the hell was Mhiki.

Billy's cell phone rang and after he answered it, he handed it over to Jack; it was of course Alex who said, "So, you out partying with your old buddies?"

Jack answered back, "I thought I told you not to call me at the office." Alex laughed and said, "How long do you think it will take to finish up your business?"

"Can't really say, it's mostly done already, just one more little detail, I'll know more tomorrow."

"Look," said Alex, "I won't keep you on the phone, just be careful and get your butt back to me ok."

"Will do," said Jack, "in the meantime try to relax and don't flirt with Will too much, you'll give the poor guy a heart attack."

Alex said goodbye and hung up. Jack looked at the phone for a moment and said, "Damn."

Dan said, "Something wrong," "No," said Jack, "I just want to get this done and get on with whatever is going to happen with my life, I know what I want to happen, but it all seems too farfetched you know, a salty, crusty old bastard like me, with a past like mine, with a woman like that, only in the movies gentlemen." Billy and Dan both smiled at Jack and Billy, in a childish voice said, "Jack has a new girlfriend, Jack has a new girl friend." Dan howled and Jack threw his empty beer bottle at Billy who just managed to duck it. All three men were laughing now. The sun was setting down the Francis Drake Passage and then Dan said, "Well guys this is real fun and all, but I have some work to do, I believe a bonfire would liven up the entertainment portion of this evenings program. I'll wait till it's good and dark and dingy over, Billy, break out a set of the NVD's and keep an eye out. I'll have coms with an earpiece so you can let me know if I have visitors on the way. It still bugs me that we can't find Mhiki, we need to go back in early in the morning and see what we can find out."

Jack said, "I think he split, I think he hopped a ride out of here, the question is where to. Tomorrow we need to check the ferry schedules and see where he may have gotten off to, but I'm pretty sure he's gone." Billy thought that over and said, "If that's the case, it's going to make it damn difficult to find his ass, he could be anywhere and we have no way to track, and or, locate him."

"A most unwelcome development," said Dan, "I'll take care of the business at hand and we can work on the Mhiki issue later." Dan made sure his radio functioned properly and also made sure he had a lighter on the offhand chance that the stove on the Power Cat would not light off on its own. When Dan was about ready to leave, Billy checked the batteries in the ANVIS-6 night vision device and made sure the unit was functioning as advertised. ANVIS-6 is the acronym for, **aviator's night vision imaging system, model # 6**. It is an amazing piece of equipment, small, lightweight and durable, and is powered by two double A batteries. It is a third generation night imaging system that turns even the blackest of night into bright green daylight by amplifying ambient light in two intensifier tubes that the wearer looks through. They can be handheld or mounted on either an aircrewmans, or infantryman's helmet.

After the men were set, Dan started out in the dingy, again taking a circuitous route to the Russians' boat. Dan boarded the boat and entered the salon and galley area, and using a red lensed flashlight began to look through the refrigerator for something that would make a good fire. Dan found a package of chicken breasts and began to look through the cabinets. It didn't take long for him to find a big bottle of cooking oil, and he also found two, one gallon jugs of alcohol for the stove. Dan took a large skillet and filled it to the brim with oil, then threw in the chicken. After that, he sat both jugs of alcohol on the counter next to the stove top. Dan began to search through the lockers on the boat and found a five gallon can of gas for the dingy and placed that just outside the salon door in the cockpit. Dan then went back to the galley and after thinking about it for a moment, used half of one of the jugs of alcohol to pour all over the blood soaked towel that was wrapped around Viktor's head. Satisfied with his handiwork, Dan lit the burner on the stove and turned the flame up all the way, and then got back in the dingy and made his was back to the Donzi.

Billy, watching with the NVD's, could clearly see the moment that Dan had lit the stove and told Jack, "There she goes, ok, he's leaving and the fire is on." By the time Dan got back to the Donzi, the men were able to see the orange glow of the fire with their naked eyes. After Dan joined them in the cockpit of the Donzi, they could clearly see open flame through the windows of the salon. Jack said, "This should be a good show." In less than five minutes, they heard the muffled, *whump* sound of the first jug of alcohol exploding and within seconds, the entire salon area was engulfed in flames. Billy looked around at the other boats with the NVD's to see if anyone had taken an interest in the burning boat yet and didn't notice anyone looking that way. That all changed in an instant when the five gallon can of gas exploded and shot a fireball almost a hundred feet in the air. That got noticed. Within a couple of minutes they could hear people yelling fire all around the mooring field and people began to move to the boat in their dingys carrying fire extinguishers. A total exercise in futility, as a fiberglass fire is nearly as hard to put out as a magnesium fire, it feeds itself and generally burns until it's all gone. By now the entire bay was lit by the flames, people in dingys were buzzing all around the boat yelling at the burning hulk trying to see if anyone was aboard. By this time, the entire upper decks had collapsed in from the heat and flames. Moments later, the starboard fuel tank exploded, nearly blowing the boat in half, the stern section broke loose and sank from the weight of the engines and a slick of burning diesel fuel began trailing behind the boat.

The would be rescuers, now turned their attention down wind of the flaming vessel and the proximity of other boats. One savvy sailor, noting the clear shot to open water down wind of the flaming mess, maneuvered his dingy to the front of the mooring ball and cut the boat loose and, in a bizarre scene, began towing the flaming hulk clear of the mooring field. Lit up by the flames, Jack could see that there were two men in the dingy, one was driving, and the other was hanging on to the mooring line. As soon as they had cleared the mooring field, the man hanging onto the line let go and the remains of the boat began to drift harmlessly into the Francis Drake Channel. Moments after the flaming mess had cleared the mooring field, a police boat with its blue lights flashing began to follow and keep pace with the now unrecognizable flaming mass of plastic. Within thirty minutes, the boat was reduced to a small glowing slick on the surface, the boat was completely gone.

Billy asked Jack, "So, what happens now?"

Jack said, "Well, nothing till morning, there will of course be some kind of investigation but it will be cursory at best. My only concern is that if they send divers down to the stern, there is a good chance they will get to meet Stephan."

Dan said, "By that time we will be out of here, but I see your point, so far, we haven't left anything for anyone to find, it would be nice to keep it that way."

Billy said, "We just have to hope they don't decide to dive on it before we get out of here in the morning." The men sat up for a while talking about what to do in the morning and then turned in for the night.

Chapter Twenty-One

Jack and company were up just after sunrise and took turns in the shower and got ready to head in. Billy said, "If you're right, and I believe you are, there's no reason to leave anyone on the boat when we head in." Jack was about to say something when Dan said, "Look, I still think we should never leave the boat alone, we have too many goodies aboard we don't want anyone to come across."

"He's right," said Jack, "one of us needs to stay and I guess it should be me, too many people know me in there and I don't want to have to explain what I'm doing here without my boat."

"Ok," said Billy, "want us bring you anything?"

"Yeah," said Jack, "Mhiki's head." Dan smiled and said "Adios," and the pair was off. Shortly after Billy and Dan had left, Jack called Alex on the cell phone. As agreed, it was Will that answered the phone. Jack filled him in on the current situation and then Will put Alex on. "Good morning," said Alex, "how are things going today?"

Jack gave Alex an abbreviated explanation and told her that he would call her later on. Jack did not mention the murders of Stephan and Viktor, and Alex was smart enough not to ask any questions, not now, or ever. She knew what type of men they were and knew that they would be taking care of business.

Alex found it strange that she was not bothered by what these men were doing. The only thing that concerned her was Jack's safety. Here were Jack and his friends, all good decent men, all had killed in their past and now, here they were hunting humans, intent on killing them. Alex thought about her grandfather, he had been an Army Ranger during

World War Two, and had survived the carnage of the invasion at Anzio where so many men on both sides were killed, and again at the landings and savage fighting on Omaha Beach in Normandy. From her knowledge of history, she knew what he must have been through, and the things he must have had to do, especially as a Ranger, the earliest of American elite forces. Yet he was the kindest, warmest, and most caring person she had ever known, and he had been a professional killer. Alex remembered one particular day, when as a child, she and her grandfather were watching a television special on the anniversary of the D-Day landings, he had told her that the children of her generation and all generations to come must learn about, and never forget the time when the world had gone mad, and of the dedication and sacrifices that good men from nations around the world had made in the name of peace and freedom, that they had killed and died in great numbers to ensure a better future for the whole world. At the time, she had been too young to really understand, but now her affection for that aging sweet old man who had seen so much death only deepened.

Will asked Alex if she wanted to go to the restaurant and get some breakfast. "No," said Alex, "I'd rather cook on the boat if you don't mind, I need something to do. I hate just sitting here like this." Will smiled at her and said, "Believe me, I know what you mean." It suddenly dawned on Alex how Will must feel, the others were out there risking their lives and he was babysitting the girl, she would consider that before complaining again.

Mhiki woke up feeling like shit, he had drunk nearly a full liter of Vodka last night and his head felt somewhat larger than normal. After taking some aspirins, Mhiki left Tortola for Norman Island; he would wait for, and then blow up the sailor and the woman and then be on his way before the Italians could find him. Mhiki would look for a mooring somewhere in the middle of the field, it would be difficult to moor the boat alone but if necessary, he could just drop the anchor.

Based on what he had learned about Norman Island, Mhiki believed it would be the perfect spot to deal with the sailor once and for all. Mhiki did not plan on any heroics, no final face to face confrontation, he would just blow the sailor up with a shaped charge, right under his bed on the boat.

The boat would fill with water quickly and sink, and that, would be that. Mhiki could linger underwater near the boat and if it appeared that the sailor made it into the water alive, he could kill him there and swim away. Mhiki was nearly giddy with anticipation. As soon as he was stationary at Norman, Mhiki would construct his new bomb. He had paid close attention to the procedure and chemical mixture ratios and was certain that he could replicate the device that Stephan had made, except this one would be three times as powerful, why fuck around, if you want to blow something up, blow it all the way up.

Billy and Dan looked everywhere and could find no sign of Mhiki. The main topic of conversation at the resort was the fire and explosion last night, and the search for any bodies. Officials were searching the area in small boats looking for bodies as no one had claimed to have been on the boat and survived the explosion and fire. Dan went to the ferry landing and checked to see which ferries may have left during the timeframe from when they had last seen Mhiki, and the last departing ferry. The guy at the dock told Dan that Road Town would have been the only destination available at that time of day. Billy asked the guy if he had been working around that time yesterday, and the guy said that he had. Billy then asked the man if he remembered seeing a guy, around fifty or so with a nasty scar on the side of his face and a messed up ear.

The man said, "Yeah, I saw a guy that looked like that, hard to miss, he seemed like he was in a bad mood or something." Billy thanked the man and Dan said, "We need to call Jack." Billy called Jack to let him know what was going on. Jack answered the phone and Billy described their search for Mhiki and what he had learned at the ferry dock. Jack told them to just get back to the boat and they would figure things out then.

After Dan and Billy returned to the Donzi, Jack said, "We need to go back to American harbor; I don't like not knowing where Mhiki is. I think we should all stick together from now on." Dan and Billy agreed and Jack called Will to let him know that they were on their way, and asked if there was still a slip open next to his boat. Will said that there was and that he would make the arrangements with the harbor master.

"Ok, it's all set," said Jack, "let's get back there and decide what to do next." Billy was driving the Donzi and had the throttles to the stops all the way. As the group arrived back at the marina, Will and Alex were standing by to catch their dock lines. After the Donzi was tied off, everyone boarded Jack's boat and began discussing what to do next. Billy said, "So, Valentnikov is loose somewhere and we have no way to find him. I can't imagine him going through all of this just to give up on you Jack, besides, he has to know that he is finished in New York, we know he's spooked now or he wouldn't have just left Viktor, and I believe he left as soon as he knew Stephan went missing."

That piece of information confirmed what Alex had been thinking, but she would not ask any questions. Billy went on to say, "He won't give up, he will be looking for the both of you Jack and you know it." There was a brief silence and Will asked, "Jack, is there any pattern or set schedule you stick to when you're out on a charter, you know like a regular route?"

"Well, not really," said Jack, "most of my charters are for a week and it depends where the clients want to go, I guess the only thing that happens with any regularity is most people want to hit Norman again before going back."

"Ok," said Billy, "if someone were to do some asking around about you, being as you and your boat are well known around here, do you think that an individual would be able to learn that?"

"I guess so," said Jack, "I am there a lot. Are you thinking what I think you're thinking?" asked Jack. Billy smiled and said, "I do believe so, we don't have to look for Mhiki, I'll bet my retirement check that he will show up at Norman Island looking for you, and I think we should all be there waiting for him. We get there and watch for Mhiki to show up. It won't be easy and he has the initiative."

Will said, "We will have to be heads up, we know for a fact that he planned to put a bomb on the bottom of your boat, he doesn't have the rebreather anymore, so he would have to buy or rent dive gear."

"I don't like it," said Dan, "we will be sitting ducks." Jack looked at Alex and said, "I don't like it either, but, Billy is right, he won't stop, we have to force a confrontation of some sort and hope for the best, he's pissed and stressed out, hopefully he'll slip up and we can exploit his mistake." No one liked the situation much, but it was what it was, and it had to end soon. After more discussion, they all agreed that Will would stay with Jack and Alex, and Billy and Dan would provide escort and cover in the Donzi during the transit. Upon arrival at Norman, Jack would tie off to a mooring ball, and then put fenders out on the port side and Billy would tie off directly to the Gulfstar, rafting up as it is called. Billy and Dan would each keep an MP-5 handy, and from now on, everyone carried a concealed sidearm at all times. Will would take the remaining MP-5 with him on Jack's boat. Jack broke out the little Czech machine pistol and put it next to him under the cockpit cushion.

After everyone was as satisfied with the plan, Jack cast off and departed the marina with Billy and Dan in close trail. There was still no wind so it would take Jack and his crew a little less than two hours to motor to Norman, Billy would race back and forth checking out other boats and be prepared for a running gunfight if it appeared any boat was making a run at PRIVATEER.

As everyone else was on their way to Norman Island, Mhiki was already there trying to pick up a mooring ball, and when he first arrived, none were available. Mhiki drove the boat around for about twenty minutes before he saw a boat leaving. It wasn't the location he really wanted, but it would have to do. Mhiki, since he was by himself, had to drive the boat up to the mooring ball, then run up forward and try to snag the mooring line with his boat hook. He missed it on his first try and as he was lining up for his second try, a young couple in a dingy came along side and the young man shouted, "Get it close and throw me your line." Mhiki waved in acknowledgement and did as the man said. When Mhiki got up to the bow, the woman was driving the dingy, and the young man was in the front. Mhiki tossed him the line and the woman drove right at the ball and held position. The young man quickly secured the line through the eyelet and handed Mhiki the other end of the line so he could secure it to the cleat.

The young man said, "I'm Jimmy and this is Jill." Mhiki, in a thick Polish accent said, "Thank you, not good English." Jimmy just smiled and said, "Whatever; have a good one man," and sped off in the direction of Pirates beach bar. Mhiki had fashioned the wig into a pony tail on the way to the island and was wearing that, and a bush hat and a large pair of shades, he looked more like an old hippie than anything else. Mhiki went below and fired up the boats diesel generator and turned on the air conditioner and sat down at the table in the salon and went to work on his bomb.

Mhiki was still putting the finishing touches on his device when Jack entered the bight at Norman Island. Unlike Mhiki, Jack did find a mooring on the opposite side of the harbor and about halfway between the Willie T and Pirates. Will went up to the bow and grabbed the mooring line while Alex rigged the fenders to the port side. As soon as they were ready, Billy maneuvered the Donzi along side of Jack's boat and Jack and Will secured the lines. Everyone climbed into the cockpit of PRIVATEER and opened a beer. Dan said, "I think we should just make it look as though we are having a party. In fact, let's throw some steaks on the grill, I'm kinda hungry." Alex said, "Sure, why not, I'll put on some music." Alex went below and turned on the stereo, and Jack and Will went back aft and got the grill ready while Billy got the steaks out and began seasoning them.

Alex asked Jack if she could turn on the generator so she could microwave some potatoes to go with the steaks. In the meantime, Dan had a pair of binoculars and was checking out the other boats.

Mhiki had finished building his device and was quite satisfied that not only would it be strong enough to sink the sailor's boat, it should fairly blow it out of the water. Mhiki went up to the fly bridge on the trawler and began looking around with his binoculars and when he saw the sailboat with the big powerboat tied up next to it, his heart almost leaped out of his chest. There, just over a hundred yards away, was the man who had ruined and disfigured him. Mhiki wanted to go kill him right now but knew that he needed the cover of darkness to perform his task. Mhiki could not believe his luck. The sailor could not know that he was being hunted; otherwise he would not be having a party on his boat. He would watch them and wait for the cover of darkness to swim underwater and plant the bomb right under the bed in the aft cabin, that would surely be where the owner and Captain would sleep. Mhiki prepared himself a light meal and began to savor the thought of returning to Paris, it had been too long since he had been there last. This would be a good time of year to do some skiing. A whole new world awaited him after he had killed the sailor and the woman.

After everyone had finished eating, Will decided it would be a good idea to do a lap around in the harbor and check out the other boats. With luck, they would spot Mhiki and formulate a plan to take him out and be done with this. Dan went with Will and the two cruised all around the harbor and when they approached Mhiki's boat, Mhiki ducked out of sight before they could see him. They decided to go ashore to Pirates and look around there.

While they were at the bar waiting to get a beer, Dan said, "He's a sitting duck like this, I don't like it."

"Me either, and I'm sure Jack ain't too happy about it either, but what else can we do." They took their beers with them and headed back out to the boat. While they were on their way back, Billy, who was sitting on the bow of PRIVATEER, had the binoculars out and was looking at all the boats around them, futilely trying to keep up with the steady stream of boats coming and leaving. Billy was looking at a decent sized trawler with an old hippie sitting on the fly bridge when he noticed something.

Mhiki had been sitting out in the heat and sun drinking steadily since he had spotted the sailor and he was sweating now and the wig was making his scalp itch. Thinking he had no real reason to be overly cautious, Mhiki took off his hat and wig and used a towel to dry the sweat out of his hair and then replaced the wig and hat.

Billy had been about ready to look around some more when he saw the hippie take off first his hat, then his hair. Billy zoomed in with the binoculars and was able to see the scar on Mhiki's face, he only looked at him long enough too be sure it was him and then put down the binoculars as Mhiki was putting his wig back on.

You slick bastard, thought Billy, if he had not seen him take off his wig, he would never have recognized Mhiki. *Got ya you son of a bitch*, thought Billy.

Billy walked over to where Jack and Alex were sitting and said, "Hi Jack, smile and walk with me down below, that's right, happy face, nothing is wrong." The two men walked below and Billy said, "He's here Jack, I just spotted him, he's on a trawler on the other side of the harbor.

He's wearing a long haired wig and a floppy hat, looks like an old hippie but I caught him taking off the wig, must be hot, anyway that's when I made him."

"You sure?" asked Jack.

"Positive, and we have to assume that he's made us too." While this was going on, Mhiki was watching Dan give Alex a tour of the Donzi. Alex preferred sailboats, but had to admit that the Donzi was nice. After Alex was finished looking at the Donzi, Jack called everyone into the cockpit and said, "Everybody keep smiling because we are being watched, nobody look at the boat and don't appear to be alarmed. Mhiki is here; he's on the trawler that's about a hundred yards away or so on the north side of the harbor. Will smiled and said, "Excellent, how do you want to do it?"

"We have to keep an eye on him, but we also have to be careful about it, if he notices us watching him, this will get difficult. We need to wait till it's dark, and this is going to be dangerous, but we assault the boat. Three of us, we use the dingy; we'll have to make like we're heading in to Pirates. We need something for two of us to hide under while the dingy driver makes a close pass by his boat on the shore side and as the dingy passes the trawler, the assault team rolls out and boards by way of the swim platform find him and fill his ass with holes. The dangerous part is we don't know what he has for weapons."

Will said, "It's a damn shame I can't just pop him in the head with a rifle from here." Billy said, "Jack, your plan sucks, however, it is as good as it's gonna get unless we make a lot of noise and that isn't really an option, at least this time we won't worry about the body, once he's found, it won't take long for the local cops to tie him in to the recent events in New York and it'll look like the Italians were just finishing up. Dan, you have anything to add?"

"Yeah, you drive the dingy and Will and I will hit the boat, Jack, you stay here and watch for Mhiki and run coms, I don't like it much either but what else can we do. He's here and so are we, it needs to end here, today."

Mhiki, as the day turned to evening had continued drinking; it was something to do. Mhiki had been unprepared for the Happy Hour cannon on the beach, but quickly dismissed it as being something normal for the bar.

For Jimmy and Jill, it was like calling the hogs to the trough; they had been lounging on the boat after a day of snorkeling and an earlier round of cocktails and were now ready to commence some battle speed drinking. The couple were newlyweds on their honeymoon and had chartered a 36 foot sailboat from the Moorings at Soapers Hole. They were both graduates of Cal Tech and had met in school, after graduation both had secured high paying jobs with the same silicon valley software development firm. That was two years ago and they had finally gotten around to tying the knot. Normally a fairly conservative couple, they were cutting loose on this trip.

From where they were moored, they had to pass close to Jack's boat and the Donzi, and when they did, Jimmy was running full throttle in the little RIB. On the two boats, people were moving around and when the wake from the speeding dingy hit, both boats pitched violently and as the wake from the speeding dingy passed beneath the Donzi, and then hit Privateer, the two boats were rolling on an opposite cycle, which is to say that as the Donzi rolled to port, the sailboat rolled to starboard amplifying the effects of the wake and yanking on the lines that held the two boats together.

Jack was pissed, he ran up into the cockpit to yell at the offending idiot, but they were almost to the dingy dock already. "Fucking idiots," exclaimed Jack, "Goddamn bare boaters, most dangerous form of marine life known to man, the vast majority of them are ok; and then you get idiots like that."

Billy, somewhat amused at Jack's apparent irritation, asked, "So, how do you know they're bare boaters?"

"For starters, that was a standard issue Moorings dingy, and second, no one that spends an appreciable amount of time on the water goes tearing through a mooring field like that; not only is it bad manners, it's dangerous." Jack looked at the way several other boats were still rolling from the wake and went back below to finish doing a com check and make sure every one was on the same page. Alex could sense the tension among the men and kept to herself, staying near Jack, but giving him his space, she could see that all of the men were clicked on now, they had transformed into the hunters.

Mhiki, who was still drinking, checked his dive gear again, and then checked his device; everything appeared to be in order. He would set the timer for fifteen minutes, which should give him time to swim back to his boat and watch the show. Another hour and he would slip into the water and shortly after, the sailor would be no more. That thought was worthy of another drink.

At Pirates, Jimmy and Jill were getting hammered, Jimmy was doing tequila shots and drinking beer, and Jill was drinking pain killers. They planned to have a couple more there, and then head to the Willie T, Jill wanted her free tee shirt and Jimmy liked the music better there, less reggae and more rock and roll.

Just as the sun was setting, Billy, Dan, and Will were getting ready. The men were all armed with their suppressed Glocks, and a knife. No one liked what they were about to do, but they had to get this done, which meant they had to take the initiative. If Mhiki was ready to repel boarders, this could go badly for Dan and Will.

Billy threw a tarp into the dingy and as the men were getting into the dingy, Billy said, "Ok Jack, he hasn't even pit his dingy in the water yet so you need to keep an eye out, if it looks like he is going to launch the dingy call us and we'll hit him hard and fast. As long as he stays put, we'll head in to the dingy dock, then Will and Dan will hide under the tarp before I head back out. If Mhiki is watching, he will only see one man in the dingy and I'll keep on going so it shouldn't arouse any suspicion. You and Alex need to stay in plain sight so Mhiki can see you. Hopefully, he'll think we went in for cocktails and you guys stayed here for some alone time or whatever. I'll call you on the radio when we start our approach to his boat, depending on what you see, give me a clear, or abort call. I guess that about covers it old buddy."

Jack looked at his friend and almost teared up, this was his problem, and he should be doing this but these men, his friends would not allow it, their mission was to keep him and Alex safe and to do that, they were willingly putting their own lives on the line, not because they had orders to do so, but because they chose to protect one of their own and the woman he was with. As Billy was departing in the dingy, Jack remembered a tee shirt he had seen once, it read, **Friends help you move—Good**

friends help you move bodies. These were such men, loyalty to one another came before any other consideration.

Mhiki had observed the departure of the dingy and assumed that they were going to the bar, this was perfect, he would go now. Mhiki was in the salon of the Trawler and put on his black dive skin and made sure his SCUBA rig was in order, he inflated his jacket type buoyancy compensator, or BC, which also serves as the mounting point for the air tank, and tied a line to it and put it in the water through the window in the salon opposite from the sailor's boat, that way, he would not be observed getting into the water. Mhiki checked explosive device which he had in a backpack worn against his chest instead of his back. The backpack had quick release clips on the shoulder straps so it would be easy to remove once he was on target. After he was sure that everything was in order, Mhiki climbed through the window and slid down the line and into the water. After Mhiki had rinsed out his mask, he slipped into the scuba rig, took a compass bearing, deflated his BC and slid beneath the surface and began swimming in the direction of Privateer and the Donzi.

Near the dingy dock, Dan and Will slid under the tarp and Billy started casually motoring in the direction of Mhiki's boat. Billy called Jack on the radio and said, "Interrogatory, status?"

Jack replied, "Clear." Billy said to Dan and Will, "Were on, go on my signal." I t had been agreed that Will would climb up onto the swim platform first while Dan covered him from the stern of the boat, then Dan would join him on the platform and the two men would sweep the boat together and shoot Mhiki on sight. As soon as that was done, they would signal Jack, who was watching, and he would call Billy in for extraction. Both men were wearing only dive fins and shorts with a belt to secure their weapons to their bodies and large dive knives strapped to their calves. They would each discard their fins before climbing onto the swim platform. They were on the target ingress now, fully committed unless they got an abort call from Jack.

At Pirates, Jimmy and Jill had run out of cash and needed to make a run back out to the boat before going over to the Willie T. Jimmy had some difficulty negotiating the floating dingy dock and Jill clung to his arm, the pair almost fell into the water twice. After finally deciding they had the right dingy, the pair boarded and Jimmy fired up the motor.

Unlike Jack, Mhiki did not know how to accurately measure distance underwater and wasn't even sure he was going in the right direction. Another hindrance Mhiki now realized, was that all of the Vodka he had consumed was making it difficult for him to focus on his compass in the dark water. Even though the instrument had a luminescent dial, he was still having a hard time staying on course. Mhiki guessed he was just over halfway there and had to surface to ensure he was on heading, then he submerged again and began to close the distance to the sailor's boat.

Jill pushed Jimmy clear of the mass of dingys at the dock and Jimmy immediately opened up the throttle on the outboard engine and began speeding through the mooring field in the direction of their boat. The dingy had no lights on it and Jimmy had forgotten his flashlight.

As Billy passed the trawler at a distance of about twenty feet, he could see that the cabin lights were on and he could see no one on deck, so he said, "Now," and the two men rolled over the far side of the dingy into the water. Billy kept going and radioed the signal to Jack, "Package delivered." Jack radioed back, "All clear." Will grabbed the swim platform and discarded his fins while Dan, kicking with his fins to keep his upper body out of the water, held his pistol pointed at the aft salon door with both hands. As soon as Will was on the platform with his own weapon drawn, Dan boarded the boat while Will covered him. When they were both ready, the two men nodded at each other and rushed into the salon.

Mhiki was getting really annoyed, he was having more difficulty remaining oriented as he closed the distance to his target, he would have to surface one more time to verify his position. Mhiki was pleased, he was only thirty feet from the boat and the sailor was looking at something else so Mhiki initiated the fifteen minute timer.

Jack was watching Mhiki's boat and observed his two friends rush into the salon when he heard the dingy running full out. Jack wanted to yell at the driver, but also did not want to attract any attention. As Jack was watching the dingy, he saw a dark shape appear right in the dingy's path. Before he could say anything, the bow of the dingy leapt up into the air forcing the bottom end of the motor and propeller deeper under. A fraction of a second after the bow of the dingy had hit the object, the lower unit of the motor and propeller hit it, almost knocking Jimmy and Jill out of the dingy.

Dan and Will rapidly swept the boat and both of their hearts sank as they realized they were alone on the boat. The two men appeared on the back of the boat and at first Jack didn't notice, he was busy watching the events right next to his own boat. As soon as he noticed Will and Dan, Jack radioed Billy and said, "Extract, now," Billy replied "Roger," and sped to the trawler. Billy positioned the nose of the dingy against the swim platform on the trawler and kept the engine in gear, holding him in position as the two men dove into the dingy. As soon as they were in the dingy, Will said, "No one home." Billy swore as he headed straight back to the Donzi.

Mhiki was aware of pain coming from his head but was somewhat confused; his mask was missing but he retained his grip on his regulator with his teeth. He could feel the water pressure increasing indicating he was sinking, he knew that he needed to kick for the surface, but for some reason, his legs were not working, nor were his arms. *Oh shit*, thought Mhiki, *the timer*. Mhiki was suddenly gripped by the horror and hopelessness of his situation, he had a live bomb strapped to his chest, he was underwater, sinking, and his neck was broken.

Jack was listening to Jimmy and Jill yell at each other as Jimmy tried unsuccessfully to start the engine again. The pair was starting to drift past Jack when Billy radioed Jack and said, "Target not at expected location." Jack didn't know what to do at the moment, He was confused by Mhiki's absence, and he believed the idiots in the dingy had most likely just killed a sea turtle and that pissed him off. Billy pulled up alongside of the Donzi and Jack said, "Tie it off and get aboard."

Alex asked, "What happened Jack?"

"Mhiki wasn't home, and I think those same idiots in the dingy from earlier just clipped a turtle, and as hard as they hit it, they probably killed it." Billy and the others boarded the boat and Billy said, "Houston, we've got a problem."

Mhiki was lying on his back on the bottom, held there by his weight belt, as close as he could guess, ten minutes had passed since he had armed the bomb. He was a dead man and he knew it, bomb or no bomb; either way, he would die right here next to the sailor. Even if he had not armed the bomb, he would drown as soon as his tank ran out of air. Mhiki screamed into his mouth piece, this was just not fair; he had not come all this way to fail, it just wasn't fair. So many years after their initial confrontation, the sailor was to win in the end. Mhiki would die alone with the knowledge of his defeat, he was not afraid to die, he just could not accept dying a failure, this couldn't be happening to him.

Everyone was back on Jack's boat and it was Dan who spoke first. "This is not good, we found bomb making materials, some cut pieces of wire and two used tubes of silicone. And, there was a line tied off in the salon hanging out a window on the far side of the boat. He's in the water now."

Jack said, "Fuck," and jumped up and ran below, as he shouted, "Everybody look for bubbles." Jack turned on the mast spreader and deck work lights, effectively illuminating a one hundred foot radius around the boat. All thoughts of caution and concealment were gone as the men, now openly armed scanned the water around the boat. It was Alex who saw the bubbles first. "Jack," she cried, "look over there." Near where the collision had occurred, were the telltale bubbles of a SCUBA rig breaking the surface. The men were all pointing their weapons at the bubbles searching for the source. Jack thought that the diver must be deep, with the illumination from the lights, they would be able to see a diver twenty feet down, and Jack also thought it was strange that the source of the bubbles seemed to be stationary.

Then it happened, in that first instant, it appeared as though a giant flash of lightning had originated from the bottom of the harbor. Billy said, "Oh shit," as they could all see the massive bubble caused by the explosion race outward and for the surface. It looked just like the old black and white films of war ships dropping depth charges. First, a huge dome of water formed on the surface, and then a massive column of water shot skyward. As the shockwave hit the two boats, everyone except Alex was thrown into the water; Alex had managed to grab one of the lifeline stanchions on her way by it. The blast had nearly lifted both boats out of the water. The stern line of the Donzi parted and the stern swung out and away from PRIVATEER causing the bow of the Donzi to dig a nice gouge in the paint and gel coat on Jack's hull. Not a single boat in the harbor was spared the effects of the underwater blast. Then, the huge column of water came back down, drenching everything and causing a second wave.

Everyone had to wait for the boat to stop rocking before they could get a grip on the boarding ladder. Alex ran to the side of the boat and saw that everyone was alright. As soon as everyone was back aboard, Billy said, "Is anyone hurt?" Alex seemed to be the only one who had sustained any injury, she had a rather large goose egg on her forehead above her right eye, other than that, they were all fine. Will, who was smiling, looked around at everyone and said, "Man, that was fucking cool." After one of those awkward pauses, they all started laughing and hugging each other.

By now, every boat in the bight had turned their lights on and excited voices could be heard from all directions. As the others stayed on deck looking at the water, Jack ran below to check his bilges and his propeller shaft seal to make sure he hadn't sprung any leaks. Satisfied that everything was ok, Jack went back up on deck. While Jack was looking at the large bump on Alex's head, Dan said, "Hey, look over there, what's that?" They could all see an object on the surface about a hundred feet back from the stern of the boat just at the edge of the illumination from the overhead lights. Billy jumped into the Donzi and grabbed a battery powered spot light. As he shined the light on the object, they could all see that it was a dive tank.

Billy and Will jumped into the dingy and raced to the object. When Billy grabbed the tank by the valve and started to lift it up, he could see that it was a dive tank, a shredded BC, and the upper fifteen percent of a shredded diver. Billy was looking at the mortal remains of Mhikiail Valentnikov, his facial features clearly revealed his identity. Billy looked at Will and smiled. Then he removed Mhiki's remains from the BC and tank and watched them drift slowly away. Billy and Will returned to the boat and told Jack what they had found and what they had done. Jack tied the BC and tank to a line on the back of the boat and said, "Any time now, we are going to have to answer some questions, questions to which, the answers will all be, I don't know."

No sooner had Jack completed his sentence when three police boats with their blue lights flashing came tearing into the Bight. Jack took Billy's flashlight and shined it at the lead patrol boat and began waving his arms. The police boat came alongside and when Jack saw the officer at the helm he smiled. "Hi there Andrew," he said to the cop. The officer looked around the boat and took mental note that all aboard were soaking wet, as were the two boats. Andrew smiled at Jack and said, "Jack Mon, what de hell ya doin, you fishin wit dynomite?"

"No Andrew, I think some diver just blew up."

"Oh yeah, what make you tink dat?"

"Well," said Jack, "this floated up right after the explosion." Jack showed Andrew the shredded BC and the tank which was badly misshaped but had not ruptured. Andrew looked at the damaged equipment and then tied off his patrol boat and came aboard. The officer asked a bunch of questions and finished by saying that they would have to check all of the boats in the morning and see if anyone was missing. Jack and his friends would not be bothered again, if need be, they could contact him, everybody knew Jack Schmidt.

After the police had left, taking the damaged dive tank with them, everyone sat in the cockpit of the boat and Billy said, "I guess that's it, all the bad guys are gone now, looks like it's back to the wonderful world of retirement for us. We will have to turn all of these goodies back in to someone and then we, will head back to the States. Alex said, "I need to know what's going on back in New York, I mean, I don't know if the cops there will want me to come back or what."

Billy said, I'll call Matthews and get all that info, Jack, I think the best thing for us to do is head back to St. Thomas tomorrow and finish closing this thing out. We can relax there while we tie up the loose ends."

"I agree," said Jack, "It takes me longer to get there so I'll leave first and catch up with you guys there."

"That should do it for now, so we will bid you two a good night." The men all went below on the Donzi after securing another stern line and Jack and Alex sat alone in the cockpit. Alex looked at Jack and after a few moments said, "Jack, can I stay, I mean, you know, here with you, for good?" Jack looked at Alex, and then looked around at the mess in the cockpit caused by the explosion and then walked to the companionway and looked at the mess below. Everything that had not been bolted down had been thrown about the boat. Jack looked back at Alex and said, "Sure, and you can start by cleaning up this mess." Alex grabbed Jack and hugged him so hard Jack thought she would crack his ribs.

The next morning, the BVI police were checking all of the boats in the harbor in an attempt to ascertain who was missing, Mhiki's remains had not been, and would never be found, a couple of roaming Black tip reef sharks had seen to that. Andrew stopped by and Jack tied off his bow line for him and Andrew and his partner climbed aboard. Andrew said, "You know Jack, funny ting, folks say you turn on all your lights just before de explosion and you all was lookin right where it blow up, how you know to be lookin there?" Andrew neglected to mention that people thought that some of the people on Jack's boat had appeared to be holding weapons just before the explosion.

"Well Andrew," said Jack, "we thought we saw a big turtle, and just after it surfaced, a couple of idiots in a dingy hit it, damn near knocked em out of the boat. I turned the lights on so we could see if the turtle was dead or not, we were looking for it when all hell broke loose."

"Yeah well, we already talk to dat couple wit de dingy," said Andrew, "and one of my boys, he look at dat motor on de dingy, had a piece of what may be from a wet suit stuck to a nick on de prop. I tink dey hit de diver, not a turtle, den, he sink and blow up. What I don't know, is why he be swimmin around here wit a bomb, you got any ideas Jack?"

"Jesus, how should I know Andrew? I'm just a charter skipper." Andrew looked at his old friend and said, "Yeah well, you know what dey say, everybody used to be someting else, be seein you Jack, you take care." Andrew took off and headed in the direction of Pirates where officers were questioning the people there, still trying to determine who was missing from what boat.

After everyone was ready, Jack and Alex got underway for St. Thomas. Today they had good winds so Jack and Alex hung out a full press of sail and were making about eight and a half knots. Alex sat next to Jack in the cockpit and was hoping that this would be the first of many such days.

After Jack and Alex had gotten underway, Billy called Timothy

Matthews on his private cell number and filled him in on the events of the last few days. Billy asked Matthews what he should do with the weapons and equipment and Matthews told him that the entire equipment package was a write off. They were to dump the weapons, equipment, and fake credentials at sea, and the three men could split the remainder of the hundred grand expense money. Bill Reynolds would have a title for the Donzi to give him, all they needed to do was fill in the name and mail it in, whichever man that wanted it, could have it. Matthews would contact Nolan in New York and tell him it was over and that the Government would appreciate it if Jack and the McTeal woman were left alone. Billy was to expect a call from Nolan later in the day.

Nolan, Brady, and Eggers were at the command center when Matthews called for Nolan. "Yes sir," said Nolan.

"Agent Nolan, it would appear that the Caribbean end of things have sorted themselves out satisfactorily, and it looks like NYPD's Organized Crime Unit will have its hands full trying to keep up with some new management changes within the Italian and Russian Mafia here in the very near future. As far as we are concerned, this is over, your two detectives can go back to Homicide, and you can go back to your regular duties. Also, if you would, let your detective friends know that I would appreciate it personally if they simply forgot about the McTeal woman completely, whatever she has, nobody wants it; also, please call Mr. Chalmers and inform him that all is well in New York, understood?"

"Understood," said Nolan.

"Very well, I believe that this is the last time we will speak," said Matthews, "I appreciate your assistance and discretion."

Nolan asked, "Do you have any message you want me to pass on to Schmidt?"

"Why Special Agent Nolan, I have no idea as to whom you refer," said Matthews before he hung up.

Billy told Will and Dan what Matthews had told him, and the men got underway for St. Thomas. As they overtook Jack and Alex, the men waved on their way past. On the way, Will dumped all of the weapons, equipment and credentials over the side with the exception of two of the sets of NVD's.

After arriving at Crown Bay Marina, the men hooked up the shore power and TV cables and sat in the salon relaxing while waiting for Jack and Alex to arrive. While they were there, Nolan called and thanked them, and told Billy to tell Alex, that as far as NYPD was concerned, she was just another tourist who may or may not come back from the islands, but if she did, no one there had any interest in her whatsoever.

The men were waiting at Jack's slip when he and Alex arrived. They all helped Jack and Alex hose down and clean up PRIVATEER, and when they were done, they all went below to the salon. Alex made a round of pain killers for everyone and sat down with the men and said, "I guess you guys should see what got this whole mess started." Alex took a large leather pouch out of a backpack and dumped its contents onto the salon table. The men could only stare in awe, no one said anything for a moment and then Will said, "Damn, their must be hundreds of them."

"Two hundred and five diamonds and ninety-six emeralds to be exact," said Alex, "nothing smaller than four carats." Dan looked at the jewels and said, "They must be worth millions."

"No," said Will, "tens of millions."

"Jack and I talked about this on the way over here and we want you guys all to have some of these," said Alex.

Billy said, "Guys, thanks, but we can't."

"And just why the hell not? If it wasn't for you guys, we would both be dead right now so I don't want to hear it."

Dan said, "Ok, I'll take an emerald." Jack looked at Alex and the two smiled at each other and then Jack sorted out five each of the larger emeralds and diamonds for each man and pushed them across the table for them. Billy said, "Jack, Alex, I just don't know what to say."

Will looked at the jewels in front of him and said, "You know, each of these piles is worth well over a million bucks, are you sure you want to just give them away?"

Alex laughed and said, "I think we can afford it Will, Jack and I will never be able to spend what we have, not even if we really tried, please take them and do something that you always wanted to, really." Billy told Jack and Alex what Nolan had told him and Alex said, "So, just like that, it's over, I can go back and take care of my things and then it's done." Dan said, "You two are free to do whatever you want, you start from here."

That night, the four men and Alex went to Tickles and got good and hammered, to anyone watching, they looked like a bunch of long lost friends catching up on old times and just having a blast. Cindy the bartender walked over to Jack and said, "Am I correct to assume that you are off the market now?"

"That is correct Madame," replied Jack. "Good, it's about time," Cindy gave Jack a big hug and walked over to Alex and gave her a big hug too. Cindy couldn't help noticing Billy noticing her, so she took the initiative and walked over and struck up a conversation.

The next day, Jack and Alex took Will and Dan to the airport, Billy won the coin toss and ended up with the Donzi and decided to hang around for a while, he and Cindy had hit it off really well. Everyone said their goodbyes at the airport and Jack, Alex and Billy returned to the Marina.

Back at Tickles, Jack suggested that they all sail over to Jost Van Dyke for the New Year's party at Foxy's, it was a short sail and they could all come back the next day. The sail over to Jost found Jack and Alex sitting in the cockpit, and Billy and Cindy sitting up by the bow almost the whole way there. When they arrived at Jost, Billy and Alex could not believe the number of boats crowded into the little harbor. Jack expertly maneuvered his boat until he was satisfied he had found a spot where no one would swing into or drag down onto him.

After they got the hooks set, Jack always used two anchors set out at forty five degree angles from the bow here; they cranked up the stereo and had a round of drinks before heading to the beach. Alex was looking around at all the different boats and counted flags from at least a dozen different countries just in their immediate area.

The group cleared customs which was located right across the dirt road in front of the dingy/ferry dock, and walked down the beach past all of the little plywood makeshift bars and tee shirt stands that are erected every year for the New Year's bash, and made their way to Foxy's. When they got there, Alex saw a black man who appeared to be in his late fifties or early sixties wearing a ratty looking tee shirt and jeans, with no shoes, sitting on a barstool playing an acoustic guitar. He was singing a song he had apparently just made up about a hideous looking hat some pink faced tourist was wearing. People all around the bar were laughing and the woman with the hat got up and took a bow when the man had finished his impromptu composition.

Jack got the man's attention and he walked over and shook Jack's hand. "Jack Mon, where you been? Thought maybe you miss the party this year."

"No way man, here, I want you to meet someone, Foxy, meet Alex, Alex, this is the man himself." Jack's friend and Alex exchanged pleasantries and then the man said, "Damn Jack, she nice, real pretty too, you shanghai her or what, she too pretty to be wit you."

Alex looked at Jack's friend and said, "Actually, I shanghaied him, poor guy never saw it coming." The man threw his head back and laughed in delight and said, "Jack Mon, you be keeping this one my friend, look I got stuff to do, good seein you mon, and a pleasure to meet you missy."

As Jack's friend left to work the enormous crowd, the group settled in at one of the tables, listening to the music, cold drinks in hand, and bare feet in the warm sand. As it grew nearer to dark and the crowd became crushing, Jack suggested that they head back to the boat.

Billy and Alex were both amazed, as packed as the beach and all the bars along it were, there still seemed to be parties going on most of the boats, neither of them had ever seen anything like this before. They stayed up well past midnight talking and just having a good time. In the morning, Alex and Cindy made breakfast and coffee. After they were done, they sailed back to St. Thomas.

When they got back, Cindy went home to check on her cat and Billy retreated to the Donzi. They had all agreed to meet at Tickles for dinner, Cindy had to work but she could still hang out some if the bar wasn't too busy.

While they were sitting at the bar, Jack and Alex asked Billy and Cindy if they wanted to come with them to Martinique. Billy and Cindy talked it over and finally agreed to come along. Cindy said that she had two weeks worth of vacation on the books and nothing better to use it on.

Two days later, at 0500, the group departed St. Thomas for their journey. Jack figured it would take about thirty some odd hours sailing straight through. As the sun began to set, Jack had everyone look to the west at the sun. It was a truly magnificent day, no clouds and no haze, a gentle sea with a fresh easterly breeze, and no land in sight.

As the sun began to set on the horizon, Jack said, "Get ready, and don't even blink." Just as the very top of the sun disappeared below the horizon, there was a brilliant emerald green flash right at the point the sun had dropped, it only lasted a few seconds but Alex thought it was the most magnificent thing she had ever seen. When she looked over at Jack, he was smiling at her and simply said, "Told ya."

Printed in the United States
56105LVS00003BA/136-183